THAT SLEEP OF DEATH

THAT SLEEP OF DEATH

Richard King

A Castle Street Mystery

THE DUNDURN GROUP
TORONTO · OXFORD

Editor: Doris Cowan
Proofreader: Jennifer Bergeron
Design: Jennifer Scott
Printer: Webcom

Canadian Cataloguing in Publication Data

King, Richard
    That sleep of death

ISBN 0-88882-229-4

I. Title.

PS8571.I52917T48 2002   C813'.6   C2002-902327-0
PR9199.4.K56T48 2002

1   2   3   4   5   06   05   04   03   02

Canada

THE CANADA COUNCIL | LE CONSEIL DES ARTS
FOR THE ARTS | DU CANADA
SINCE 1957 | DEPUIS 1957

ONTARIO ARTS COUNCIL
CONSEIL DES ARTS DE L'ONTARIO

We acknowledge the support of the **Canada Council for the Arts** and the **Ontario Arts Council** for our publishing program. We also acknowledge the financial support of the **Government of Canada** through the **Book Publishing Industry Development Program** and **The Association for the Export of Canadian Books,** and the **Government of Ontario** through the **Ontario Book Publishers Tax Credit** program.

Care has been taken to trace the ownership of copyright material used in this book. The author and the publisher welcome any information enabling them to rectify any references or credit in subsequent editions.

J. Kirk Howard, President

Printed and bound in Canada.♻
Printed on recycled paper.

Dundurn Press	Dundurn Press	Dundurn Press
8 Market Street	73 Lime Walk	2250 Military Road
Suite 200	Headington, Oxford,	Tonawanda NY
Toronto, Ontario, Canada	England	U.S.A. 14150
M5E 1M6	OX3 7AD	

THAT SLEEP OF DEATH

foreword

Those of you who are familiar with the topography of McGill University will recognize that there is no such edifice as the Elwitt Building. I created the building, and named it after my late thesis advisor and friend, Sanford Elwitt, as I wanted a certain layout of offices and corridors unavailable in any existing building on the McGill campus.

I also took the liberty of adding a few streets to the Montreal urban landscape. There is no du Collège Avenue in downtown Montreal and anyone familiar with the city will notice that the street bears a resemblance to McGill College Avenue. There are at least two other streets in the novel that do not exist but I leave it to the discerning reader to discover them.

I must thank Maeve Binchey for inspiring me to write this mystery. In a talk she gave at the Ritz Carlton Hotel she urged the audience of over three hundred people to write a novel. "It's easy," Ms. Binchey told us. "Write ten pages a week and in thirty weeks it's done."

She added that she expected to be thanked in the forewords of the three hundred novels that were certain to result from her talk. She somehow neglected to mention that six or seven rewrites would be required following the thirty weeks it took to write the first draft.

Novelists, and especially first-time novelists, require a great deal of advice. I would like to thank all those who willingly gave me suggestions that I hope improved the manuscript. I would especially like to thank Barbara Kerr and Jan Whitford. Barbara read an early draft of the manuscript and freely gave me pages of notes, all of which improved the story. Jan Whitford spent many hours and many e-mails discussing the plot and characters with me. If this mystery novel fails to live up to the high standards set by Jan and Barbara the fault is, of course, mine.

Louise Dennys took time from her busy schedule to read and discuss the book with me and I wish to thank her for her time and helpful suggestions. My friend and colleague Robert Cajolet helped me to ensure that when the characters spoke French they did so correctly.

Doris Cowan made me understand that editors do more than find grammatical errors in manuscripts — a lot more. Her ideas were consistently excellent. She challenged me to find ways to improve the book and I hope that I lived up to her expectations. She performed miracles of literary alchemy on a daily basis.

I would like to thank Jennifer Bergeron for meticulously copyediting the manuscript. She sought and destroyed all the annoying typographic and grammatical errors that play havoc with the pleasure of reading.

Finally, my brothers Joel and Norman and my son Nicholas are constant sources of joy and support and I thank them for that.

This book, like so much else in my life, is dedicated to the memory of my mother, Laura Schecter King.

chapter one

If I had known when I caught the shoplifter that it would lead to my becoming involved in a murder investigation I might have let him go. I think.

The bookshop I co-own with my business partner Jennifer is called Dickens & Company. Our store is in the heart of downtown Montreal and I know many of our regular customers by sight. But we get a lot of impulse walk-in trade as well, some of it up to no good, so I keep my eyes open. I like to practise my observational skills. I'd never seen this guy before. He was skinny, clutching his backpack to his stomach, wearing a pale blue wind-breaker zipped up to the neck, a good seven inches shy of six feet with a bad complexion. We have a library security device and the alarm sounded as he tried to rush out the door. He didn't actually make it out. I happened to be standing nearby and I just stepped over and grabbed him as he tried to shove past some incoming customers.

I don't know why but shoplifters tend to fall apart when they're caught. They just give up. I held on to him and politely asked him to let me look in his backpack. There were three books inside, all of them with our store's price stickers and none of them paid for. I took him into the stockroom at the back and called the cops. The shoplifter was desperately offering to pay for the books, begging me to take the money and call it quits. My policy is not to get into conversation with these hapless souls; there's too big a risk I'll feel sorry for them and let them go. So we waited for the police to arrive and he kept on talking. I guess he thought my silence was a bargaining position because he offered to double the price of the books if we could forget the whole thing.

Luckily the cops arrived before this guy offered me serious money.

Usually it takes about twenty minutes for a couple of patrol officers to arrive. But this time the cops were in the store almost before I could hang up the phone. And there were three of them; two in uniform, one in plain clothes. The uniforms stayed with the shoplifter in the stockroom to do the paperwork and to issue the warrant for fingerprinting and booking. The third cop, quite spiffily dressed in his plain clothes, accompanied me back into the store. His grey trousers had a neat crease, his paisley tie was done in a half Windsor, his black loafers were shined and his blue blazer looked new, though not particularly expensive. He was a bit taller than me, which made him a shade over six feet.

"Catch many shoplifters?" he asked.

"Not really," I said. "Our security system is pretty good, so the smart thieves go elsewhere. Students know the system because it's the same one as they have in libraries. Every once in a while we catch some dummy who doesn't know what he's up against."

"How does the system work?"

"Magnets," I told him.

"Magnets?"

By this point in the conversation he'd only uttered a dozen words but it was clear he was French Canadian. His English was almost completely unaccented, but he pronounced the words with a slightly different emphasis. It's just a difference in syncopation, something I've noticed in people who've been fluent in both languages from an early age. I was glad we were speaking English. He probably guessed, correctly, that my French would be painful for him to listen to.

"Yeah, there's a magnetic strip hidden in the books," I explained. "If we don't de-magnetize the book at the cash the alarm rings when the book, and the person carrying it, leaves the store."

"Are you the owner?" he asked.

"One of two," I said. "My name is Wiseman. Sam Wiseman, and my partner is Jennifer Riccofia."

"Gaston Lemieux. Nice to meet you." Then he added, in a kind of mumble, "Detective sergeant," and extended his hand so that I could shake it. Which I did.

I was curious. "Is it a new policy of the police to send a detective along on a shoplifting call?"

"No. The force has this training thing where division people ride with patrol officers. They want us to keep in touch with what's going on in the city. And the patrol officers get the benefit of my years of experience." I thought I could hear a shade of irony in his voice as he said that, but I couldn't be sure. "This is my last day of this duty for this year." He didn't add "Thank God" but he sure implied it.

While we talked, his eyes were on the books, and he started off around the store, taking a good look at the displays. It wasn't clear whether he was looking for evidence or checking out the merchandise. When we got to the fiction section, he pulled *The Luck of Ginger Coffey*, by Brian Moore, off the shelf and started to read it.

This was unusual behaviour for a police officer, to say the least. "What do you do normally?" I asked.

"Murder," he replied, putting the book back. "I'm attached to the homicide division." He selected another book and leafed through it. This one was *The Eustace Diamonds*, by Anthony Trollope, Penguin edition. "I used to read murder mysteries and detective novels but they were too much like work. Lately I've started reading Dickens," he said, replacing the Trollope on the shelf and picking up *Dombey and Son*. He looked at me and gestured with the book in his hand. "Your store's name is 'Dickens and Company.' You must have everything written by Dickens."

"Well, almost everything. But really we called the store Librairie Dickens & Compagnie because of the language laws. We only carry English books and the Dickens part of our name is our way of getting that message across."

"I see," he said.

I hoped I hadn't offended him by mentioning the fact that in Québec only French company names are allowed on the outside of commercial establishments. The difference of opinion on this subject between English and French Quebeckers is sometimes quite sharp.

Apparently he didn't mind my frankness. "Dickens is becoming one of my favourites," he said. "Along with Balzac." He ran his fingers through his black hair, replaced the book (a depressing novel even by Dickensian standards) and picked up another one. "I'll take this one," he said, handing me a copy of *Nicholas Nickleby*. "I'm told it's one of his best."

Hmm, I said to myself. Did he expect me to give him a free book? For a moment we stood silently look-

ing at each other in the middle of the store each with a
hand on the book. Then he caught on, and laughed.

"I didn't mean 'I'll take it,' I meant I'd like to buy it."

"I knew that," I said, trying to cover my embarrassment. We walked over to the cash and he paid for the
book. "Don't forget to de-magnetize it," he said. " I don't
want to set off your alarm."

By this time the uniformed cops were finished with
the shoplifter and had escorted him out of the store.
One of them came back in and asked Lemieux,
"Êtes-vous pret? Nous avons fini."

"Oui, un petit moment. Attendez-moi dehors."
Turning to me he said, "Nice talking to you. The next time
I come I hope it will just be for more Dickens."

We shook hands again and he left.

And that was how I met Gaston Lemieux.

I have always considered myself pretty well integrat-
ed into Québecois society — for an anglo. When I meet
francophone writers, especially those whose books had
been translated into English, we always have a lot to talk
about: the differences between the French and English
book businesses, rights, marketing, publishers, bookstores, and of course books. My partner Jennifer Riccofia
and I have a great relationship with the French-language
booksellers, because we don't compete with them and
we're able to help them track down English books for
their customers.

But the more I hang out with Québecois the more I
realize how cut off I am. When it comes to talking to regular people, people with whom I don't share a professional connection, I've often found that we have almost no
common vocabulary. We don't watch the same television
shows or read the same magazines or listen to the same
music. So this detective sergeant with an interest in
Dickens was a surprise.

As soon as the cops and the shoplifter left the store I got back to some of the chores of running a bookstore.

I have a photograph of myself and Jennifer Riccofia that was taken at the party we held for our grand opening. Jen and I are standing at the front of the store, leaning against the window so that the name, Dickens & Company, is just above our heads. My left arm is circling her narrow waist and she has her right arm around my waist. Jennifer isn't tall: she just comes up to my shoulder. We are leaning against each other so that my head is resting on hers. We both have curly hair, mine is brown and hers is red, and the light streaming in the window gives us an innocent, happy, almost angelic look.

I used to have the photo tacked up on the bulletin board in our office, but everyone who saw it thought, I guess from the way that Jen and I are smiling in the picture, that we were married. I got tired of explaining that we are not, in fact, husband and wife, so I had the picture framed and set it on my desk in a place where only I can see it.

We met about eight years ago when I was the manager of one of the stores in the Classic Bookshops chain and Jennifer was the Montreal and eastern sales representative for Murray & Kerr, a publishing house based in Toronto. We're same age, thirty-five. We became friendly — at one time I thought I would like to be more than that, but we somehow jumped that stage of our relationship without falling and landed on friendship.

We were soon seeing each other once or twice a week for lunch or dinner or a movie. We talked about work a lot of the time. I was getting restless managing a chain store and I told Jennifer about my frustrations. She was discontented, too, tired of the travelling and more and more convinced that she was too far from the centre of publishing activity, Toronto, to advance her career. But she loved Montreal and wasn't prepared to trade it for the head-office culture of Toronto. It wasn't long before our weekly crab sessions turned into planning sessions for the type of bookstore we both dreamed of owning. And pretty soon we started talking seriously about joining forces.

Six years ago, with money begged, borrowed, saved and in my case inherited (not a large fortune, just an education fund set up by my Zaide Moishe), we opened Dickens Company Bookstore in downtown Montreal. So far, neither of us has regretted our decision; things have worked out very well. Dickens & Company is in the black and Jennifer and I are making a living, not getting rich, but we're happy.

Our lives as booksellers developed a regular pattern. Jen looks after the buying and hires and fires (rarely) the staff. I take care of accounting and marketing. I also spend a lot of time worrying about our inventory and how we are going to pay for all the books we keep ordering. Jennifer is used to my whining and mostly ignores it.

A week after the shoplifting incident, I was going over a stack of invoices trying to calculate our inventory level.

"Do you realize how much money you've spent on books over the last three months?" I asked her, showing her my stack of invoices.

"A lot, I imagine. Some wonderful books came out and we had to have them. Don't worry. They'll sell. They always do, don't they?"

I had to admit she was usually right but worrying about money was part of my nature. Jennifer wasn't like me at all in that respect. She was always more or less sane about the business and didn't seem to mind reassuring me at regular intervals.

"Sam," she said, "you worried about the same things last year and we had our best year ever. We even made more than a nominal profit. Everything will be OK."

She was right, of course. Jennifer is the ideal bookstore partner. She can read vast amounts of publishers' catalogue copy and from that morass determine which books to buy and in what quantities. She's intelligent, sure of herself and her opinions, and also a good listener. The publishers' reps who call on her quickly learn to respect her. As for me, well, having me around is good for Jennifer's ego, I guess: it means there was always someone around who is more absent-minded and disorganized than she will ever be.

About three weeks after the shoplifting incident, Gaston Lemieux walked into the store. Despite my pride in my memory for faces I didn't recognize him immediately. He was off duty and wearing casual clothes, which of course are very different from a policeman's "plain clothes."

This time he bought *Bleak House*.

We talked about books for a while, and I suggested that we go and get a cappuccino at the café around the corner on Sherbrooke.

"Why not?"

I told Jennifer I'd be back in a half hour or so. Gaston and I went out out into the warm late-spring afternoon, and strolled around the corner to my favourite hangout, the Café Paillon.

The place is owned by Jake and Jackie Paillon. They are European, although I don't know what country they come form. They speak English and at least three other languages that I recognize, French, German, and Italian, and a few that I don't. I'm pretty sure that Jake was originally Jacques and that Jackie was Jacqueline, but I've never figured out when or why they anglicized their names. The café has ten tables and a bar with six stools; it's frequented by students and faculty from McGill University. The prices are low and the place isn't overdecorated. The white walls are covered with framed prints, chosen for their colours, not their artistic school. Impressionists are mixed with Warhols and Picassos. There's a corkboard near the door where people advertise articles for sale, apartments for rent and events to attend. The ambiance is friendly and low key.

After sitting down at a corner table, Gaston and I ordered coffee and continued the politico-conversational dance that we'd started when I told him about the bookstore's name. All English- and French-speaking Quebeckers do this when they first meet. Each has to make sure that the other is not totally intolerant. Each has to make sure that the other understands that ethnic and cultural differences are something to be celebrated, and surmounted in the name of friendship. Once we get past all that, the phonics of Quebec politics, we usually discover more interesting things to talk about.

Gaston, it turned out, was like me — more interested in broad policies than in local issues. He was interested in the justice system and I was interested in the politics that govern the cultural industries in Canada. We talked about politics and the police (but not the connection between the two — I sensed that he was much too conservative for that kind of speculation).

He was one of two children of an upper-middle-class French-Canadian father and English-Canadian mother. That explained his fluency in both languages. His sister was a lawyer, as was his father. Gaston had begun law school at the Université d'Ottawa, as he was expected to do, but he had dropped out.

"I was more interested in the application of law than in arguing about it. So I became a cop," he said. He didn't seem to want to talk about himself much. But I was curious.

"Why didn't you become a politician?"

"I was too impatient for that, " he said. "And I don't have the right outgoing personality."

"Do you think you'll ever go back and finish your law degree?"

"My parents keep hoping for that!" He shrugged his shoulders, looking a little uncomfortable at my questions. But then he relaxed, apparently realizing that my interest was genuine. "They think I'm sure to get tired of police work, and come back and join the family law firm." Then he started to laugh. "They've been hoping for that more than fifteen years now. I'm not about to give up my career on the force."

"Families are like that," I said. "Mine too, but in my case it was my grandfather. He wanted his grandchildren to become professionals. He didn't specify what kind. He just wanted me not to be a cab driver like my father. It's probably a good thing he didn't live to see that I ended up as a bookseller. He would have considered it not much better than driving a cab. But I've never regretted it."

Over the next few months Gaston got into the habit of dropping by the store every two or three weeks to buy a new book. He was reading his way through Dickens at a steady pace. We'd always talk and fairly often we'd go around the corner for lunch or just a coffee. After a we had exhausted politics we moved on to a subject we both found more exciting: police work.

I had never got over wanting to be one of the Hardy Boys and took unabashed pleasure in discussing his cases with him. He would tell me about his work with a novelist's sense of the drama of murder. He rarely focused on the gory parts of the crime; he wasn't much interested in the blood and guts of murder beyond what they provided as clues for solving the crime. He saw criminal investigation as a big puzzle, an intellectual challenge. In some cases he expressed more sympathy for the perpetrator than for the victim. "He beat her once too often and got what he deserved," he said of man shot to death by his wife. Of a man who'd killed someone in a fight he commented, "you can only push a guy so far before he explodes," or "people should be very careful when they drink." He didn't excuse the murderer, exactly, but he tried to understand how he reached the point of killing someone. But despite his sympathy he was relentless in his pursuit of the criminal.

I loved those sessions. We could talk over his cases endlessly. He enjoyed laying out the puzzle for me and he was interested in my insights. On a couple of occasions he flattered me by telling me that my comments had helped him to bring a case to a successful conclusion.

This emboldened me to take the next step, and I began to ask (nag, actually) to be allowed to accompany him on an investigation. He never said no but he always managed to put me off until later. "When a mystery more appropriate to your talents comes along," he said (whatever that meant), "I'll be sure to call on you."

As it turned out I discovered what should have been obvious: the easiest way to become involved in a police investigation is to become involved in a crime.

chapter two

Book retailing used to be a fairly simple profession. You ordered books; you sold books. Even the chain bookstores that appeared in the sixties and seventies didn't change things very much. Some customers still preferred the pleasure of browsing in the local independent bookstore.

But in the nineties the so-called superstores blew the old ways to bits. Now, to compete, bookstores have to be huge or at least combine books with a café or a cyber-café and lots of comfortable living-room furniture (I sometimes suspect that the superstores were invented by furniture companies).

Jennifer and I dreamed up various schemes and services to attract and keep customers. One of her more successful ideas was providing some of our clients with credit and delivery services, mostly professors at the universities and lawyers who operated in the high-rises that surrounded us. They phone in an order and we deliver the books to their home or office, at their expense.

I'm less enthusiastic than Jennifer about this system, because it's too successful, and I'm always the one who has to go and collect the money. Most people pay with a credit card, but there are a few who use this service to return to the good old days of the nineteenth century. They refuse to give their credit card number out over the phone or protest that they don't trust the mail.

What they really want is a personal visit to settle their accounts. That is the part of the plan I dislike. It flatters them to get this personal service but it humiliates me. I have too much pride to play the role of a tradesman who comes to the back door, ledger book in hand. Jennifer always points out that the program pulls in decent money, keeps our customers happy, provides a service the chain superstores don't, and I can just put up with it.

So it was early on a beautiful warm Monday in mid-September that I made my way to McGill University to collect outstanding accounts from three English professors and one history professor. I decided to make the history department my first stop, because the man I had to see, Harold Hilliard, tended to be pretty efficient.

I could at least start with someone I liked.

Hilliard had long been one of my favourite clients. He was a high-maintenance customer who demanded and appreciated special attention. His taste in books was excellent — in many ways it mirrored my own. He was sophisticated without being arrogant and he knew what he wanted. What made me especially like him was that he never tried to tell me what books we absolutely had to have in the store. Too many people think everyone will be interested in what interests them.

Professor Hilliard would appear regularly, wearing an expensive brown tweed jacket, and leave me a list of

seven or eight books. The list would be neatly typed and
it would always include his name, mailing address at
McGill, and his office phone number. Booksellers are
grateful for such attention to detail.

"All of these books were reviewed in the last couple
of years," he would tell me and when I looked over the
titles they would always include the best recent books in
history, biography, literary criticism and — believe it or
not — modern business practices. I didn't understand
the value of business books to a historian but that is
what made Professor Hilliard such an interesting customer; his tastes were eclectic.

I would pack up the books on his list that we had in
stock, and special order the rest. When they came in, I'd
take a walk over to his office

On that bright September Monday I knew that if his
records agreed with mine, and they always did, I'd be
out of his office with a cheque for $519.96 within fif-
teen minutes. Some of his colleagues were not so organized. I heard the same excuses over and over: "How can
it be that much? Are you certain?" "I thought I returned
that book." "I'm sorry, I don't have my my cheque
book." Or sour grapes: "It really wasn't as good as the
review said it would be."

Professor Hilliard's office was big and comfortable.
You have to be pretty senior or important to get an office
like that. It was on the main floor of the history department, which itself occupied most of the southeast corner
of the Elwitt Building.

When I arrived the reception area was empty.
Even the normally vigilant secretary/receptionist,
Arlene Ford, was absent. Pleased that I wouldn't have
to waste time stating my name and my business to the
other underlings, I marched right up to Hilliard's
office door and knocked.

I didn't get the customary "Come in," in answer to my knock, but the door was ajar. I thought I would just peek in to see if there was any sign of Professor Hilliard. The door swung halfway open in response to my gentle push, but then it stopped. Something was blocking it. I put my head around the door to see what was in the way.

I got the fright of my life.

Professor Harold Hilliard was lying on the floor with his head in a pool of blood. I could only see him from the waist up; the rest of his body was behind the half-opened door but I was pretty sure he was dead. I read somewhere that when faced with a panic situation the normal human reaction is fight or flight. I did neither. There was no one around to fight with and I was frozen in the doorway and couldn't have moved if I wanted to, and believe me, I wanted to. I don't know how long I spent glued to the doorsill transfixed by the gruesome scene.

The sound of a woman's voice shouting, "What do you want?" and the angry click-clack of high-heeled shoes on the vinyl tile floor snapped me out of my daze and I turned to see who was screaming at me. It was Arlene, the department secretary. She was an elaborately turned bleached blonde about thirty-five, who favoured brilliant blue eyeshadow and a shellacked-looking French twist. Suspicious and unfriendly at the best of times, she was now marching down the hall toward me with outrage in her eyes. Clearly, she was not pleased to find me at Hilliard's office door. She would be a lot less pleased if I didn't stop her before she discovered the bloody scene for herself.

"Wait a minute," I said stepping toward her to block her entrance to the office. She gave me a mean look and reached past me to pull Hilliard's office door closed. But as she did so she caught sight of the body and the blood.

Then she screamed and recoiled, practically knocking me off my feet.

She whirled around, grabbed me and tried to shove me up against the wall. "What have you done to him?" she yelped. Then she backed away from me toward the safety of her desk. Fight *and* flight.

"Me?" I asked incredulously. "Nothing. I just found him."

Her eyes were drilling into me. I noticed that her black mascara was clumped on her lashes. "Stay right there. I'm calling security."

I decided staying right there was not really necessary and followed her back to the reception area. While she was on the phone I sat in one of the chairs in the waiting area and thought about the situation.

I had spent enough time with Gaston Lemieux to know that it was important to give a clear and accurate description of events when reporting a crime. I knew that the police spent much of the early part of an investigation trying to sort out the vague and contradictory statements of witnesses. I did not want to be that kind of witness and I made careful mental notes, so that I could give a detailed, coherent statement to the police when they arrived. By that time it had occurred to me that in a few minutes I might be meeting my friend Gaston in unusual circumstances.

Within less than two minutes of being summoned, three McGill security people came barrelling in through the big main doors. The self-important little guy in charge had a walkie-talkie in one hand, a cell phone in the other, and a pager clipped to his belt. He was prepared for any communication emergency, but I could not see if he carried a gun.

"Miss Ford," he said. He had a strong upper-class-twit-of-the-year British accent. "You say a dead body has been found?"

The two uniformed security people remained at the door to the department to ensure that no one not authorized to do so entered.

"He found the body," the secretary said, pointing an accusing finger at me.

The campus cop turned and took a couple of steps toward me so that he was almost standing on my feet.

"Who are you?" he demanded. He was maybe five-six in his army boots, but so was Napoleon. He had a thick moustache and a Sixth Dragoon Fusiliers regimental tie. He carried "aggressive and efficient" to extremes.

I stood up, which forced him to back up a pace or two. "Wiseman, Sam Wiseman. I came to see Professor Hilliard on a business matter and discovered him dead." I didn't like his officious manner, so I asked, "Who are *you*?"

"I'm Julian Alexander. Head of security."

He turned back to Miss Ford and asked, "Have you ever seen this man before?"

She looked at me warily. "He's been here once or twice."

He stood at attention and barked at us as if we were a large group rather than just two people. "You are both witnesses to a serious crime and you will have to remain here until the police arrive. Until they get here I'm in charge." I was pretty certain that he didn't have to deal with murders on campus every day, but I still thought his act was a bit much. I guess we all deal with stress in different ways.

I sat back down in one of the guest chairs and Miss Ford sat at her desk as Alexander called the police on his cell phone. He didn't dial 911. He punched in a seven-digit number that must be known only to security people. He gave a brief description of the situation, said "yes" a couple of times, hung up and slipped the phone into his jacket pocket. On his walkie-talkie he informed someone in the security office that there had been a murder, instructed him to tell a couple of senior people of that fact and ordered him to treat this information as "extremely confidential." My guess was it would be all over the campus in twenty minutes.

"The police will be here in a moment or two. You will be required to give statements at that time." He parked himself against a wall opposite my chair so that he could keep an eye on both me and Arlene Ford. We weren't much in the way of suspects but we were all he had.

As we waited for the cops to arrive I noticed that there were no professors around. It was just a little before nine-thirty and the only faculty member present was dead. Where were the others?

It took the police about ten minutes to get there. When the two uniformed cops showed up Alexander immediately took them to a corner to give them his report. I watched the three of them talk and glance over at me and Arlene Ford. One of the cops then secured the scene with yellow plastic barrière-de-police tape.

As I watched him do so I heard a familiar voice behind me. I was in luck. Gaston had been assigned to the case! I turned around to greet him and I'm embarrassed to report that I had a big smile on my face. I had finally become involved in a police investigation, and I was thrilled. At that moment I was happier at the possibility of being in the middle of a murder investigation than I was sad about the poor victim lying dead in his office.

"Sam," Gaston said, with a tone of surprise in his voice, and I quickly wiped the smile off my face. "What on earth are you doing here?"

"I was here to see Professor Hilliard. I discovered the body," I told him, standing up as if I was making a formal report.

"So," he said, and the slightest trace of a smile flashed across his lips. "You may be able to help me with this matter. Once the scene of the crime is secure I'll want to talk to you." He motioned for the two uniformed cops to join him, and they went into Hilliard's office. I took pleasure in the fact that he excluded the Alexander from their conversation. I could hear their low voices but I couldn't make out what they were saying.

A few minutes later he emerged, and went over to thank Julian Alexander for his help. The police would take over now, he explained. The security chief looked so miffed that Gaston, thinking better of it, asked him to remain in the department as the senior representative of the university. Alexander was appeased at once. He arched his back, puffed out his chest and raised himself on the balls of his feet, so impressed was he with his own importance.

Then Gaston came over to me. I'd been going over the details of what I had seen and I was ready with my report. Finally, the detective skills I had developed as a bookseller would be put to good use! Customers ask for that book they "heard about on the radio the other day, the one about the woman who fell in love and moved away. I think the author's last name began with a B." With those few skimpy clues a good bookseller will be able to narrow down the search and find the book that the customer wants. It takes clever questioning, an ability to absorb and retain details about lots of different books, intuition, and sometimes inspired guesswork.

And I knew I was good at it. I told Gaston exactly what I'd seen, quickly and thoroughly, leaving nothing out. I was tempted to embellish my heroism in the few minutes after I discovered the body, but I had to report accurately that I had been frozen to the floor with shock. This was actually the only thing that had prevented me from stepping into Hilliard's office and messing up the crime scene. I didn't tell Gaston that.

"Sam, it is important that you write up all that you have just told me," Lemieux said when I finished my oral report.

"I can do that," I said looking around for a pen and pad. "If you can get me something to write on ..."

"Not here. I want to keep the witnesses separated for the moment. I'll meet you at the usual place for a coffee as soon as I get things moving here. Figure an hour, maybe an hour and a half."

I didn't want to leave but I calculated that the best way to remain involved in the investigation would be to follow Gaston Lemieux's instructions to the letter. As I left the building I passed a group of cops carrying lab equipment and two men dressed in the light grey suits of the coroner's office wheeling a gurney in the direction of the history department.

I considered what my next move should be. Now that I had my foot in the investigative door, I wasn't taking it out until I got right inside the house. I walked across campus to the McGill University Bookstore to buy myself a notebook and a pen in order to write up my notes. I could have written my report quickly and returned to work until it was time to meet Gaston, but I didn't.

I strolled very slowly along Sherbrooke Street, enjoying the special atmosphere of Montreal in the autumn, to the Café Paillon, "the usual place" where Gaston asked me to meet him. I chose a table near the back and got to work over a double allongé. When I finished writing I still had at least half an hour before I could reasonably expect Gaston to arrive. I let my mind wander.

How could I make myself indispensable to this investigation? It occurred to me that I could suppress some information for a short while and then report it at an opportune moment. It didn't take me more than a minute's reflection to reject that idea. I didn't have much in the way of evidence to suppress, and besides, I knew Gaston well enough to know that wasn't the best way to curry favour with him. After reviewing my options I decided that the role of amanuensis was my best bet. My notes were a good start and I would be ready to perform whatever "literary" chores came my way.

Gaston arrived at the café at about eleven o'clock. Another double allongé for me and a regular coffee for him.

We traded information. I told him that the history department had appeared deserted when I arrived and stayed that way while Arlene and I waited for the cops to arrive. He told me that the faculty were either at their nine o'clock classes or just hadn't got to work yet. Professors who didn't have early classes tended not to arrive much before ten o'clock. And after security was called Julian Alexander's men didn't allow anyone into or out of the building.

Arlene Ford was actually there but not at her desk; she had gone into the common room just off the reception area, intending to make coffee. She heard me go down the hall and knock at Hilliard's office door. She came out to ask why I hadn't waited at reception and she saw me react to seeing the corpse.

I gave Gaston my notes and he gave them a cursory once-over before he folded them neatly and slipped them into his pocket.

"I found something at the scene that I need your help with," he told me. "The victim was clutching this in his right fist." He reached into his outside jacket pocket and pulled out an evidence bag with a crumpled piece of paper in it. He smoothed the plastic bag out on the table in front of me and I saw that the piece of paper was a Dickens & Company special order form. "I was hoping you could tell me if this has any significance; other than the obvious, of course."

We use a standard numbered form for all special orders, noting information about the book and the customer's address and phone number. In this case the order number was 5643, nothing significant in that as far as I could see. The book on order was *Cambridge History of England,* Volume 3, *The Sixteenth Century* and the name of the customer was Professor H. Hilliard. There was no address, just a phone number. I turned it over to see if there was anything written on the back, but it was just a regular customer copy of a special order form.

Gaston leaned forward, both elbows on the table, looked me straight in the eyes and said, "This is serious, Sam. So listen carefully. What I have here is a man who discovers a corpse and just about the first thing we find, and find it clutched in the hand of the dead body, is a piece of evidence that points to that man — you. How do you explain that?"

"I don't. I can't." I stammered.

"Was Hilliard expecting you?" I felt my tension gauge shoot up. Gaston was cross-examining me and it was making me nervous. "Well, not *expecting* me. But I came to see him about once a month to collect outstanding invoices." I paused to catch my breath, which was becoming laboured. Gaining control of myself, and developing an unexpected sympathy for those who find themselves in the clutches of the police, I continued. "You can't believe I had anything to do with his death other than finding the body. You know me. Why would I kill him?"

"You're right. I know you and I don't believe that you're a murderer and I certainly can't see any motive for you to kill Hilliard. But, and this is an important but, I'm not the only one who sees the evidence and the other homicide detectives don't know you and might be less willing to believe you. So please, look into the order and see if you can get some information about it that is not apparent at this moment. Because this evidence makes you a suspect."

I copied the information from the order form into my notebook and said nervously, "You bet I will. But, really, I can't see anything special about this order. We order hundreds of books each week for our customers. This looks like one of many."

I tend to ramble a bit when I'm nervous. It helps me to think without letting on what I'm thinking about. In this case my thoughts were: now I have another motive beyond curiosity to stick as close to this investigation as possible. I have to make sure that I don't end up in trouble for something I didn't do. I wanted to investigate a murder, not be accused of it.

We were about to leave when one of the most beautiful women I have ever seen walked past our table on her way out of the restaurant. As she approached us the woman suddenly broke out in a big smile. I smiled back, thinking that I must know her from somewhere. A customer, maybe? But would I forget a customer who looked like this amazing vision? Now her elegantly ringless hand was descending onto Gaston's shoulder. "Guess who!" she said, laughing

Gaston, startled, turned and jumped out of his chair. "Gisèle." They hugged and did the Montreal two-cheek, all the while telling each other, in French, of course, how pleased they were to see one another. I got up, hoping to be introduced without delay.

"Sam," he said. "This is my sister, Gisèle."

"Plaisir," she said, shaking my hand. I wanted to say something sophisticated but all I could do was mumble something in French and stare at the tall, slim, black-haired beauty whose firm, cool hand I was shaking. "My friend Sam Wiseman," Gaston told her.

We all sat down again, she beside Gaston, and they launched into a rapid conversation in French, which I didn't attempt to participate in. The gist of it was *What a surprise to see you, what has been going on, I was just leaving, so were we, do you have time for coffee, no, I'm in the middle of a case, how is Papa?* I tried not to eavesdrop on the siblings and to admire Gisèle without staring. I had an overpowering feeling that I wanted to run away with her to a desert island where we would spend the rest of our lives.

I gathered from various references in their conversation that she was a lawyer, working for a law partnership whose offices were just up the street. It was obvious from the easy animated way they talked to each other, in beautiful informal French, that they had a very close relationship. It was nice to see a warmer side of Lemieux. They agreed that it was too bad that they met so rarely. Gaston asked his sister to pass his love on to their mother and said that he would call her in a few days.

Then Gaston was back on his feet, saying that we really had to go. He looked at me inquiringly, "At least, I have to get back, but perhaps Sam would prefer to take another coffee?"

Gisèle then turned her dazzling smile on me for a moment and all my senses cut out. It took a moment for me to realize that she was apologizing to me and saying no, she couldn't stay either as she had a client coming to meet with her in twenty minutes

In truth, I feared that if I stayed another second with Gisèle not only I would make a fool of myself by falling in love with a woman who was obviously far too beautiful for me, I would also miss out on the rest of the investigation. "I'd better go along with Gaston," I said. Then glanced at him, anxiously, hoping he was expecting me to accompany him. "To ensure that I didn't leave anything out of my report."

Just then Gaston's beeper went off. He lifted it off his belt and looked at the little display screen and said, "We've got to go. The lab team is almost ready to move the body. I want to take one last look at the scene before we lose control of it." He reattached the beeper to his belt. We said our goodbyes, paid and left the café. Gisèle went off in the opposite direction, back to her law office.

"Your sister is delightful," I said, feeling that the comment was totally inadequate.

"Yes, she is very charming," he replied vaguely. He was lost in thought.

Part of me was hoping that we would drive back to the McGill campus in an unmarked police car, sirens blaring and with one of those flashing red lights stuck on the roof — sort of like Kojak. But Lemieux was a pretty low-key guy. We walked.

The day was still fine and as we went along I tried to get Lemieux to advise me on proper etiquette at the crime scene but he barely replied to my questions. He pretty much ignored me for the ten or fifteen minutes it took us to reach our destination.

chapter three

Back at the history department, things had cooled down in some ways and warmed up in others. Arlene Ford was sitting at her desk, from which vantage point she could see everything that was going on. To her right she had a view down the corridor to Professor Hilliard's office. She faced the door to the department so she could see who came and went, and she seemed a lot cooler than when I saw her a couple of hours previously. Her anger had subsided, and she seemed to be actually flirting with Julian Alexander. Someone had brought them tea and muffins, and Alexander was sitting on her desk, keeping an eye on things. But mostly keeping an eye on Arlene.

Ms. Ford saw us enter and cleared her throat and signalled to Alexander with a little thrust of her head to warn him that we were back. The head of security slid off the desk and turned to face us. "Everything is under control," he reported. "Some faculty tried to gain admission to the premises but I turned them away until you give the OK. I've also kept the dean of arts and the vice-chancellor up to date." I half expected him to complete his presentation with a snappy salute and a click of his heels. Where do they find these guys?

Arlene Ford was tensing up again. I could tell by the way she was avoiding eye contact and aggessively straightening up the papers on her desk.

"Thank you," Lemieux told Alexander. "Please keep the area sealed for now. When the lab crew is finished I'll start interviewing people. Right now my colleague and I are going to take another look at the murder scene. It will be helpful if I can speak to people who knew Professor Hilliard. That would include the two of you, of course," he said, nodding to Arlene.

"I can't say that I knew him more than to say good morning to." Alexander seemed almost obsequious towards Lemieux, a superior officer. "I'll be more than happy to tell you anything I can. If possible, though, I'd like to speak to you privately." The nasty look he shot me from under his bushy eyebrows and the way he had half turned his back, excluding me from his conversation with Gaston, made it clear exactly who he didn't want present.

"Don't worry about Mr. Wiseman," said Gaston mildly. "He's assisting me in the investigation. I've confirmed that he was here on business."

"But—!" Arlene Ford jumped up, outraged. "This man claims to have come to the university to see Professor Hilliard. So he must have known him too. Isn't it possible that he is hiding something? No one knows when he arrived in the building!"

"Mr. Wiseman is not a suspect," said Gaston in the same unruffled tone. "Mr. Alexander, did you note the names of the people that have been turned away?"

Security Chief Julian looked surprised that he would be expected to do anything except play the heavy. It didn't seem to have occurred to him that he could do something helpful at the same time.

"I know who they were. I'll have a list typed for you in a minute," said Arlene. She was still giving me the evil eye, but she was anxious to impress Gaston.

"That won't be necessary. Here they all are now," Alexander said.

A mob of professors — perhaps a pride of professors is a better term — had appeared in the entranceway and were shoving their way in. One of the uniformed cops was vainly trying to hold them back. Giving up he called out to Lemieux, "Je m'excuse. J'étais à la porte mais ils ont poussé ..."

"Are you in charge here?" the leader of the gang snapped at Lemieux.

"Just a moment, please." Gaston, speaking to the cop, said, "Retournez à votre poste. Ces gens vont sortir dans quelques instants. Quand ils sortiront prends leur noms et coordonnées."

The cop left the office. Lemieux turned and appraised the man who had asked the question. He was an over-height, overweight academic type of about fifty with messy grey hair and a beard to match, wearing baggy brown corduroys and a shirt that may have once been red. "Yes, yes, I am in charge. I'm Detective Sergeant Lemieux. With whom do I have the pleasure?" Gaston let the question hang and extended his hand.

"I'm Mac Edwards. I'm the chairman of this department and I need to get to my office. So do my colleagues." The colleagues chimed in with a chorus of *yeah*s and *me too*s. "But your guard dog here," Edwards pointed at Julian Alexander, "says we have to wait. Some of us have been waiting for more than two hours. What's going on?"

"This is a crime scene. Mr. Alexander had no choice but to keep people away from it. There has been a murder."

"Murder!" Edwards exclaimed. A ripple of disbelief ran throught the group. "He didn't say anything about murder. He didn't give us any information. That is, we knew there had been a death, but we thought it was a burglary or ... Who was murdered? Not a member of the department, I hope. I mean," he added hurriedly, realizing his statement might seem a little callous, "or a student, or a staff member?"

"Professor Harold Hilliard was murdered in his office. We are examining the scene," said Gaston.

I watched the group of faculty very carefully to see how they reacted to this news. If any one of them was not shocked it might indicate that he or she had guilty knowledge of the crime. But they all looked like they had been socked in the solar plexus. The collective gasp of breath was audible. Some looked a little more stunned than others but as far as I could tell they were all sincerely upset at the news. They had that vulnerable look people get when they have a personal connection with the victim of a crime. They looked as if they felt unsafe.

"Can you tell us what happened?" asked a woman from the back of the crowd in a soft voice.

"Professor Hilliard's body was found at around nine-thirty this morning. I can't tell you any more except that he did not die of natural causes. We're trying to establish what happened. I'm going to want to interview all of you." I noticed that Lemieux wasn't disclosing very much in the way of detail.

An ancient professor who looked well past retirement age, cleared his throat and asked, "Do you have any suspects?"

There was a long pause while Lemieux looked at each one of them in turn. I suppose he was gauging how best to answer the question. After all, one of them could be the murderer. "We are still in the evidence-gathering stage. I can say that some of the evidence has been instructive. For the rest it requires further analysis."

"When will we be allowed to go back to our offices?" asked an auburn-haired woman with a nasal American accent.

"When we're finished," Lemieux said briefly.

"And when will that be?" she enquired. "We have work to do, classes to prepare, papers to grade, and appointments to keep." She was getting wound up to give us a lecture on the importance of the academic contribution to the modern world.

One of her fellow historians, a lanky guy in a tweed blazer, blue cotton shirt and a striped necktie interrupted with, "She's right. When are we going to have access to our offices? In an hour, a day, a week?" The rest of them were muttering angrily and I half expected some kind of uprising, since they were all historians; well versed in the history and value of rebellion.

But then another of the group, a short bespectacled fellow with a loud emotional voice, suddenly shouted, "What on earth is wrong with you two, with all of us. One of our friends has just been brutally murdered and all we worry about is our offices? Are we that insensitive, that selfish?"

There was an embarrassed silence. I think the embarrassment was as much at the unseemly outburst as it was at the rebuke.

"Nicholas is right," said Mac Edwards. He sounded like a man who was used to telling a group what to do. But at least he understood the value of becoming conciliatory when he saw that belligerence wasn't going to work. His voice now sound ingratiating, if somewhat insincere. "We should get out of the way and let the police do their job and not worry about our offices and papers for the moment. They'll be here when the police are finished. We should begin planning some sort of memorial service." Turning to Lemieux he said, "Let me know if there is anything I can do to help. Notification of the family, that kind of thing."

"Thank you for your co-operation," Lemieux responded. Was I wrong to suspect the trace of irony in his voice? "Will you all please stay on the campus for the moment. Leave your names with the officer outside. I'll need to speak to each of you. Is there somewhere that I can find you when my team is finished here?"

"There's the faculty club," someone murmured.

"Yes," proclaimed Edwards. "We'll wait for you at the faculty club." The professors straggled out of the department office at a funereal pace.

The corpse had not been moved. We had to step over it to get into the office. The pool of blood was drying on the floorboards. Lemieux and the other cops seemed untroubled, but I was new at this. I suddenly felt more than a little queasy at being in the presence of a violent death.

"Look but don't touch," said Gaston to me in an undertone. I didn't bother being affronted, but he should have known I wouldn't touch anything. I'd examined many a crime scene in books, analyzing the clues right along with the presiding sleuth. Besides, I didn't want my fingerprints on anything, or I'd really be in trouble.

The room was a mess. There were books and papers all over the floor. Three cops were filling up bottles, glass specimen plates, test tubes, and glassine envelopes with crime scene evidence, and stowing them neatly in large sample cases. Out of the corner of my eye I observed that they were giving me the curious once-over. I tried to look cool and official.

Harold's (I'd always called him Professor Hilliard when he was alive, but that no longer seemed necessary) desktop was wiped clean, as if someone had swept everything off the desk onto the floor, and his phone was lying on the floor, the receiver off the hook and making that annoying staccato bray they emit when they're neglected. One of the uniformed officers saw me looking at it, smiled at me, took Harold's coat off the coat tree and dropped it over the phone, smothering the noise.

The star of the show, the late Professor Harold Hilliard, was lying on the floor, partially covered by some books and papers, in front of his desk. His head was surrounded by a halo of coagulating maroon blood. He had a surprised, open-eyed look on his face but I couldn't see any wounds on his head. I did see a small iron statue with a marble base lying on the floor not far from Hilliard. The base of the statue was flecked with blood and some other stuff — bits of his skull and brains, I suppose.

Lemieux, following my gaze, said, "Yes, that's the murder weapon." Turning to one of the uniformed cops he snapped out an order, which was quickly obeyed, to bag it. Lemieux took the plastic bag from the cop and examined the statue. He snorted a short laugh and handed the bag to me. I looked it over and saw why he laughed. Engraved in the base of the statue was the name of the figure: Hegel. It was a bust made of some heavy metal and it was just the right size and balance to be an excellent murder weapon. Hegel's head was the handle; the murderer must have gripped it and whacked the victim with the marble base.

Death by Hegel. More than one student, me included, had suffered this fate figuratively; Hilliard had met it literally. I handed the statue to the uniform cop, who took it from me and returned to the corridor outside the office, where he was joined by a second. The CSU cops had finished packing up their stuff and were on their way — to another crime scene? the police station? home? I really had no idea where they waited to be called to crime scenes.

I forced myself to look at the body. Except for being dead, the victim was a nice-looking man. His hair, the part of it not matted with blood, was neatly trimmed but not short. He was wearing a blue blazer, a blue button-down shirt open at the neck, and expensive-looking khakis, brown loafers, and grey socks. Alive he had probably been very proud of his wardrobe. Dead, it didn't matter.

"Well, we know what killed him. Now we have to find out why. He was killed before the office was searched. That much we know."

"You mean, because the books are on top of him rather than the other way around?"

"That's right," said Gaston with an approving nod that told me I was catching on. We were still standing near the door at this point and I took a tentative step into the room. "Just a minute," said Gaston, putting a hand on my sleeve to hold me back. "Before you start poking around, take a good look at the office. This will be our last chance to look at the scene of the crime as the murderer left it. This room has the personality of the killer."

Lemieux could see that I didn't understand what he meant.

He explained, "Someone came in here, and for one reason or another killed the professor. The killer was also obviously looking for something and wasn't careful about it. We don't know what he — or she — was looking for, or if he found it. But the way he searched is in some way consistent with his personality. Because the searcher did such a sloppy job we can assume two things. He was in a hurry and knew what he wanted. He expected to find it in some obvious place — on the desk or behind some books."

"So he tossed everything off the desk onto the floor looking for it."

"Right. And pulled the books off the shelves to see if it was behind them. In other words, either it was too big to be concealed *in* a book or it was something Hilliard would have kept out in the open."

I contemplated the wild disorder on the floor around my feet. "Do you think there was a fight? He came here for something. Harold said no or wouldn't play along, and so the guy got mad, killed him, and ripped the place apart?"

Gaston didn't even have to think about that one. "No. The murderer was focused and efficient. He did come here to get something. You're right, there. And this something was important enough to kill for. He may not have been planning to kill Hilliard at this time but he was prepared to do it as a last resort. He could have brought the weapon with him or known it was here. We have to find out who Hegel belonged to. We have to establish whether the crime was premeditated or the result of an angry impulse. Maybe the murderer wanted to leave his options open and didn't bring a weapon. Or chose to use a weapon that couldn't be traced back to him. I lean towards that interpretation myself. What do you think?"

Impressed by this display of professional expertise, I really had no opinion.

It was a nice size room, longer than it was wide. On one of the long walls there were windows that looked out over the campus. The desk was a little to the right of the door as you came into the office. Standing in the doorway you faced the first of the three windows and a couple of chairs for visitors. You had to turn your head to the right to see Hilliard's large desk; it was much bigger than anything the university was likely to issue to professors these days. So either the desk dated from earlier, more affluent days at McGill or it belonged to Hilliard. I wondered whether Hilliard had money. I considered asking Gaston whether he thought money could be a motive in this crime. But I was getting ahead of myself. And I was afraid Gaston would give me a precisely worded explanation of why I was wrong.

Behind the desk was a comfortable-looking high-backed leather chair. Behind the chair was a narrow table, about a foot wide, pushed right up against the wall. Everything that had been on the table was now strewn all over the floor; it had been wiped clean like the desk. The rest of the space was filled with floor-to-ceiling bookshelves. There were books on the upper and lower shelves but the middle shelves, from about my waist to just over my shoulders, were empty. The books and papers that previously resided there were dumped onto the floor.

From force of habit I started to look over the books that were left on the shelves.

I was standing behind the door peering at the bookcase when I overheard the cops gossiping about this and that just outside in the corridor. In my sleuth mode, I automatically started listening to them, just to pick up whatever information I could. Sidling closer, I inclined an ear as I surveyed the room. Although what I expected to learn from a bunch of cops I don't know. At first they gave recent sports events a verbal rehash. The only hockey being played was exhibition games, so it was much too early to get into any kind of real coach-bashing or debate over the Canadiens' prospects for the season. Without sports, conversation quickly turned to shop talk. The main topic of conversation was none other than the guy in charge — Gaston. It didn't take long to figure out that these cops didn't really like him. They thought he had too high an opinion of himself, the kind of guy who believes, as one of them expressed it, "his farts don't stink." They found Gaston too bossy and not willing to be one of the guys, *un des gars*. I was embarrassed and I hoped that Gaston wasn't aware of the conversation, but I understood why they felt the way they did.

Gaston could be a bit on the cool side, and in Montreal it's always a good idea to be able to hang out; to be able to *jaser avec les gars*. Gaston was not that type of person.

And my information-gathering was not adding to the murder investigation. The cops' conversation turned to people and events I knew nothing about, and I went back to my consideration of the books.

Hilliard's collection of history books was excellent. I noticed a series of books that all had the same design on their spines. A set, but not in order or even all shelved together. I gave them a closer look and realized that they were the volumes of the *Cambridge History of England*. Volumes one, four, six, and five, in that order. Looking around, I located volume two on the floor by the desk.

"Look at this," I called to Gaston. "He has all the volumes in the *Cambridge History of England*. All except one, apparently. The one he requested from the store."

Gaston came over to examine the books with me. For a moment he looked meditative and I wondered if I was making a fool of myself. Obviously if Hilliard's set was was missing one book, he would order that one.

But Gaston was taking the matter seriously. "Maybe the way in which it came to be missing is a clue. Did the killer come here for this book? But then, why not just take it and leave — why mess up the office? Was the book hidden? I wonder if it was the object of the search."

"But is anyone so desperate for a book on sixteenth-century Britain that they would kill for it?" I mumbled.

Gaston was still thinking. "Obviously, the book was missing before he was murdered. Maybe he was trying to tell us something by clutching the order for its replacement in his dying grip?" Even the calm and cool Detective Sergeant Gaston Lemieux was capable of a dramatic turn of phrase. Maybe the murder scene brought it out.

"I'll check into the order when I get back to the store." I was ridiculously pleased that there was something I could actually do to further the investigation. "I'll find out when he ordered the book and if anyone remembers anything else about the order," I promised.

"Good," said Gaston.

I decided it was time I took a closer look at the body. Feeling very brave, I threaded my way through the mess of papers and books, back to where it was lying. I had never seen a corpse outside a casket before (and precious few of them in caskets). It would have been nice to see the initials of the murderer's name written in blood, but no such luck. I did notice, though, that there was a telephone wire not far from the body.

"Did you see this?" I called, and Gaston stepped over the body to come and look.

"What?"

"A phone wire."

"That's interesting. But where is the phone?"

"Here." Forgetting the no-touch order, I picked up the coat revealing the the phone on the floor. The distress signal had stopped and the instrument was quiet.

"Is it connected?" He knelt on the floor, put the receiver back in its cradle for a moment, then lifted it to his ear. "Listen," he said, holding it out to me to demonstrate that there was a dial tone. Then we both looked at the disconnected wire lying on the floor.

"Well, maybe there's another phone somewhere." I bent over to pick up the wire, but this time I remembered not to touch it. I straightened up.

"Where does it plug into the wall?" Lemieux asked.

We both looked around to see where it went. He pointed to a phone box on the wall to the right of Hilliard's desk, about three feet off the floor. There was a small plastic envelope stuck to the box with a printed card inside it.

"It wasn't connected to a phone," I said. "It was for his modem, for his computer."

"Then where is the computer?" Lemieux asked.

Without moving we both turned in a slow circle, looking for a computer. We were looking for something that was pretty large and would not be buried under the books or papers on the floor. No computer.

"Well, it's missing. Maybe stolen," Gaston said.

"Maybe Hilliard interrupted the thief and got killed trying to defend his computer."

"Maybe." He didn't sound convinced.

Two guys dressed in dark suits came into the room with a stretcher.

"I think it's time to bid adieu to our victim," said Gaston.

At that moment the uniformed police officer came up to Gaston and handed him an evidence bag with keys in it. It jangled as he held it up to the light and shook it. It looked like an unexceptional collection of keys to home and office. I looked quizzically at Gaston.

"This will just take a minute, Sam," Gaston responded to my unasked question. Gently, he frisked the body and looked in the pockets of the blazer and trousers, then stood and nodded to the unifirmed cop. "Rien de plus." I was fascinated. I had assumed that the thorough body search was something he would leave to the coroner.

"The crime scene people look for the victim's keys before they do anything else."

"Why?"

"To ensure that the murderer hasn't got them. If the keys are missing it usually means that the murderer intends to visit the victim's home. You'd be surprised at how many times we catch people just by beating them there."

He handed the bag back to cop. "Keep them with the rest of the crime scene evidence." He signalled to the two guys from the coroner's office to remove the body. One of them pulled a lever under the stretcher, lowering it almost to the floor. Then they heaved the body up onto it with one practised move, and worked the lever to crank it up to waist level again, where it was easier to manoeuvre, and wheeled the stretcher out the door.

Then he turned to me. "Sam, let's you and me go talk to the department secretary again. Maybe she knows what the professor's computer looked like and what kind it was."

chapter four

Arlene didn't seem any more pleased to see us this time, and Julian Alexander was still hovering, as if to protect her.

"Are you guys done?" she asked.

"Almost," Gaston answered. "I'm having the body removed now and we're going to seal the office for a while and I may want to question some of the other professors, but first I have to ask you a question. Do the professors have computers in their offices?"

"Computers?" she said as if she had never heard the word before. "Why do you want to know about computers?"

"Just answer the question, please. Did Hilliard have a computer?"

"Yeah, he had one. One of those small ones. A laptop. Why? What does that —" Suddenly she gasped and covered her mouth with her hand. Her eyes opened wide in dismay and then her face crumpled as if she was about to cry. The two men from the coroner's office were wheeling the late Harold Hilliard out of the history department. They were behind us so I had to turn to see them. She pulled back as if she had been shoved. She looked so distraught that I was afraid that she was going to pass out. She stumbled and the chief of security caught her and held her close to him, his arm around her shoulder for support, and mumbled some comforting "there-theres" to her. She breathed deeply for a moment in order to regain her composure.

"Did he have a regular computer?"

"No. If you're asking if the university supplied computers to the teaching staff, the answer is no. Not in Arts anyway."

"Well, do you know what his computer looked like? And if he kept it in his office?"

"It was usually on his desk. The university supplies Internet access and he sent and received a lot of e-mail."

"So the last time you saw his computer it was in his office?"

"Yes."

"In that case, it may have been stolen. Could you come into his office and take a look? We may have missed it. We were looking for a big one."

"I don't want to go in there."

"The body is gone and we'd like your help, if you don't mind."

"I'll go with you," Julian told her.

It was clear that she was very upset by the murder of someone she worked with and would have rather been anywhere else. But she also realized that she didn't have much choice but to co-operate so she got up and marched into Hilliard's office. She moved so fast we had to trot a few steps to catch up to her. Once inside the office she stopped abruptly and we almost bumped into her.

"It's not here!" she said and turned to go back to her desk. Because we were so close to her, she virtually fell against Lemieux. He reached out to the doorframe to keep from falling and she grabbed him around the waist to keep her balance. When they realized that they were tangled together they each jumped about two feet in the air to separate.

Lemieux recovered his composure first. "Could you take a closer look? You can't tell from here if it's missing or not."

Arlene flashed him the look of someone who has just been told that there was a problem with her gum surgery and that it would have to be done again, and went into the office. She looked under the desk and the table and moved some of the piles of paper with the toe of her shoe. Finally she said, "It's just as told you. It's not here. Can I go now?"

"Yes, but please stay at your desk. There are a few more questions I need you to answer." Turning to Julian and me, he asked, "What do you think? Did Hilliard take his computer home with him last night and leave it there, or was it stolen this morning?"

"If it's been stolen I may have to make a separate report. All thefts should be reported to the security office," Alexander informed us.

"Whatever," said Gaston.

"I'd bet on stolen. But can't you check to see if it's at his house?"

"Thanks, I'll do that." Gaston bared his teeth at the university cop. I guess it was meant to be a smile. "Thank you for keeping order around here during the crime scene investigation. You can tell your faculty that they are welcome to return to their offices now. Except for Hilliard's, of course."

Julian gave him a crisp military nod and strode off.

He made a special point of stopping to say goodbye to Arlene, and I couldn't hear what they were saying, but there were lots of smiles exchanged and I think he patted her hand as he took his leave.

Casting a last glance over my shoulder at my friend Harold's office, which I would probably never see the inside of again, I saw the cop closing the door and starting to tack up yellow passage-interdit tape across it.

Arlene was sitting at her desk, pretending to be deeply absorbed in some papers she was typing into her computer. She looked harried. Her morning at a crime scene had taken its toll. Her normally well-coiffed hair was in disarray, probably from running her fingers through it nervously. Gaston went over and stood in front of her desk. Unwillingly, with her fingers on the keyboard, she looked up. "We'll need your assistance, Ms. Ford," he said. "No one is to go into that office. Will you see that they don't?"

She gave him the briefest of nods, and began to turn away.

"And I'd like to ask you a few questions. It won't take more than five minutes. "

"Okay," she said with a tone of resignation in her voice. It seemed that the hostility was finally draining out of her.

I took up a position on the opposite side and behind her, leaning against the wall. Present, but not intrusive, out of the line of direct visibility.

"What time was it when you arrived at the building this morning?"

"Around nine, maybe a bit after, just like every other morning."

"Was there anyone else here when you came in?"

"No. Well, just Sarah and Allan. Sarah Bloch and Allan Gutmacher. They are graduate students here. I saw them in the common room having a coffee when I walked by." She pointed to a room just off the main entrance to the history department.

"I thought you said the coffee had not been prepared?"

"They brought their own. The graduate students tend not to drink the department coffee. There's an etiquette problem. They worry that if they start making coffee it will become their job to do it every morning. Some of the professors are pretty arrogant and tend to treat graduate students like servants. So they bring their own coffee in and avoid the problem altogether."

"I see," said Lemieux. "Are they always in that early?"

"Only on Mondays and Fridays when they have ten o'clock seminars."

"Did you see anybody else?"

"I did pass Jane Miller in the corridor. But she was walking away from the department. Probably heading to her office."

"Do you mean that she could have been coming from here?"

"There's no way I could tell that. The corridor outside the history department — that corridor," she said, pointing out the department office's door, "cuts across the hallway where the professors' offices are." Gaston and I both looked. We could see what she meant. Traffic in that corridor could come from three directions.

"Does she teach here?"

"Yes. She's married to the dean of graduate studies, Fred More."

Gaston thought for a minute, then asked, "Do you feel up to giving me a statement now?" Indicating the common room, he continued, "Could we do it in there? Or would you rather wait?"

Arlene stared at us for a while. She was obviously trying to decide which was the lesser evil: talk to him now and get it over with or put it off and have to face it later. Finally she sighed and said, "All right. But give me a few minutes. I want to freshen up and make the coffee. No one ever did make the coffee."

"I can do that for you," I said, trying to be helpful and also to ensure that I would be included in the questioning of Arlene Ford. "Just show me where the stuff is."

While he waited for Arlene to return from the ladies' room, Lemieux talked to the cop on duty, and I went into the common room. At the far end there was a counter with a coffee pot, coffee makings and a small bar sink. Most of the room was taken up by a large conference table. I noticed that there were two brown bags on the table and two empty, or almost empty cardboard coffee containers from the Second Cup café. I wondered what was in the bags so I took a peek and I found that each of the two bags contained another, unopened coffee from Second Cup. These cups were full, untouched and quite cold.

"A lot of people try to avoid making coffee around here," I mumbled to myself. Just as I finished making the coffee, I realized the significance of the four cups at the other end of the table. I called Gaston into the room and showed him what I had discovered and quickly explained what I thought the cardboard cups signified.

"I'm sure the secretary said that the two graduate students were drinking coffee here when she walked in at nine o'clock. That would explain the two empty cups. But the two full cups mean that they arrived at different times, each bringing a coffee for the other, which means that for a while, one of them was here alone with Hilliard."

"... and therefore could have murdered him," Gaston finished my thought. He stepped out of the room and beckoned to the CSU cop. A couple of seconds later he was taking a bunch of Polaroids of the table with the bags and cups on it, just the way I had found them. Lemieux then carefully removed the cups from the bags and had the cop take some more pictures of them. He then gave all of it to the CSU cop to take away with him.

Just before the CSU cops left, Gaston called his forces over for an impromptu staff meeting — a staff dressing down as it turned out. Lemieux told them, in a clipped, cold tone of voice, that he expected nothing less than total professionalism from them at all times. He did not really care who they liked and didn't like so long as they did their jobs properly, at all times, without gossiping about the department in public places. He considered it a lapse of police discipline for them to chat about it where members of the public might hear. That included times when they were standing guard or packing their equipment or whatever. In other words, Gaston had overheard their conversation criticizing him for not being one of the guys.

The cops mumbled something about being sorry but I could tell from the hostility in their eyes that this exchange only proved to them that what they thought about Lemieux was correct and they would soon be reporting this tantrum to their friends and colleagues.

I thought maybe Gaston was overreacting, and I was having a hard time reconciling this military-sounding commander with the thoughtful, humorous person I knew. But I also knew how serious he was about discipline and the chain of command. I was beginning to see how the police force functioned. And that a thoughtful loner with an intellectual bent, like Gaston, would have to develop a pretty tough shell of some kind to prosper in such an environment.

Ignoring their hostility, Gaston asked the CSU team what they had found in the way of prints. He was told that they had found more than enough to keep them busy trying to sort them out and make identifications for weeks. The leader of the team gave Gaston a brief run-down of where they had looked for prints in addition to Hilliard's office. They had checked all the other offices and discovered that the doors were locked. Fingerprints were taken from all the door handles. It was unclear what they expected to find but at least they would have prints for comparison purposes. Finally, they gave the common room the once-over. The place must have been cleaned the night before because they found very few prints on the table and none on the coffee-making equipment.

"So, what you are saying," Gaston summarized, "is that there were lots of people in that office at various times and it will be difficult to determine who was there when. Correct?"

"Oui. Vous avez raison," he was told. "Mais nous allons faire notre possible."

Lemieux dismissed his troops and turned to stand in doorway to the common room; I was just inside. He turned to me and said, "Too many fingerprints are as bad as too few. But those coffees may be significant."

I was living a boyhood fantasy — playing cops and robbers, with real police. It had occurred to me that Lemieux probably first approached me to help him collect and interpret evidence because on the face of it, it did seem that I might be involved in the murder. If I had been the murderer he would have to trick me into revealing myself somehow, and it would be better for him to keep me convinced I wasn't a suspect. But I was pretty sure that he didn't seriously think I killed Hilliard, and I was part of the investigation now. I wasn't going to let him out of my sight if I could avoid it. I was having fun — and not only that, I wanted to be sure that suspicion didn't fall on me again.

Arlene Ford came into the common room just as the coffee was finished. "That smells good," she said. "And I need another cup right now. "

Seizing the chance to be of service (and to stay to listen to Gaston question her) I rushed over to the counter and said, "Sit down and I'll get you a cup. How do you take it? You like yours black, don't you?" I added, looking at Lemieux, who had just entered.

He sighed, sat down at the table and said, "Yes, black, thank you."

"Milk, please," Arlene told me and I poured coffee for them and a cup for myself and took a place in the corner of the room.

Arlene looked a lot better, more relaxed. She had brushed her hair and pulled it back in a ponytail. We could see her not-blond roots but we also saw that she had washed her face and not replaced her heavy make-up. She was prettier without it. Her smile seemed more natural, less forced without the faded lipstick. She also smelled delicious: a tantalizing combination of spice and musk. I wanted to compliment her on her scent but I thought better of it. She also seemed to have come to terms with the fact that her unpleasant morning would turn into an unpleasant afternoon unless she made the best of the situation. I could see in her grey eyes that she had decided that she had no real choice but to answer questions and that she had best co-operate and get it over with.

Gaston settled in his chair and said to Ms. Ford, "Okay. Let's begin."

"I already told the other police what happened."

"I know. But I'm going to want more details. I need to know more about the victim. To start: Do you happen to know his address? I'm going to want to search his apartment."

"It's 3519 Lefebvre, just a couple of blocks up the hill. His apartment is on the top floor."

"Thank you," Lemieux said and made a note of it. That was interesting. I knew he had looked at Hilliard's correspondence tray and his university staff emergency information and was already well aware of the professor's home address. "How long had you known Professor Hilliard?"

"I started working here about twelve years ago and he was here when I started so I've known him for twelve years."

"Was he well liked? Did his students like him?"

"His students? No, I wouldn't say he was popular with his students. He was impatient and never forgot that he was the professor and had authority over them. He never made any effort to be friendly with his students — with most of them anyway. He was a hard marker and rough on the kids who tried to hand their assignments in late. If one of them left a paper for him with me I had to write the date and time I received it on the first page so no one could slip a late paper in on him."

"What did you mean when you said that he made no effort to be friendly with his students, 'most of them, anyway'? Did he have some friends amongst the students?"

"Friends?" Arlene repeated the word as if she wasn't sure of its meaning. "No, I don't think he had any students as friends, exactly."

Lemieux, zeroing in on the way she emphasized the words "friends" and "exactly" and he asked, "Well, did he have any kind of relationships with any of his students, other than professional? Any kind at all?"

"I don't think I should answer that question. There are rumours, but that's all."

I could see Gaston's eyes focus tightly on Arlene. His question hit a target. It was not yet clear how many points he was going to get. "Rumours won't hurt him now and they may help the investigation. You do want to help, don't you?"

"Yes. But, well, oh, OK. He made no effort to be friendly with most of his students but he did try to get very friendly with some of his women students."

"I didn't think teachers still did that." I remarked, remembering my own student days in a less sensitive time. "Wasn't he afraid of being charged with harassment?"

"If he was he never showed it. I don't know if he was ever charged with anything. He was careful in that he never tried anything here, in his office."

"Then how do you know that he came on to his female students?" I asked. I thought I knew Harold pretty well, as a customer, at any rate. But I did not know the person Ms. Ford was describing, and I began to wonder whether her hostility to him had some basis in her own feelings.

"Certain of his women students would visit him in his office and then go out with him for a meal or coffee. They never spent all that long in his office but coffee breaks could take a long time and who knows what happened when they met him late in the day as he was leaving? I'm pretty sure he was up to something with some of them — and I'm not the only one who thinks so. He had a reputation."

Arlene was looking down at her hands as she told us this but now she glanced up, first at Gaston, then at me. Maybe to see whether we believed her. I tried to keep the skepticism off my face. Hilliard was undoubtedly demanding as a customer and I supposed that was the way he was as a person and a scholar, but he had always seemed to me to be a fair-minded sort of fellow, not the self-absorbed predator that Arlene Ford made him out to be. I made a mental note to share my suspicions with Gaston.

"Was he involved with anyone at the moment?" he was asking her now.

"I don't think so. For a while I thought that he was interested in Sarah Bloch. But I was sure she wouldn't break up with her boyfriend, and she didn't."

"Sarah. Who was here this morning?" Lemieux asked, flipping back through his notes.

"Yes. Sarah Bloch and her boyfriend Allan. They're graduate students and teaching assistants here. I already told you."

"Did he have any interest in women closer to his own age?"

"I don't think so. Not since Jane Miller at any rate."

"Jane Miller? That's another familiar name." Lemieux had his thumb in his notebook where he had recorded the names of the people he would be wanting to see the next day and he flipped back to that page and said, "She's the other person who was here this morning. Seems strange that three people who had some kind of relationship with the deceased were here early this morning. Tell me about his relationship with Jane Miller."

"Well, he actually seemed serious about her. She was an undergraduate here and after she got her PhD at the University of Toronto he was instrumental in getting her her job. The department does not like to hire its graduates for their first jobs. It prefers that they get some experience elsewhere. Jane is really ambitious and she got Harold to help her. He was chair of the hiring committee and made a strong case for her. The committee went along with it. They seemed very involved with each other. We all thought they might even get married.

They started going out soon after she started here full time and they were together for about two years. They seemed to love each other almost as much as they loved themselves and their careers, and believe me that's saying something. Then about two years ago they suddenly broke up and Jane started dating Fred More. She married him about a year and a half ago. Harold changed after that. He was always pretty arrogant and self-centred. He thought his Harvard PhD made him superior to everyone else. After he broke up with Jane he got even harder to deal with. He went back to his old ways of hitting on the women students. And also, that's about the time the rumours about Jane started."

"Rumours?" Lemieux prompted.

"Yes. Suddenly there were these rumours that she had stolen, you know plagiarized, part of her thesis. No one really believed them, but things like that can really hurt someone's career. I suspected Harold was the source — to get even with Jane. Hell hath no fury like a man scorned, right?" She gave a dry chuckle at her own weak joke.

"I see. So now we have three possible motives. Love, unrequited or over-requited, jealousy, or robbery."

"Robbery?" asked Arlene.

"The computer," responded Gaston. "His computer is missing. Can you describe it?"

"It's just a laptop. It's white, Japanese, Toshiba, I think. He jokingly called it Clio. I think he wrote Clio on the top of the case."

"Cleo? Like Cleopatra?" asked Lemieux.

"Not Cleopatra; the goddess of history." Arlene explained.

"She was the muse of history. It's spelled C-l-i-o." I piped in.

"Very clever," Gaston commented. He turned to Arlene and said, "You've told me a bit about his relations with some of the people around here and how his students felt about him. Can you tell me how his colleagues saw him?"

"Well, other professors liked him a lot better than the students did. Male professors, that is. Women didn't trust him. Men were a little in awe of him. He had a Harvard PhD and he published lots of articles and book reviews. He was extremely good at getting grant money so he could do research in France. His field was the French Revolution. And even though he was full of himself his male colleagues tended to think highly of him. It's a guy thing I guess."

"I take it that you didn't think much of him."

Arlene looked at Gaston for a minute or two before she responded, as if she was trying to decide how to answer the question. Finally she took a deep breath, exhaled it, then said, "Look, he's dead and I don't want to say things about him when he can't defend himself. But I didn't think much of a forty-two-year-old professor who tried to take advantage of his women students. Some of them were only eighteen years old. He could be a real sleaze. You said you had three motives for killing him. Forget robbery. No one would have killed anyone for that computer. Maybe you should be looking for a husband or boyfriend of one of his women ... friends. I'm sorry," she said softly. "It's been an awful day. Someone I worked with for twelve years has just been murdered and I've said some horrible things about him. It's too much. I want to go home."

I looked around for a Kleenex in case she started to cry but could not find any. She breathed deeply a few more times, trying to get her emotions and tears in check.

"You're right. I'm being insensitive. That's often the case in a murder. We forget the feelings of the living in order to avenge the dead," Lemieux told her. "Can I have someone drive you home? Or is there someone I can call to come and pick you up? I have just one or two more questions for now. Anything else can wait."

"I can get home under my own steam. Just ask your questions so I can go."

"You said that the two graduate students, Allan and Sarah, were having coffee when you came in this morning."

"That's right. They usually come in together. I think they usually go everywhere together."

"Could anyone have been here before them?"

"Very unlikely. They were usually the first in. They seem to have a routine. They come downtown by métro and stop off at the Second Cup on du Collège for their coffee on their way to campus."

"I see," Lemieux said. "Can you describe them for me?"

"Describe them? Sarah is a natural blonde, about five feet four or five inches tall. Pretty, I suppose, but not gorgeous. She could be if she did more with herself, but she doesn't." Arlene started to sniffle and she fished around in her bag for a Kleenex. But instead of using it on her nose or the corners of her eyes where tears were starting to form, she tore at it while she squinted her eyes as if she were trying to bring a picture of Sarah and Allan into focus. "Allan is tall," she continued. "Close to six feet, with dark hair and a permanent sour look on his face and a chip on his shoulder."

"Why would that be?" Lemieux enquired.

"I think it's because he doesn't really fit in around here. He's much further to the right politically than almost anyone else around here; Hilliard had conservative opinions, too, in some ways, but Allan is way more aggressive about it. Frankly, I don't know what Sarah sees in him. He is bright enough, but sarcastic. I never took to him, but who knows? There's no accounting for taste. He may be really nice to Sarah. He seems a domineering type to me. Is that all?"

"Yes, thank you. Please give me your phone numbers so I can call you if I have any more questions."

Arlene gave him her phone numbers and she left.

"Well," Lemieux said to me. "What do you think?"

I told Lemieux what I thought of her description of Hilliard. I recounted some of my experiences with the man, which were entirely positive. As I told him what the victim was like in life I realized that had he and Lemieux had a chance to meet they would have liked one another. They had similar tastes in books and they were similar in another ways as well. They both believed that there was an order and structure to things and they both looked for it. Maybe that's why Hilliard was a historian and Lemieux a cop. "But in general I agree with her," I concluded. "No one is going to kill a person for a computer."

"That depends what's on the computer, mon ami. And we won't know that until we find the computer. This is turning into a very modern case. Cherchez l'ordinateur."

Lemieux got up and walked over to the common room windows. He looked out at the campus for a while, then turned back to me. "I understand what you are telling me. I am not prepared to accept everything she says at face value. I'm sure she is lying about something. Most people who are involved with a murder victim panic and try to conceal something, often something completely innocent. But I don't at this point know what she is lying about or why." He paused and thought for a moment and then continued. "Usually in murder cases it takes a day or two to find the people we need to interview. Here I have a wealth of people to take statements from. And now, I suppose I had better tackle that gang at the faculty club, and then try to find out if our two students arrived separately or together this morning, and if anyone knows when they left."

As we left the Elwitt Building Lemieux asked me, "Do you know where the faculty club is?"

"I'll walk you over." Didn't he understand that I would stick to him like a burr as long as the case was unsolved?

He looked at me with amusement. "Don't you have a job to go to?"

"I did. Maybe I still do. I'll check into that later." But it crossed my mind that I should really call Jennifer. She isn't cute when she's angry. I decided to face that later.

chapter five

The McGill University Faculty Club is an old greystone building on McTavish Street. Probably a former residence of one of the charter members of Montreal's Golden Square Mile. The building is well maintained and hasn't lost any of its solid bourgeois glory.

We walked up the steps and into a red-wallpapered foyer. To our left was the lounge, where I could hear the professors idly discussing the things all academics talk about when they get together—sports and real estate. (With their intimate friends they discuss appointments, other people's salaries, and tenure.) To our right was a flight of stairs that led up to private dining rooms and meeting rooms. Lemieux and I must have looked out of place because before we could walk into the bar to meet the faculty members we were approached by an old man in a uniform — one of the legion of retired armed forces personnel who spend their golden years earning some extra money acting as officious guardians at private and semi-private clubs across Canada. "May I help you?" he asked.

Lemieux flashed his badge. "I'm here to see the group in there." He tilted his head to the left, indicating the professors sitting at a table in the lounge. The hussier just about saluted at the sight of Lemieux's badge and stood back to let us pass. "I'd like to speak to them privately. Is there an empty room somewhere in the building I could use?"

"I'm sure there is," the hussier said, backing up to his desk to check an appointment book. "There's a room available upstairs. It's the third door to the left on the next floor up. I'll ask your guests to meet you there. You'll need this." He handed Lemieux a key to the room and gave us a minute to start up the stairs before he went to tell our guests — as he termed them — where to meet us.

The room was a lovely dark-panelled salon with a large conference table surrounded by comfortable-looking leather chairs. It was well equipped for meetings, with a stack of pads and pens on the table. One wall was covered with shelves filled with old books, giving the place the feel of the private library it probably once was.

Lemieux took the eleven o'clock position at the conference table facing the door with a set of high windows with heavy blue velvet drapes behind him. I stood by the door waiting for our professors to arrive. As they settled themselves around the table I took a pad and pen and sat off to one side ready to keep out of sight as much as possible and to take notes in order to be helpful.

"All right," said Lemieux. "My first question is an obvious one. Could each of you please tell me when you last saw Professor Hilliard alive?"

"I saw him at lunch last Friday," said Ron Michaels, the guy with the tweed blazer and regimental tie.

"Tell me about it," Lemieux prompted.

"Carla Schwartz and I" — he gestured to his right where Carla, a mouse-faced little woman, sat — "were having lunch right here in the faculty club. He was here as well. He was alone at one of the back tables. Almost hidden."

"That's right," added Carla Schwartz. "I didn't see him at first. He was way off in the corner. I think he was with Jane and Fred More. Jane Miller is one of our colleagues and Fred More is the dean of graduate studies," she explained.

"No, he wasn't *with* them," Sally Howard piped in. "I was here before he arrived and he came in alone. I asked him to sit with me but he said he preferred to be alone and headed to the back. Fred and Jane came in later. They were near his table but they weren't together."

"Was that unusual?" asked Lemieux. "To avoid his friends?"

"Not really," Sally explained. "Sometimes we use lunch to catch up on reading or marking or whatever. Jonathan, on the other hand, came in while I was lingering over coffee and he was pleased to have my company."

Jonathan Marreton, the white-haired gentleman with an equine face, treated us to a courtly smile and said, "Absolutely. At my age I accept all the invitations I get from pretty young women. I don't get many. It was odd though. Hal and Fred and Jane sitting very close to each other, but I don't think two words passed between the three of them during the entire time they were here."

"You were close enough to hear them?" Lemieux asked.

"Not to hear them," Marreton answered. "But certainly close enough to notice they weren't talking, or even looking at each other much."

"Can you think of any reason why they wouldn't be on speaking terms?"

Lemieux's question was followed by a silence. A silence that suggested that the members of the history department knew of, but did not want to mention, a reason for the Hilliard and the Mores not to speak to each other.

"I already know that professors Hilliard and Miller had a relationship before she married," Lemieux prompted.

"If you know, then you know the reason they weren't speaking," Carla Schwartz put in.

"That's not exactly true, Carla," Sally Howard said. "Sure, there was a — well, a coolness between Hal and Fred and Jane when they first married but they got over that years ago. Hal and Fred never became friends but they could be cordial to one another."

"Sally's right, Carla," Ron Michaels said, supporting his colleague. "I wouldn't say that Hal and Jane were buddies but whenever they passed one another in the department or whenever they ran into one another at college function they would chat. I think that they still enjoyed each other's company — intellectually, that is. And Fred was always a little protective of Jane, but still friendly."

"They may have been sweet as pecan pie when in a group but I can tell you that when they thought no one was watching they were as cold as ice," Carla said, defending herself.

"When you say, 'they' who do you mean? Hilliard and Miller or Hilliard and More?" Gaston enquired.

"Hal and Fred, certainly," Marreton said. "But I don't think that I ever saw Hal and Jane share much of a conversation beyond good morning."

"That's not true," Michaels reiterated. "I saw

them chat any number of times when they were in the department."

I could see why Gaston wanted to interview the professors as a group. He could get at the contradictions in their stories, something that would have required seemingly endless back-and-forth meetings if he had decided to interview each of them separately.

"Maybe so, but I can tell you that I was coming into the club as Fred and Jane were leaving," Mac Edwards said. "And they were both as silent as death. They barely mumbled hello as I passed them at the door."

"I see," Gaston said. But I wasn't sure what it was that he saw. It sounded to me like Hilliard sort of got along with his ex-lover, but only in public and that he and the ex-lover's husband did not get along at all — and made no effort to pretend that they did.

"Was Hilliard well liked?" Gaston asked.

"Well liked by whom?" Edwards countered.

"His colleagues? His students? Were any of you close to him?" Gaston probed.

"I suppose that I was as close to him as anyone in the university," Nicholas Wheatley responded. "We would have lunch once a week or so and we tended to attend the same conferences and colloquia. I was on a panel with him a couple of years ago and we spent a fair amount of time working on our papers together."

"I think the detective meant, were any of us actually, really, friends of Hal's, friends beyond our connection as departmental colleagues, and the answer is no," Carla informed us. "He was never what you would call extroverted. After Jane he didn't show much of an interest in any of us. I don't know what he did for a social life."

"Did any of you see Professor Hilliard at any other time during the day yesterday or this morning?" Gaston asked, changing subjects.

"I saw him in the early afternoon," boomed Wheatley. His voice was the one that had actually showed concern for Hilliard when we first met. "He was coming into the department as I was off to class. He seemed lost in thought. I'm not sure that he even saw me as we passed."

"Did any of you see him after that?" Gaston asked.

A chorus of noes.

Lemieux looked around the table slowly and said, "Thank you for your help. I may need to see some of you again. But you're free to return to your offices and your students." I tore my notes off the pad and folded them into my pocket.

Outside, Gaston and I joined the throng of students heading south to Sherbrooke Street. The information we'd gathered in the faculty club from the professors didn't convey anything to me, and I wasn't sure Gaston had detected any useful leads in it, either. The rush of students reminded me that we still had to determine whether Allan and Sarah arrived at the history department singly or together.

At the corner of Sherbrooke and McTavish, Lemieux turned to me to say goodbye and head off, probably to do some more detecting — without me. But before he could speak I jumped in: "Listen, why don't I go over to the Second Cup and ask them about Allan and Sarah? I really don't mind and I can report to you later."

"You have no official status," he reminded me. "You can't go around asking questions as if you were a police detective."

"I know," I said, smiling at him as winningly as I could. "That's the beauty of it. I'll pretend that I know them or that I'm a professor and that they lost some exam papers and I'm looking for them at the café, sort of retracing their steps to find the missing papers."

He looked dubious.

"I'm going there anyway, it's on the way to the store, and it will save you some time."

"It's very unorthodox," Gaston said slowly.

"I'm sure I'll have no trouble getting some information."

I could tell that he was beginning to see the merits of my idea. "Well, I suppose ... I've got to write up my report and get a beat constable over to Hilliard's apartment to make sure no one goes in before I get a chance to search it. It would save me some time."

I waited.

"Okay," he said at last, " you can do it, but remember, *do not* represent yourself as a cop. And if it looks like you're in over your head just leave and let me know and I'll take care of it myself. Understand?"

"Perfectly." I had no intention of trying to pass myself off as a cop. And how could I possibly "get in over my head" as he put it? I was going to check out a café, not get into a gunfight.

"Meet me at Hilliard's place at seven this evening and let me know what you find out about our two students. Do you have the address?"

"Yeah, 3519 Lefebvre. I'll meet you in front at seven."

Lemieux headed east and I crossed Sherbrooke to walk over to the Second Cup.

Knowledge is power, and in a pinch, information is power. I knew that if I could unearth some really useful information he would see me as a truly helpful comrade in arms and not as a pain in the ass trying to push my way into a police investigation.

chapter six

I realized that I had been out of the store for a long time so I figured I'd better make an appearance.

When I walked in, Jennifer was at the service desk talking to a customer. She saw me come in and flashed me an amazingly dirty look. The customer never noticed that the relaxed, knowledgeable person she was talking to was forming the intent to commit mayhem. Even I would have thought, except for that that one furious glance, that Jennifer was laid-back and cheerful, leaning against the information desk. I looked around, realized that there was no other staff member in the store and there was a customer waiting to pay for a couple of books at the cash counter. I hurried over to over to the cash to make myself useful ringing up the transaction.

When I looked back a moment later the customer was folding her special order forms into her purse and thanking Jennifer, who was now standing in a fighter's stance with one foot slightly ahead of the other, shoulder-width apart, hands firmly planted on hips.

All this time, I'd been so enthralled with my morning's adventures that it hadn't crossed my mind to call her, and now I was in big trouble. I knew how much she hated being left to handle things on her own. I realized I'd been depending on the fact that we had two staff members working that day. But they didn't seem to be around.

The second the door closed behind Jennifer's customer, her face was twelve inches from mine and her eyes were firing poison darts that made me flinch away from her. I was drawing a deep breath for the apology that was clearly required, but she didn't wait for it.

"Where were you? We have a business to run here. Lorraine had an urgent dentist's appointment and I finally had to let Yvonne go out to lunch. You can't just disappear. People call for you. What am I supposed to tell them? Random House called. They want a cheque or they won't ship. Why didn't you pay them?"

"I'm sorry," I began. "I should have ..."

"You should have done a lot of things, but you didn't think, did you?"

It was worse than I thought. It wasn't just my unexplained absence. The Random House guy was always very nice and friendly on the telephone, but they do have rules, which I try not to break, but sometimes things get behind. Jennifer hates it when I forget to pay our suppliers. She worries that I'm withholding payments because we don't have any money and we're going bankrupt. No matter how much I explain that I'm only managing the cash flow and that the publishers know that they'll get paid eventually, it still drives her crazy when she has to take a call from our most important supplier's accounting department because I'm not there to deal with it. Part of my job description is to protect Jennifer from accounts receivable clerks.

"I'm sorry. I sent the cheque. They'll get it in a day or two. I should have called this afternoon. You won't believe what I was doing."

"OK, I'll bite. What were you doing? Other than avoiding work, that is."

"I was working on a murder case with my friend Gaston Lemieux. You know, the cop who reads Dickens."

"Come on, a murder case? Couldn't you just say that you wanted the day off? I wouldn't have minded. Really. But a murder case. Do you really think I'm going to believe that? You're a bookseller, not a private detective."

"Jennifer, *I discovered the body*. The murder was at McGill, in the history department and you know the victim."

"Me? Who?"

"Professor Hilliard. He orders, ordered I should say, a lot of books here."

"Harold Hilliard was murdered? I did know him. I can't believe it. I've never known anyone who was murdered before."

"No. Me neither," I agreed. "Did you ever talk with him? I quite liked him."

"Well, I didn't."

Jennifer was one of the easiest people in the world to get along with so Hilliard must have had a pain-in-the-ass aspect to his personality that I never saw. Although I had certainly been hearing about it this morning. "Why not?"

"I suppose I should speak kindly of the dead but he was a lech. He was way older than me but he used to come on to me."

"Really. Wow. I never knew."

"I know," she said. "I don't tell you about every guy who comes on to me. But never mind that. Tell me about the murder. And don't leave out any details. If you're going to desert me for hours and hours the least you can do is let me share the fun vicariously."

"When Gaston got to the scene, he asked me to help because, believe it or not, and this is the weird part, one of the clues is from the store."

"This store?"

"Hilliard was lying on the floor, dead, and just try to guess what he was holding clutched in his fist?"

"Sam, be serious for a minute. How can I possibly know that?"

"He was holding one of our special order forms. Lemieux thinks it may be important, but we can't figure out what it means. It almost got me into big trouble. First I discover the body and then the first clue points to me!"

"Gaston Lemieux thinks you're capable of murder?" Jennifer asked incredulously.

"No, of course not. I was lucky he was there because another cop, one who doesn't know me, might have been more suspicious. But the order form may have special significance. I want to check to see if there is anything about the order that will be helpful to the investigation."

Jennifer got to a computer terminal before I did and asked, "Do you remember the name of the book? I'll look up the order."

"I have the order number," I found it in my notes and read it aloud to her.

"Here it is," she said from the computer. "*Cambridge History of England*, Volume 3, *The Sixteenth Century*. A pretty straightforward book order. Oh, wait a minute. This is unusual. The book wasn't ordered by Hilliard, it was ordered for him. Jane Miller-More paid for it and left instructions to call Hilliard when it comes in."

"She teaches in the history department too," I said. "But I don't see why Hilliard would use his last remain-

ing strength to grab a book order form. If he was holding it when he was clubbed on the head he probably
would have dropped it. Somehow he grabbed it as he
was falling or just after he fell. But you can see why they
wondered about me."

"Why would you kill him if you went there to collect money?"

I told Jennifer the rest of the story, and when I got to
the part about the missing laptop and how Gaston and I
had wondered if anyone would really kill for a not-that-
expensive computer, Jennifer, who is really a smart cook-
ie, immediately interrupted, "Wouldn't that depend on
what was on the computer? Maybe Hilliard had something in a computer file they wanted to suppress."

"We thought of that," I replied loftily, although it
was really Gaston, not me who made the connection.

Just then Lorraine, one of the two assistants, came in.
Jennifer put her to work on the cash and tidying the displays at the front of the store. She then disappeared into
the office. I followed, wondering if I dared tell her I was
leaving again immediately, after my prolonged absence.

Jennifer was putting on a jacket, and putting a book
into her large handbag. "I'm going out for lunch and a
read," she said. "It will help me get over the stress of
having to run this place all by myself."

"Why don't I buy you lunch, as an apology?"

"Sam, you don't have time for lunch. You have to
investigate a murder."

She flipped her hair at me as she turned and walked
out the door. I couldn't see her face but I knew she was
smiling at having got the last word.

There was a time when Montreal was the only city in
Canada in which you could get a decent bagel or cappuc-

cino (although not usually at the same place). The Montreal diaspora has now spread its culinary culture thoughout Canada in the same way that the European diaspora brought it to Montreal in the first place. The displaced Montrealer's need for good cappuccino combined with the modern business practice of franchising everything into large chains has led to the creation of a hundreds of cappuccino bars across Canada. Second Cup is one of those franchise operations. Amazingly, their coffee is quite good and I've been known to spend time at one of their locations when I'm not at the Café Paillon or one of the other independent cafés I frequent.

After making sure that Lorraine and the other bookseller, Yvonne, were not going to be leaving the store for any more appointments or headaches, I headed over to the Second Cup on avenue du Collège, to see whether anyone there could tell me if Allan and Sarah had come in that morning, together or separately. When I walked in, there were two young staff members chatting behind the counter, both wearing the Second Cup uniform—a black polo shirt with black slacks and a black apron with the corporate logo on it. There weren't many customers at the tables. It was too early for the coffee-break crowd from the offices nearby and too late for lunch, and of course the after-work people who don't hang out in bars wouldn't be there till much later.

I zigzagged around the café looking under tables and chairs as if I had lost something. I was able to give what I'm sure was a convincing performance, because I do have a tendency to misplace things, and have more than once had to search theatre aisles, buses, and classrooms for lost possessions. After a fruitless search for my imaginary missing papers, I approached the counter and the young woman, whose name badge identified her as Ellen, asked cheerily if she could help. Her male colleague, Tom, stood at the espresso machine waiting for Ellen to call out my order so he could fill it.

"Actually, you can help me," I told them. "But not with coffee."

Tom must have thought that I was hitting on Ellen because he moved closer to her in a protective way. Ellen, more trusting than Tom, asked, "Tea?"

"I may have lost something," I told them. "A large manila envelope full of term papers."

Ellen clucked sympathetically and looked under the counter. "Nothing seems to have been turned in today," she said. "I'm sorry."

I pretended to be very disappointed, furrowing my brow and sighing, then, "Maybe you can help anyway," I said, acting as if I'd just thought of something.

Ellen was all attention. It was clear that she was a Second Cup employee who took the company's customer relations policy very much to heart. Tom, on the other hand, was beginning to look exasperated.

I played for sympathy, the absent-minded professor who is helpless in the real world. "You see, it wasn't actually me who lost the envelope. It was one of my colleagues from the university. My teaching assistant" — I decided on the spur of the moment to go for broke and pretend to be an academic who was high enough on the totem pole to have a teaching assistant. I sure hoped Tom and Ellen didn't ask for identification — "lost or misplaced the envelope. He said he would find it but I can't really wait for him to get off his duff and do it. My students need their marks." (I hoped that at least one of them was a student and would be impressed by my concern.) "He told me he met his girlfriend this morning for coffee and may have forgotten the papers in the café but then he ran off to a class without telling me what café he meant. It could have been here or the Paillon."

"I wasn't here this morning," Tom said. "I started at noon."

"I was here," Ellen offered. "It's a split shift day for me. What does your TA look like?"

I described Sarah and Allan as best I could, and suggested that they might be regular customers who stopped by at about the same time every morning.

"Oh yeah," Ellen said. "I know who you mean. They're students at McGill. I am too and sometimes I see them on campus. They're always together."

"You remember them, out of all your customers? You must have a very good memory," I flattered.

Tom still seemed to be wondering why I was questioning Ellen with such interest. He had to leave us to wait on a customer, but I noticed he was keeping a beady eye on me as he ran the espresso machine.

"No, no," Ellen was saying, "my memory is terrible, really, but there was something else about them, about him, that made me notice him." She hesitated. She seemed embarrassed by the "something else." My curiosity was definitely piqued. Did she have a crush on him, or what?

"What was that?"

"If it's busy and he has to wait, he'll read one of the newspapers." She pointed to a rack of daily newspapers on a wall adjacent to the coffee bar. "Even when he's with his girlfriend, which is most of the time, he'll get involved in a newspaper and ignore her."

I had yet to meet Allan Gutmacher but I had already formed an opinion of him as rude, politically unenlightened and self-centred. "And that made you remember him?" I prompted.

"Well, no." Another embarrassed pause. "It's kind of silly, but he, I think his name is Allan, sometimes takes things."

"Takes things?" I asked. I was there to investigate a crime and already I had uncovered criminal activity. I had Gutmacher dead to rights — on sugar stealing. "What did he take?"

"The newspaper!" she blurted out. "Well, not the whole paper, just the section he was reading."

"And what would that be?" I queried.

"Usually the editorial section of the *National Post*."

I didn't want her to get the impression I was grilling her, but I had to find out whether Allan and Sarah had been here this morning. I tried to think of a subtle way to phrase the question, and failed. "Did they come in this morning?"

"They usually do," Ellen told me.

"But are you positive they came in together *today*?" I repeated. Really, my information-gathering technique needed work.

Ellen didn't seem bothered. Her round, freckled face brightened. "Yes, I'm sure."

"And do you remember if one of them, that is, Allan, was carrying an envelope? It would have been quite large."

Ellen stopped to think. "Wait a minute, I'm wrong. They didn't come in this morning. That is, not together. He came in first and waited a bit, for her, I suppose, then he bought two coffees and left. Later she came in and she also bought two coffees. I guess someone slept in or something. I didn't see any envelope. He has a briefcase but he didn't leave that here. I'd have noticed a briefcase."

"Do they usually have their coffees here or do they buy them to go?" I asked.

"Oh, to go. They always buy them to go."

"And you're sure that he came in first?"

"Yes. Then her about half an hour later."

"Thank you," I said. "Obviously, he was here, but he must have left the students' papers somewhere else." I put on a glum expression.

Ellen said, "I'll have another look." She crouched down and looked under the counter again, doing a really thorough search for my missing papers. When she popped up again she had a sympathetic look on her face. "I'm sorry, there's nothing back here."

"I'll bet he left them at home," I said. "He may not have misplaced them at all. He could be just trying to get some extra time to mark them." I pasted a smile on my face and looked at Ellen and said, "Thank you. You've been very helpful."

So, I thought to myself as I turned to leave the café, Allan did have opportunity and perhaps a motive to commit murder. I would be able to bring Lemieux another suspect when I met him later. I was feeling so pleased with myself that I forgot to look where I was going and I tripped over a briefcase leaning against a chair near the door. To prevent myself from falling over I instinctively reached out to grab something for balance, and found myself clutching the leather-jacketed shoulder of the guy whose briefcase I had just kicked.

"Hey, buddy," he exclaimed aggressively, pulling away from me and getting ready to defend himself.

"Sorry," I said, embarrassed. "I didn't see you. I was thinking about something. Sorry."

I have a mortifying tendency to blush and I knew my face was probably a deep red by now. Oh, well, it all contributed to my fumbling professor act.

"OK, but watch where you're going."

He was sitting with a laptop computer open on the table. I had almost knocked him, and it, onto the floor. What the hell, I thought, maybe I literally stumbled on Hilliard's missing computer. Then I felt foolish: there were laptops all over the place, how likely was it that this was the one that had been stolen?

"I'm glad I didn't knock your computer over," I said to the guy. "What kind is it?"

He looked at me for a minute trying to figure out what I was up to. First I almost knock him down and then I start poking my nose into his business. But pride of ownership won out. "It's a Mac," he said, looking pleased. "I just got it." I was pretty sure that the secretary had said that Hilliard's computer was a Toshiba.

"Expensive?" I asked, trying to keep the conversation going in the hope that I might learn something of value.

"Not if you know where to shop," he told me in a conspiratorial tone of voice. I wondered what that meant.

"Really? I'm kind of in the market for one myself, but they're so expensive. Where did you buy it?" I didn't know where the conversation was going, but I thought that I would play it out and see.

"Sometimes you can get a deal, if you know what I mean."

I was beginning to understand. The guy had bought a hot computer. Maybe I wasn't so far off the mark.

"Right," I said joining in the conspiracy and sitting down in the chair next to him. "Maybe I could afford one if I got a 'deal'." I did my best to look sincere so that he would trust me with information.

"You a cop?" he asked in a low voice, almost a whisper.

I didn't want to risk the two staff members hearing our conversation and blowing my cover so I whispered back, "No. I'm a bookseller."

"Oh, well then," he said. Obviously that explained why I would need to get things cheap. "I'll tell you where I got it. But you didn't hear it from me."

"No problem."

I sensed that my new friend enjoyed playing the part of a shrewd operator. He leaned over and said in a low voice, "Go down to the Brasserie Lachance. Do you know where it is? It's on Peel. Look for a guy named Ronnie Pepper. Convince him you're not a cop and he'll do business with you."

"How will I recognize him?"

"Think of a guy who never got past his Elvis years and you'll spot him, no problem. And one more thing: his office hours are five to seven. No earlier, no later. Get it?"

"Yeah, thanks," I said. "I'll let you know how I make out."

"No, you won't," he told me and winked. He actually winked. I played along and tapped the side of my nose with my index finger.

"Right," I said, and left the café. It was just about three o'clock. So I went back to the store to make amends to Jennifer by catching up on some paperwork and phone calls until it was time to leave to find Ronnie Pepper.

chapter seven

The Brasserie Lachance is on Peel Street on the west side of the block south of Ste-Catherine Street. It is an oasis of architecture in a desert of black aluminum-fronted fast food restaurants. The Brasse is situated in a 125-year-old two-storey red brick building that housed the Windsor Tavern during the last quarter of the nineteenth century. At some point as the city of Montreal grew up around it, the name was changed to the Peel Street Tavern. When the men-only taverns of Québec came to a legislated end, it became the Brasserie Lachance, either because the owner of the place was a M. Lachance, or because he had a sense of humour and this was his comment on the beer-serving business.

The brick of the building was maroon, almost black, with age and soot. The heavy wooden doors were slightly off alignment and you had to kind of lean into them to get them to swing open. You could still just barely make out the words "Windsor Tavern" in the tiles of the entryway floor. The interior of the Brasserie was finished in dark wood and mirrors. A century of smoking and drinking had helped the wood to age to a rich dark matte and to fade the mirrors.

I'm not much of a pub-crawler. I had only been to the Brasse a couple of times when I was a student. The overall atmosphere of the place when I knew it had been warm, friendly, and noisy. At that time it was popular with students and workers and a bunch of old guys who looked like they were born at around the time the building went up and who were rooted to its foundations.

Things had changed over the fifteen years since I had last been there. The old guys were still there but now they were surrounded by a mob of grey-business-suited men and women from the high-rise office towers along René-Lévesque Boulevard. The students and workers were gone. I had expected a near-empty beer joint, where Ronnie Pepper would be easy to spot. I didn't know how I would find him in that crush.

I needn't have worried. He stood out like a red velvet suit in a boardroom. He was sitting alone at one end of the bar. About my age, he had an elaborate Elvis pompadour, a black leather jacket, black stovepipes, and mod boots like the ones the Beatles used to wear, a white shirt and a thin Frank Sinatra tie from the fifties. The guy was a sartorial history of popular music. I pushed my way through the crowd and sat down beside him.

I ordered a beer. Ronnie Pepper was holding a half glass of beer with both hands, his elbows propped on the padded bar.

"You Ronnie Pepper?" I asked in an undertone. I was trying to act ultra cool but I had a slight fear that I just looked ridiculous.

"Who wants to know?" he asked back. His voice was so low I could barely hear him and it took me a moment to understand what he had said.

"Wiseman. Sam Wiseman." I stuck out my hand to shake his.

He just looked at me, waiting, ignoring my outstretched hand.

"Well, I know a guy who bought a computer, and I need one. He said you might be able to help me out."

"So you're a guy who knows a guy," he said. "What makes you think I have a computer to sell you?" I don't know how he managed to make his voice so quiet and yet so penetrating. He wasn't whispering but he sure had the volume turned down. I guess in his line of work it was a security precaution.

My usual way of dealing with strangers is to try to present myself as likeable and trustworthy. It's almost an instinctive reaction of mine and I could feel myself trying get Pepper to like me now. What a waste of time. The look he was giving me made me abandon that plan in a second. I decided to give free rein to my nervousness; after all, I wanted to convince him I was just an innocent out to get a good deal on a computer.

"I need a computer and I haven't got much money and, like I told you, I met a guy who told me that you might be able to help me out."

"A guy," he said. "This guy have a name?"

"He wouldn't tell me," I confessed.

"But he didn't mind telling you my name, though, did he?"

Ronnie Pepper turned his back to me and pulled a cell phone from an inside jacket pocket and called someone. I couldn't hear a word of the conversation and I thought I had struck out. Dejected, I got up and was about to walk away when he turned back to me and said, "Hey, where are you going? Do you want a computer or not?"

"Yeah, sure I do. I was just stretching my legs," I said nervously.

"Well, stretch 'em by walking out of here and down to the corner of Cypress. Turn right and you'll find an alley. Another right into the alley until you get to a dark van. The guy in the van is expecting you. His name is Albert. What did you say your name is?"

"Sam," I said.

He went back to his conversation. I waited politely for further instructions. When he closed up his phone and put it away, he turned back to the bar, and seemed surprised to see me still there. "Didn't you understand me?" he asked.

"Yeah, Cypress, the alley, Albert," I told him.

"Then ..." he prompted.

I understood that there were no more instructions, no code words or signals. "Thanks," I said.

"Yeah, right. Whatever," said Ronnie Pepper, and turned back to his beer.

I worked my way through the corporate crowd to the door, wondering how may of them bought their Yuppie toys from Ronnie. I realized that he and I had something in common: we were both retailers. He obviously understood the three important rules of retailing: location, location, location. He'd set up shop at this brasserie because it gave him access to a constant stream of rich young consumers — exactly the kind of people I wanted entice into Dickens & Company. It was an uncomfortable feeling, this insight that I was like Ronnie in at least that one way.

I turned onto Cypress but when I got to the alley I stopped to review the situation. It was dark in there, shaded by the buildings on both sides. I wondered if I was walking into a set-up to be mugged. I almost walked past the alley to Stanley Street and safety, but after a moment of arguing with myself I went into the alley.

About fifty yards ahead of me, in the darkest part of the alley, I spotted the van. I approached warily. As I got closer I could see that there was nobody inside. Where was Albert? I edged along the side of the van. A stream of cigarette smoke was coming from behind it.

Suddenly Albert emerged, a cigarette hanging from the corner of his mouth. "Oui?" he said. He managed to look menacing and nondescript at the same time. His cloth cap cast a deep shadow over his eyes and he was both taller and wider than me; he had on dark slacks, a white shirt, a dirty paisley tie, and a windbreaker. His "oui" slipped from between lips that barely moved and were not smiling.

"Je m'appelle Sam," I mumbled nervously.

"Bonjour, Sam," he said. "Je m'appelle Albert. Plaisir." He reached out and shook my hand warmly and a smile crossed his face. I breathed a sigh of relief.

"Tu cherches un ordinateur?"

"Oui," I answered, feeling more confident.

Albert opened the back of the van and stood aside so I could climb in. There was a lot of merchandise back there. Clothes on hangers, sound equipment, lots of CDs, and some computers. I checked out the computers, but there were very few laptops, none of which were Toshibas. Most of them were desktop models and they looked pretty ancient. While I was there I took a quick look to see if there were any books. I was glad I didn't find any. I don't know what I would have done if I had found some with a Dickens & Company price sticker.

I stepped out of the van and told Albert that I was looking for a Toshiba laptop. I asked if he had seen any in the last day or so or if he was expecting one. He eyed me suspiciously and told me that he couldn't remember seeing any Toshibas but that the laptops sold fast and he had no way of knowing what he would have in the future.

I didn't press the issue. I was about to leave when he put a heavily muscled arm around my shoulder and asked, "As-tu besoin d'un système de son? Un veston en cuir? J'ai des bonnes choses en cuir."

"Pas présentement." I backed up a step to discreetly free myself from his arm. "Merci pour ton aide. Je reviendrai si j'ai besoin quelque chose."

"À la prochaine," he said using the international merchant's farewell phrase to a customer.

I turned and hurried out of the alley.

chapter eight

It was quarter to seven by now, time to meet Gaston at Hilliard's apartment building. I walked up Stanley to Sherbrooke and then on to Lefebvre. The place was about nine blocks from the store, straight up the mountain.

Lefebvre is a quiet, tree-lined, gentrified street with brownstones and greystones which were originally the townhouses of the upper-middle class. In the fifties and sixties these houses became rooming houses for the poor, transients and students. In the eighties, yuppies eager to reject their parents' suburban lifestyle reclaimed these houses and turned them into single-family townhouses and condominiums. Hilliard's condo was on the top floor of a converted apartment building, just north of Milton. It had some lovely art deco touches on the archway over the front door, which had been carefully restored.

I had the address in my pocket but I didn't need it. There was a blue-and-white police car parked in front, and Lemieux and its driver were standing on the sidewalk talking. Lemieux saw me as I approached. He lifted a hand in greeting and said, "I'll just be a minute." I took this to mean that he didn't want me to join his conversation. While I waited I gave the street a quick study. There were for sale signs in front of almost all of the condominiums, but none of the private houses. I really had no idea what this meant but I was so into the mode of sleuthing that I automatically made a mental note of whatever I observed. I figured it must mean something.

Gaston came up to me, interrupting my speculations. "Let's find the concierge."

As we entered the building, I started reporting my various discoveries. "I checked the book order in our computer and it turns out that Hilliard's book order wasn't actually his. It was ordered for him by Professor Jane Miller-More. Maybe he meant to point an accusing finger at Miller-More. Maybe she at least knows something."

"Good work, Sam." Gaston was looking around the small lobby for some sign of life. The area was small but there was room for a couple of chairs and a low table. There was a glass door to the building facing the front door and adjacent to it on the left was a smaller wood door. To the left of the wood door was the name board but there was nothing on it that indicated where the concierge was to be found.

I thought he hadn't really been listening to me, but now he glanced over, and said, "We'll have to find out from Professor Miller-More what that's all about when we interview her." The guy was always thinking about at least two things at once. "Right now we have to find somebody to let us in."

I was pleased that he was using the first person plural form in planning his next steps. That meant I was still included in the investigation. He was surveying the the names on the building mail directory as I began to fill him in on my adventures with Ronnie Pepper and Albert.

Suddenly I had his full attention. He was looking at me as if I was out of my mind. "Listen, Sam," he said sharply, "leave the police work to me. You are not to do things best left to my team. Understand?"

"Understood," I responded sheepishly, smarting a little from the rebuke.

I guess he realized he had sounded like a superior officer, scolding me, and he relented. "It's not that I don't appreciate your help, but I have people who are trained to do that kind of work."

I was staring at the names on the board, and I forgot to be miffed when I noticed that one of the names, Grant, was followed by the letter A. "Look," I said, "I'll bet this guy is the super. He doesn't seem to have a whole floor like the rest of them. It's probably the basement apartment."

Gaston said, "You're right," and rang the bell. When after a few minutes there was no answering buzz he tried again. I turned aside and cupping my hands around my eyes, put my face to the glass front door to see if the super was in the hallway or something. He chose that moment to push open the side door, which hit me in the back.

"Oui. Est-ce que je peux vous aider? Can I help you?" In typical Montreal fashion, he asked the same question twice, once in each language. He was an older man, about sixty, neatly dressed in khaki work clothes, and very clearly francophone despite the surname; there was probably an Irish Catholic grandfather or great-grandfather somehere in his distant past. Gaston turned to him and showed his identification. "Bonjour. Monsieur Grant? Je suis avec la police et nous voudrions voir l'appartement du professeur Hilliard."

"Je regrette mais le professeur n'est pas là. Je ne l'ai pas vu depuis ce matin."

"Je sais. Malheureusement, il y a eu une tragédie. Le professeur Hilliard est mort."

The super put his hand over his heart and kind of stumbled backward so that he was leaning against the door he had just come through. "Non, non, ça ne peut être vrai," he stammered. "Je l'ai vu ce matin."

Although the rest of the interview between the concierge and Lemieux took place in French I'll spare you my bilingual rendering and translate their conversation.

"When did you see him this morning?"

The concierge quickly recovered his composure. "Early. He always left early. He and I, we both liked to get off to a good start to the day. I usually saw him in the morning as I was sweeping up."

"Yes," Lemieux said, neutral politeness concealing what I guessed was impatience. "What time was it when you saw him this morning?"

"As I told you, it was early. About seven. Maybe a bit later but certainly before seven-thirty."

"Do you know where he was going?"

"To work I guess. He's a professor over at the university."

"Why do you think he was going to work? Did he say something?"

"Where else would you go at that time? Anyway, he was dressed for it and he was carrying his briefcases."

"He carried more than one briefcase?" Lemieux asked and I could see by the look in his eyes and the slight change in his tone of voice that he thought that this was significant.

"He had his big brown one and his small black one."

"What was the size of his small black one?"

"About like this." Grant answered holding up his hands to show us a shape of about a foot and a half long and a foot high.

"About computer size." I said in English.

Lemieux looked at me and nodded. To the concierge he said, "Has anyone been here this morning? Anyone ringing the buzzer, or just hanging around?"

"No. Only your guy in the patrol car's been parked outside since 9:45 this morning."

"I think it's time we saw the apartment. Do you have a key?"

"Of course I have the key." As he said this he rattled a large ring of keys he removed from his front pants pocket. "Come."

Hilliard's name was beside an apartment number given as Cinquième/Fifth, meaning the fifth floor, I assumed. Mr. Grant opened the lobby door with one of the keys on his ring, a Medico. We use Medicos at the store as a security precaution because they can't be copied, so I recognize them when I see them.

The concierge set off at a quick march and we had to almost jog to keep up with him. In fact, I almost got hit by the door again as I rushed to get through it before it closed. Grant walked to the rear of the building and waited for us in front of a small elevator. He used another key from the ring, a very small one, to buzz for the elevator. There were no call buttons, which I thought was a bit odd. How would an unexpected guest get up to the apartment? Then I realized that was the point. You would have to be let in and the person you were there to see would have to send the elevator down for you. Pretty clever security.

Gaston Lemieux must have had the same thought. He asked the concierge, "Doesn't this building have stairs?"

"Of course it does. Every building does." I think the concierge was beginning to think we were quite stupid; imagine not knowing that buildings have stairs. "They're behind that door." He was pointing to a fire door at the end of the ground floor hall. "It can only be opened from the inside on this floor. For security. You understand?"

The elevator arrived and we got in. There was just enough room for the three of us and I wondered how the tenants moved furniture in on this thing but I didn't ask for fear of appearing really, really thick. I assumed that there was some sort of freight elevator and left it at that.

The elevator doors opened onto a small vestibule on the fifth floor. This area, accessible only to invited guests, was in effect Hilliard's front yard.

The walls were covered with black wallpaper with an abstract design. To the left of the door there was a wooden chair, also black. There was an empty black boot rack to the left of the chair. To the right of the door was a large black vase with a purple abstract design painted on it. The design was floral in nature and there were large green palm fronds in the vase reaching almost to the ceiling. The effect was about 200 percent too stylish for me. In spite of the black walls and accessories there was a lot of natural light coming from a skylight just above the right wall. The place must have been a cave at night when there was no natural light. I only knew Hilliard from the books he read and I had formed the impression that he was an affable conservative sort of a person. The decor of the vestibule was cold and showy and if I were to form an impression of him based on his sense of design I would probably imagine him to be cold and showy as well. I guess he was like the rest of us, made up of various characteristics, some of them contradictory.

Opposite the elevator was the door to Hilliard's flat. The concierge was turning over keys on his enormous, jingling key ring. How he kept them all straight I could not imagine. The guy must have quite a memory. Maybe the keys were marked in a way that I could not perceive. Some of them had coloured plastic rings around their heads but all the keys seemed to be placed randomly on the large key ring.

Thinking about this made me think about the keys that fell out of Hilliard's pocket. As I visualized the keys I remembered that Gaston had said that if the victim's keys were found it meant that the murderer didn't steal them. Suddenly, I realized that he was wrong. I remembered that there were no Medico keys, nor was there a little elevator key for that matter, on Hilliard's key ring. I was absolutely certain of it.

I pulled Gaston aside and said a word in his ear.

"Well done, Sam," he told me. "That's very observant of you. That means we can expect a visitor. If he or she hasn't been here already. I'll make sure the cop parked in front is extra vigilant."

At last the concierge selected a key, another Medico, and opened the front door. Inside Hilliard's condo, the decoration was, if anything, less warm and less inviting than its vestibule. It was all shades of white, and after the blackness of the vestibule I was almost blinded by sunlight reflecting off the various snow and cream and parchment colours. As my eyes focused I realized that the room we walked into was the living room. There was a white six-foot-long sofa against the wall to the left of the door. Across from the sofa were two easy chairs covered in the same fabric, with a blond wood table in the centre of the room. The wall behind the sofa, and the two walls adjacent to it, were painted eggshell white. There were white pine end tables at each end of the sofa holding ceramic lamps which were the colour of white chocolate with white-gold fissures decorating them. The lamp shades were the colour of old-fashioned linen bed-sheets. The floor was covered with a sand white carpet. The ceiling was titanium white, which made the room look big and bright. The wall across from the sofa was probably painted the same eggshell white but I couldn't tell because it was covered from floor to ceiling with bookshelves that ran the length of the wall, about ten feet. To the right of the door was the other half of the skylight I had noticed in the vestibule. The effect of all the light and white made me think of an operating room. It was was nice to look at for about ten seconds but you would need sunglasses to live there. I couldn't wait to get a look at the rest of the place.

"Tabarnoosh," Gaston muttered.

"Yeah," I responded. "This guy sure was neat. It's like a showroom." I half expected the furniture to be lined up in alphabetical order.

I wandered over to the bookshelves to look at the books. You can tell a lot about people by the kind of books they buy. I've learned that people talk about the books they read about in the *New York Review of Books* or the *Sunday Times* but the books they actually buy and read are often a different story. Hilliard was probably one of those people who read what they said they read. The shelves were full of books on history. What amazed me was that the books were organized by topic and period and alphabetized by author or editor. Amazing. More than that, the books were lined up so that the spines were all even and appeared to have been dusted regularly. I wanted to run my finger along the tops of the books to check for dust but I thought that it would be tacky, what with the owner of the books being freshly dead and all. It didn't seem fair to come into a murder victim's house looking for clues to the crime and end up judging him as a housekeeper.

"What do we do now?" I asked.

"We arrange for some privacy," Gaston whispered to me. He turned to the concierge and said, "Thank you very much for bringing us to Professor Hilliard's apartment. We'll let you know when we leave so that you can lock up. I'm going to seal the place when I leave so only the police will be permitted to enter. If anyone else wants access to the apartment you'll have to get my permission. If you notice anyone, anyone at all who does not belong here, trying to get in to the building or this flat call me immediately. Here's my card." Gaston pulled a business card from his blazer pocket and handed it to Grant.

Mr. Grant looked at the card and looked at Gaston. He didn't want to leave but he didn't want to challenge the police either. So he did kind of a nervous little dance at the doorway. He half turned as if to leave and then he turned back to face us as if he was going to say something. He said nothing and backed up a step, stopped, turned to leave, stopped and turned to face us again. He probably would have kept this up until he got dizzy and fell over if Gaston hadn't realized what was happening. Putting on his most reassuring professional manner, he spoke kindly and slowly: "Mr. Grant, I know you've had a shock, but we'll take care of things now. We'll stop by your apartment as we leave so you can lock up." He put his arm around the man's shoulder and gently turned him towards the vestibule and the elevator.

The concierge took one last look over his shoulder and stepped into the elevator. Gaston bumped the apartment door closed with his shoulder and looked around the living room again.

"Well, nothing seems to be out of place."

"That's an understatement."

"So apparently our mysterious visitor has not been here yet. To be on the safe side we'd better wear these.

So we don't disturb any fingerprints or some other evidence." He produced a couple of pairs of surgical gloves from an inside jacket pocket and we both put them on. From the wrists down we looked like a couple of surgeons in search of a patient.

"No computer anywhere," I said, scanning the place.

"Evidently," Gaston answered. "But that's not all we're looking for. We're also looking for clues of a more general nature. Anything that will help us to understand our victim and help us to figure out who killed him."

"Maybe it was the president of the Messy People's Society," I joked.

Ever the diplomat, Gaston ignored me. "It certainly doesn't look as if anything has been moved in a while which means that the killer hasn't been here or knew that the thing he —"

"Or she," I piped in.

"— was looking for isn't in this room. Or the murder had nothing to do with anything Hilliard had and only to do with Hilliard himself."

A wide range of possibilities, I thought to myself.

"Before we start let's check out the rest of the place to see if I'm right."

It took me a moment to see where the rest of the place was. The wall opposite the entrance from the vestibule was cut with an high, arched opening that led to a hallway. The wall of the hall was also painted eggshell white so it almost blended into the living room wall. There was a large painting floating somewhere in my field of vision and it was only after I oriented my sense of perspective to the space that I perceived that it was hanging in the hall beyond the living room. The painting had a white background, the colour of baby's-breath flowers, with very pale faded-red and bleached yellow brushstrokes to create an abstract drawing. It kind of reminded me of a dying computer screen saver. I knew that there had to be a bathroom and kitchen somewhere but I couldn't see where.

I followed Gaston and saw that there were doors, two to the left and two to the right of the back wall, concealed behind the short alcove walls.

One of the doors was on the back wall itself and the other one was adjacent to it. We went through the second door on left and found ourselves in Hilliard's study.

I swear this guy had more books in his house than I had in my bookstore. Three of the four walls of the study were lined with floor-to-ceiling bookshelves except where there were doors for closets. The fourth wall was mostly filled with a window. An easy chair and hassock stood in the corner with a lamp behind and a small table beside the chair. A comfortable place to read. The room was dominated by a large oak desk in its centre.

This room was all done in brown tones. The desk was deep brown oak, the reading chair and ottoman were café-au-lait brown, the wall-to-wall carpet was earth brown, so as not to show the dirt I guess, although I couldn't imagine any dirt actually getting into this place. There was an old, comfortable-looking, cracked brown leather chair behind the desk. The desktop was clear save for a desk blotter, a telephone, and a banker's lamp in the upper left hand corner. No computer. I could imagine working very comfortably in this room. I was tempted to move in.

Gaston walked into the room and opened the closet door. We found a couple of file cabinets in the closet and banker's boxes on an upper shelf. Gaston pulled open a file cabinet drawer and found files, all neatly arranged in hanging folders identified with small tags in plastic holders. We looked at the first one and it said History 541.1/Notes (Teaching) followed by History 541.1/Notes

(Reading) followed by History 541.1/Exams (Mid-Term) and so on. This was one organized guy.

"We'll check out the other rooms to get a sense of the layout of the place and then we'll search with a bit more focus," Gaston said as he walked out of the room with me at his heels. "In particular, please keep your eyes open for a telephone jack for his computer. Like the one you found in his office. I want to know if he used his computer in the same way at home as he did at work."

We walked into the kitchen–dining room area. There was no wall separating the two rooms so there was easy access between them.

One of the walls in the dining room was exposed brick and the colour scheme followed the brick tones. The carpet was russet and the table was a square and reddish brown. There were four matching chairs at the table, one on each side. To the left of the door there was a credenza made of the same wood as the table and chairs, obviously a set. There was nothing on the lacquered tabletop except my reflection. Fingerprints would have been obvious on its gleaming surface but there were none. There was light streaming in from a large window in the wall across from the table.

The kitchen was a standard white kitchen with grey counter tops. It was serviceable, with a stove, fridge, dishwasher and cabinets but none of the accoutrements a person interested in cooking would have had, no interesting spices or kitchen gadgets in sight. Only a coffeemaker, toaster and microwave. Everything else was behind closed cabinet doors.

There was a wall phone in the kitchen but so far as I could see no additional jack for a modem. I didn't think Hilliard would hook his computer up in the kitchen anyway but I was told to be on the lookout for an extra phone jack and I was.

We went down the hall to the final two doors. One led to a small guest bathroom and the other to a large corner bedroom. In keeping with his one colour per room approach Hilliard had chosen beige for his bedroom. The carpet was the colour of wet sand and the walls a bit lighter, the colour of dry sand. There were windows on two walls. The duvet on the queen-size bed was the colour of bronze and the drapes matched it. There was a brass lamp on each of the night tables and one of the tables was piled with books and magazines. The other was bare except for the lamp and a phone. Again, no evidence of an extra phone jack. The light in the room was golden because the sun was setting now.

I wasn't surprised to find that Hilliard's clothes were neatly arranged in his closet. Groups of suits and sports jackets and blazers neatly hung on wooden hangers and arranged by colour. Sports shirts were on plastic hangers and dress shirts folded in their dry cleaner plastic packages and stored on shelves.

Hilliard's bathroom was large and had all kinds of special stuff. A whirlpool tub, a shower with shower heads on two walls and various levels, a hot lamp in the ceiling, two sinks, two magnifying shaving mirrors and a long set of mirrors over the sink that concealed an equally long medicine cabinet. One end of it contained lots of soaps, a shaving brush, shaving cream in a wooden container and a razor, colognes and some over-the-counter medicines. The other end, over the second sink, was empty. Most people's medicine cabinets are overflowing with junk. Hilliard's was neat and only two-thirds full. From the selection of pharmaceuticals and grooming products I got the impression that Hilliard was more concerned about how he looked than how he felt.

Gaston seemed lost in thought as he wandered back into the living room. Turning to me, he asked, "Well, my friend, what do you make of all this?"

Seizing this chance to impress him with my observational skills, I jumped in. "It may be unfair to the recently departed but it looks like this guy had a single-minded, compartmentalized approach to life. One colour per room. Everything organized and in order. Nothing out of place. The only place I noticed anything personal was in his bathroom. He had a lot of, well, what can you call them, beauty products for men. Most guys have one after-shave, one toothpaste, and so on. Hilliard had several of each. Plus different kinds of soaps and cleansers. It looks to me like our victim was as self-centred, tight-assed, and monochromatic as his apartment. But I'll bet that the bedroom got a lot of use."

"What makes you think that?" Gaston asked.

"He lived alone yet the bathroom was designed for two," I explained. "Two sinks, two shaving or make-up mirrors and a whirlpool bath built for two. And empty space in the medicine cabinet for guests. Believe me, this guy liked to control things and make them go his way. But you know, there is one thing out of place."

"What would that be?"

"The smell," I sniffed the air. "There is a very slight but distinct trace of perfume." The scent was somehow familiar to me, but I couldn't think what, or who, I associated it with.

"You are right. But there are no perfume bottles."

"Which means that the perfume, and its owner, were here recently. But here's no sign she ever lived here. Her presence cleaned out of his life just like whatever was her end of the bathroom cabinet."

"You're probably right that his personality was, what did you call him? — Monochromatic and self-centred? Having a sense of what he was like will help us interpret the evidence. I would guess that the reason for his death had something to do with his lifestyle, that's for sure." He wandered over to the sofa and sat down, still focused on his thoughts. I sat down on one of the chairs and my mind wandered as I waited for him speak again. I wondered whether his sister Gisèle was as brilliant a lawyer as he was a police detective.

Gaston snapped me out of my daydream. "This place is neater and more organized than any home I've ever seen. His office was total chaos. So either the murderer came over here and tidied everything up, or he or she messed up the office looking for something. I think it's the latter. There hasn't been time for this kind of tidying up, but wrecking a place can happen very fast. That means that the murderer got what he wanted at Hilliard's office and so didn't have to search his home. We are pretty sure he took the computer; he may have taken other things too. I'm also sure that he hasn't been here, partly because he would have been in hurry and would have made a mess like in the office, and partly because I've had this place under surveillance from the moment I got the victim's address. It's unlikely he could have got in here and out again without being seen."

"So what you're saying is that we're no further ahead than we were before we came here."

"In a way, yes. But that doesn't mean there's nothing here to help us. Let's look around and see if we can find something useful. Let's assume that the murder is in some way connected with Hilliard's work or with someone he knew at work. I'll bet that when he worked at home he worked in the study."

This seemed kind of obvious. I wanted to help but I had no idea where to start. Going through all the books looking for a note or something would take hours. I couldn't look for fingerprints. I didn't know what to do.

Gaston must have got an idea because he stood up and went into the study. I followed and watched as he circled the room until he found the connection for the phone on the desk. "That's what I'm looking for. There are two jacks here and the phone is plugged into one of them. So the other one is probably for the computer." He pulled out one of the drawers of the cabinets in the closet and started carefully flipping through the files.

"That's true," I said. "Now all we have to do is find the computer." I was a little disappointed in myself for not finding the phone jack. So far I hadn't been much of a help.

I sat down at his desk and opened one of the drawers. I was hoping to find an envelope marked "To be opened in the event of my death" but all I found were pencils and pens, a note pad and that kind of thing and the three pennies I think you'll find in every single desk drawer in the world. I opened another drawer and found a stack of manuscripts of books and articles he had written.

I can't explain why I did what I did next. Perhaps it's because I'm a snoopy, suspicious person. Perhaps it's because I'm a slob and I tend to hide things in order to make my desk appear neat. If I had a big clean desk blotter like Hilliard's I would probably conceal stray notes or papers under it. I lifted it up and there, stuck to the desk, was a yellow Post-it note with some writing on it.

"I think I found something!" I was excited.

"Don't touch it," he said, getting there just in time to stop me peeling it off the desk. I pulled my hand away as if the note were radioactive.

We looked at the note. It wasn't clear what the scratchings on it referred to.

"Ham, roman numeral three, and a one," I read. "Or Ham, I, I, I and the digit one."

"Is it a shopping list? Three somethings of ham and one of something else?"

"I don't think so. A shopping list is usually done in regular, you know, arabic numbers and usually contains more than one item. Anyway, why would he hide a shopping list? It's a reference to something he wants to remember. Bible and play references are usually written that way. Like Genesis chapter 4, verse 21 or *Macbeth* act II, scene 1."

Then we both got it at the same moment. "*Hamlet!* Not *Macbeth*, *Hamlet!*" we exclaimed together."

I was extremely proud of myself for finding an important clue. "Hamlet, act three, scene one. That's great! But what does it mean?" I had no idea. I was hoping that Gaston, more experienced than me at these things, would recognize its significace.

But he was as puzzled as I was. "I don't know," he said. "I have to admit I never read *Hamlet*. I've seen it performed in French. I don't remember act three scene one particularly. Do you?"

I hadn't read *Hamlet* since college and couldn't remember the last time I saw the play. It was embarrassing. One thing Gaston ought to have been able to count on from me was my knowledge of all things English and literary. "There must be a copy of Shakespeare around here somewhere," I said hopefully. "We can check it out and see what the significance of the note is."

"We can't take anything off the shelves until the lab detail has checked the place out for fingerprints and such. But you must have a copy at home or in your store. Read it and let me know what significance *Hamlet* has to a murder —"

"Murder in Shakespeare?" I interrupted, giggling. "You must be kidding."

Gaston wasn't amused. "Let me know by tomorrow."

Homework, I thought to myself. I imagined detective work as being more exciting than a freshman

English homework assignment. But I knew Gaston was serious and I decided to read *Hamlet*, at least act 3, that very night.

"Let's go," said Gaston. "I don't think there's anything more for us to do here. We'll have to let the CSU team go over it now."

We left the apartment, and while I called for the elevator he took out a yellow sticker the size of a loonie that said POLICE! ACCÈS INTERDIT, and pasted it over the keyhole of the lock, then pulled the door shut.

As the elevator descended he said, "I want to see the concierge before we leave. I have one more question to ask him."

The concierge was waiting for us when we got off the elevator and it was clear from the way he was leaning against the wall that he'd been waiting there since he left us.

"I've sealed the apartment," Gaston told him. "For the moment only the police can enter it. But I have one more question. Did Professor Hilliard have a housekeeper?"

"Sure, he had a housekeeper. You don't think a busy man like him had the time to clean his house, do you?"

"Do you know her name? Did she have a key? Do you know when she was here last?"

"Not so fast," Grant pleaded. "Her name's Betty. Her last name is one of those English names that is so hard to pronounce. Smitt or something like that."

"Do you mean Smith?" I asked.

"*Oui*, that's right. Smitt."

"How did she get into Hilliard's condo?" Gaston asked.

"She had a key of course. But sometimes she forgot it and I let her in."

"And when was she last here?" Gaston patiently repeated his last question.

"Thursday. She came every Thursday."

"Do you know where she lived?" Gaston asked.

"I don't know. Maybe in Westmount."

I wasn't sure if he meant she really lived in Westmount or if he thought all the English lived in Westmount and therefore that is where someone named Betty Smith would live.

"How do you know she lived in Westmount?" Gaston asked.

"She told me," Grant said with an exasperated tone. "How else do you think I would know? We talked about how long it took her to get here and she said she was lucky she only had to come from Westmount and it was only one bus."

"I don't suppose you know her address, do you?"

"No, just Westmount."

"I'll have to find her then," Gaston said.

"Someone named Smith who lives in Westmount. That shouldn't be to hard. I'm glad I only have to read Shakespeare."

"We'll find her," Gaston said with a smile. "Do you want a lift? I'm finished here."

It was just after eight. I accepted his offer and told him he could drop me on the corner of Hutchison and Fairmount in Outremont. There was someone I had to meet. A date, I guess you'd have to call it.

chapter nine

One of the advantages of running a bookstore more or less in the middle of a college campus is the constant stream of beautiful young women that pours through the door. It's also one of the disadvantages. They get younger every year, of course. Teachers notice that too, I'm told. They also get sillier and sillier. And some of them get silly at the sight of an eligible male in his thirties. I don't know what they see in me, but they seem to find an old geezer like me more attractive than young men their own age; it makes me retrospectively resentful, remembering how their exact counterparts snubbed me when I was twenty. On the other hand, I'm only human. And male. It's sometimes very hard work resisting their blandishments. Jennifer finds the whole spectacle highly amusing. She calls me the "freshies' choice."

Susan was a bit different, though. Definitely not a freshie. The words *terse* and *tough* were invented for her. She was also terrifically attractive, with long, straight black hair and brown eyes so dark they were almost black too, and the kind of perfect Italian skin that comes from the genetic imprinting of hundreds of generations living by the Mediterranean for thousands of years. She looked as if she just got back from a tropical vacation.

She showed up in the store a few weeks ago, zeroed in on me, and handed over a reading list. "I have to read some fiction. Can you help me find these?"

She said "fiction" with the feeling that most people reserve for the words "root canal."

"What's wrong with reading novels?" I asked. "I do it all the time. It's fun."

"Yeah, maybe. I put off an English course till my last semester and now I have to do it to graduate. It's not for fun."

Obviously, her major was not English. I helped her find her novels. Her scorn for them as made-up stories was very clear.

Her no-nonsense attitude was a bit scary, but I tried to defend literature. "Maybe you won't find them all that awful. Anyway, I've read a lot of novels, and these ones aren't bad."

"Yeah, right," she said.

"Really. It would be a shame to blow graduation because of a couple of novels. And after you graduate, in what? Economics? Nuclear physics?"

"Biochemistry."

"Once you're a graduate biochemist you'll never have to read fiction again."

"We'll see," she said. I realized she thought I was hitting on her, and she was making it clear that she could see right through my approach. It was at that point that I actually began to feel like hitting on her.

"Where do I pay for these?"

I pointed her toward the cash counter was she stalked off to pay for her books.

After she paid she took a few minutes stowing the books away in her large, serious-looking briefcase. As her back was turned I took the liberty of admiring the athletic curve of her long legs in black stockings and miniskirt. Only to be caught in the act as she abruptly turned and looked at me with narrowed eyes. For a moment I thought she was going to smack me like an outraged 1950s movie heroine. Instead, taking her time, she came up close and without cracking a smile, she said, "Isn't this the point where you ask me out for a coffee or something to eat?"

For a few seconds I literally couldn't speak. Then, I'm sorry to say, I laughed. I thought she was putting on her tough-girl act either to scare me away or for some kind of joke. I was horrified when her face changed and she suddenly looked as if she was going to cry. A minute before you might have taken her for a wised-up twenty-five-year-old. Now she looked about sixteen, and mortified.

"Well, thanks a lot," she said in a choked voice, and rushed out of the store.

Of course I ran after her.

Over the next few weeks we became — I think the only word for it would be *entangled*.

Susan was one semester away from graduating with a degree in chemistry. She was an American from Rochester in upstate New York, who decided to move to Montreal and McGill University because she figured Montreal was about as far from Rochester as you could get in terms of urban culture and still be in North America where she could go to university in English. I was half correct about her Mediterranean background. Her mother was Greek and her father was from Ithaca, New York.

Her interest in science, it turned out, was genetic. Her mother was a chemist who came to the United

States from Greece to work in the Kodak labs in Rochester, which was where she met her future husband, Susan's father, who was also a chemist at Kodak. Her family was kind of a living Kodak moment.

After Gaston dropped me off I ran to Susan's apartment, late, and she was irritated. Did I mention that all the women I'm drawn to have hot tempers?

"Do you know how long I've been waiting? Do you think I've got nothing better to do than wait around? You're lucky I had lab notes to rework or I'd have been long gone, buster! Haven't you ever heard of the phone? It's a new invention. You find them on every street corner these days."

I loved it when she talked like Katharine Hepburn, but she was right, I do have a problem with punctuality. When I get involved with something I tend to forget that people are waiting for me — usually Jennifer, but now Susan too.

There's no question Susan was a lot of fun to be with. Part of the fun was that she was not terribly interested in the things that interested me. I would talk about a book I had read or about something that I had seen on the news and she would not know what I was talking about. But she had an incisive scientific mind and she didn't accept the things I said just because I said them. She questioned my assumptions and I enjoyed the intellectual challenge of talking to her, though in my heart of hearts I knew it wasn't a basis for a real relationship. I didn't particularly like having to explain why I read what I read, why I liked the movies and plays I liked. The trouble was, the more doubts I had, the more assumptions she seemed to be making about the permanence of our relationship. I knew I would have to disentangle myself, but I wasn't sure how.

Susan wasn't interested in things abstract, the humanities or the arts. On our second date I had made the mistake of taking her to see a Goya exhibit at the museum. She gave me an anatomy lesson at each painting. She explained that the figures were completely out of shape, much too elongated. When I told her that Goya had astigmatism and he painted what he saw, Susan argued that what he saw was not the way things were in the real world and why didn't he get eyeglasses or find another line of work, something where poor eyesight wouldn't be a problem. I knew from this experience never to see a Picasso exhibit with her.

"Sorry," I said. "But I have a good excuse this time. I'm involved in a murder."

"For your sake I hope you were the victim."

"No, really. I'm involved in a murder investigation," I repeated, pointedly not laughing at her joke.

"That's the lamest excuse I've ever heard! You were delayed because you had to commit a murder? Please! You can do better than that."

"I didn't commit murder. I'm working with the police to solve one. Let's go get something to eat and I'll tell you all about it."

"This better be good," she said as she slipped on her jacket and stepped out into the hallway. But she was beginning to believe me. I could tell. And she was beginning to be curious.

There is a café/bakery on every street corner in Montreal. And the corner of Hutchison and Fairmount, about half a block south of Susan's apartment, was no exception except that the Opera Café was a cut above the others in the neighbourhood. I don't know why they called it the Opera Café. They played jazz, mostly blues, on the café sound system and there was nothing even remotely operatic about it. But the coffee, sandwiches, and salads were great and there was always a plat du jour if we wanted something more substantial.

I ordered grilled chicken breasts and Susan had her usual salad. Cappuccino, which I would need to keep me awake to read Shakespeare, followed the food. During the meal I told Susan about my day. She started off pretty skeptical but soon got involved in the mystery. "Do you think you'll find the computer?"she asked.

"We know he had it when he left his condo to go to work and his office was a mess so we have to assume that something was taken and we can't find the computer so it seems likely that that's what was taken."

"Most people put their computers right on their desks. Especially if they carry them around. What I mean is: if the professor carried his computer around with him he didn't hide it. So why would someone mess up the office for something that was right there in plain sight?"

I don't know if Gaston had thought of that; he sure didn't mention it if he had, and I know that I was so wrapped up in the chaos of the murder scene I hadn't considered the obvious. Since the computer was missing we just assumed that the office was trashed in the course of the robbery. But we also knew that Hilliard had not put up much of a fight so the office was not destroyed in a struggle. We didn't put two and two together to realize that the murder, the theft of the computer, and the trashing of the office could have been related sequential events. We assumed the three actions to be part of one continuous event.

Susan had a way of cutting through the illogical clutter of a situation and exposing its central core. She was a lot better at dealing with real-world problems than abstract ones.

"God!" I exclaimed, almost shouting. "We missed the obvious. Hilliard was killed, the computer was taken, but the murderer must have been looking for something else. Obviously something related to the murder and the computer but we don't know what that was and we don't know if the murderer found it."

"Or it, whatever it is, had nothing to do with the computer,"she said and smiled the smile of people who easily cut to the kernel of a problem but don't have to actually solve it.

"Then there's all this business about Shakespeare," I said.

"*Shake*speare." She might have been saying "*dog* turds," if you went by the childish distaste in her voice.

I ignored her tone and told her about the note hidden under the desk blotter. "I'm not sure what it means. Lemieux wants me to read the play tonight, or at least scene one in act three, to see if there is anything there that helps us."

"What makes you think the note is a clue?"

"The fact that it was so carefully hidden and so neatly written seems significant. We can't be sure it has anything to do with the murder. In fact I'm pretty sure it has nothing directly to do with the crime. How could Hilliard know to hide that note in case, some day, he happened to be murdered, in which case the cops would find it and understand it and arrest the murderer? If he knew he was going to be murdered, why not just hide the name of the murderer under his desk blotter? Or better yet, do something to prevent the murder in the first place and avoid the messiness of an untimely death. No, I think the reference to Hamlet has some significance for Hilliard alive, which when we understand it may help us figure out why he was murdered. And I think that Lemieux thinks so too."

I didn't realize it at the time, but what I explained to Susan was prophetic. Gaston and I struggled to understand the significance of the reference to Hamlet to the crime. Neither of us realized for quite some time that the significance of act 3, scene 1 of *Hamlet* was right on the surface, there for anyone to see the moment they abandoned their traditional way of looking at things.

While we were finishing our cappuccinos Susan snuggled up to me and said, "You know, Sherlock, in a way it was a good thing that you were late. It gave me a chance to finish my lab notes so I can devote the rest of the evening to you."

I was strongly reminded of what I liked about Susan. But something about the way she said "Shakespeare" had sent a chill through me. And suddenly a vision of Gisèle's face floated in the air somewhere, just out of reach. I was certain that Gisèle loved and appreciated Shakespeare.

"I can't," I said a little too bluntly. I felt badly that I was brushing her off so I softened my tone and continued, "I have to read *Hamlet*. I can't say that I'm looking forward to it. It's a really long play and I don't know if I'll be able to get through it in one night. But I've got to try or I'll be bounced off the case."

"Oh, well," Susan sighed. "If you prefer murder to me, I guess ..." She let the sentence trail off and sighed again.

I didn't prefer murder to Susan, but I was beginning to fear that she was taking me a little too seriously. The odd reference to her sister's wedding, and how happy it had made her mother, made me suddenly determined to go home and solve a crime rather than get into an extended evening that, no matter what delights it might offer, could also lead to a conversation about our relationship.

I paid and we left the restaurant. I walked Susan home and then headed to my place.

chapter ten

I stretched the fifteen-minute walk home into thirty minutes. Not because I wanted to think but because I wanted not to think. To stretch the walk from Susan's apartment to mine meant taking the scenic route through lower Outremont. Upper Outremont is the enclave to the Québecois ruling class just as upper Westmount is the home of the English-Canadian ruling class. (I always suspected that Outremont was named by the denizens of Westmount as the name literally means "beyond the mountain," not a appellation a group would apply to itself.) Lower Outremont, although mostly populated by Québecois, is more polyglot than the section on the mountain.

I never get tired of exploring Montreal neighbourhoods. No matter how many times I walk the same streets they never lose their charm and mystery, especially the area north of chic Laurier Avenue and south of dowdy St-Viateur. It's a neighbourhood of large, solid brick and stone single-family homes and the uniquely Montreal triplexes. The residents are a mix of the francophone Québecois bourgeoisie and a large Hasidic community. The Hasidim, dressed in their traditional black clothing, and the Québecois in their fashionable black styles manage to coexist, mostly without conflict if not in actual harmony. Maybe it's because both groups have a certain sense of separateness that this happy coexistence is possible. Who knows? As I pass the the houses I try to imagine what life must be like within. Sometimes through an unshaded window I see a well-stocked library and I imagine I'm looking into the study of an intellectual, a professor at the Université de Montréal perhaps. Other times I see a dining room heavily furnished with a table, chairs and china cabinet all of polished dark wood and I imagine the happy shabbas that must be celebrated around that table.

It was a beautiful, clear, cool autumn night and I consumed a peaceful half an hour wandering the streets of lower Outremont before I cut back to Park Avenue and home.

I wanted to clear my head so that I could read *Hamlet* without imagining a clue to Hilliard's murder on every page. I knew that looking at the play that way would lead to sloppy thinking. The note had been left before the murder and I had to guess what significance the act and scene referred to in the Post-it might have had to a living breathing history professor. Of course *Hamlet* is so littered with murder — murder for revenge, murder for ambition and lust, or through mistaken identity, suicide, assassination and murder by treachery — that it would be hard not to think of homicide, poison, and swords, while reading it.

I was refreshed by the time I got home. I felt that I could take on all of Shakespeare's tragedies and I began to look for a copy of *Hamlet*. My house is the exact opposite of Hilliard's. His books were so well organized they were practically card-catalogued; my books, and I have thousands of them, are shelved randomly. I had to remember where things were in order to find them. Not always an easy task. I had a paperback copy of *Hamlet* somewhere but couldn't find it. At last I resorted to a fat *Collected Works* ; it was big and easier to locate than a slim volume. I took it to the sofa in my living room, got comfortable and began to read. I skimmed the first two acts and concentrated on the third and read bits from the rest of the play. I had to read it slowly and more than once before I got into the rhythm and beauty of the Elizabethan English.

The thump of the book hitting the floor woke me up for a second. I shifted my position and felt myself slipping into a dream. I was lying naked on a high rough oak table. There were candles in ornate bronze candle holders at each of the corners of the table. The candle holders were covered in the colourful wax drippings of hundreds of previous candles. Lady Macbeth, who I realized was Susan, approached the table. She was wearing a black hooded cloak and as she walked slowly toward me the cloak opened and I could see that she was naked under it. As I fell into a deeper sleep I remember thinking to myself that I was about to have an erotic dream about Susan and I felt myself getting hard. Lady Macbeth/Susan moved to the foot of the table and threw her head back causing the hood to fall off. She shrugged her shoulders and the cloak fell to the ground. She stood for a moment, her glorious body looking golden in the flickering candle light. She began to walk around the table and as she moved away from the foot of the table she turned into Ophelia and her cloak turned into pale blue. I could see the two goofy gravediggers from *Hamlet* leaning on their shovels beside a freshly dug grave. I became paralyzed with fear and couldn't speak. As Ophelia/Susan moved around me she stroked my body but I couldn't move. Suddenly, Ophelia/Susan had a sword in her hand which she held over her head and chanted, "For whom dost thou glisten, my wanton blade?" She brought the sword to her face and kissed it. "For me? Or for thee?" She then raised the sword over me, sharp point down, and I tried to scream to wake myself up but couldn't. She walked slowly around the table repeating these lines and I noticed that the gravediggers were slowly digging the grave deeper. I couldn't escape. Ophelia/Susan was standing directly above me now, and the sword began to descend. A terrified squawk woke me, breaking the spell of the dream: it was me trying to yell in my sleep.

I sat up, sweaty with terror, and realized that I had fallen asleep in my clothes. My heart was racing and it took me a moment or two to catch my breath and calm down. I looked at my watch and realized it was four in the morning.

I peeled off my clothes and, picking up Shakespeare from the floor, I stumbled to the warmth and protection of my bed, hoping to leave the nightmare in the living room. I truly did not want to know what it meant. But once there I couldn't sleep; a second wind swept over me in a burst of nervous energy, and I got up again. It's true, solving murders can keep you up at night. I read through most of *Hamlet* and half of *Julius Caesar*. At six o'clock I took a nap.

chapter eleven

At seven-thirty that same morning, feeling a bit spaced out but wide awake and ready to take on the day, I showered and dressed. I made it into work by about 8:15.

Our store is designed to give the customer a feeling of comfort and privacy. There are upholstered chairs scattered around so that customers can browse comfortably and the free-standing shelving units are over six feet high so that people don't realize that they are in a store with lots of other people in other aisles they can't see.

They can be heard, however.

I was at the service desk preparing and signing cheques, so that Jennifer wouldn't have any more embarrassing experiences with publishers' accounting departments, when I heard two familiar-sounding voices drifting over from the history section. At first I didn't recognize the voices but I sure knew what they were talking about. The murder.

"Hi," said a woman's voice. "I didn't expect to see you here."

"I don't teach till one so I thought I'd browse for a while," answered a man.

"Isn't it awful about Hal?" the woman asked and my ears pricked up. Stealthily, I moved around the book-shelves so that I could see without being seen. It was Macauly Edwards, the chairman of the history depart-ment, talking with Sally Howard, one of the professors. Gaston had interviewed them at the faculty club. I tiptoed back to the service desk and eavesdropped.

"Do you think anyone in the department could have done it?" Sally inquired.

"Well," he returned in a tone of slightly embittered amusement, "I can think of a couple of possibilities, can't you? It could have been, well, the obvious person. Or someone somewhere else in the university. But I think suspicion is going to fall on us first."

"Us? We didn't do anything." Sally Howard sound-ed a little concerned, a little panicky for someone who didn't do anything.

"I don't mean you and me," Edwards explained. "I mean members of the department. Luckily no one said much to the cops about what's been going on."

Not for long, I thought to myself.

"What do you mean?" asked Sally.

"I don't want to talk about it here," said Edwards. "I'm meeting Carla for coffee at the Patisserie Belge. Join us and we'll talk about it there. It's more private."

They left the store. For a moment I wasn't sure what to do. It didn't take me long to realize that I had to fol-low them to get the information they didn't give when Lemieux interviewed them. I asked Nicole to cover the service desk, found Jennifer and told her what I was about to do. She was less than thrilled, and told me I should plan to hire some extra staff while all this was going on, and pay them out of my own pocket, because she was getting tired of covering for me. Then she gave me the evil eye, making sure I felt as awful as possible. She was right, of course, and I tried to look shamefaced to appease her, but nothing could have stopped me at this point with such a hot lead to check out.

I left, with her snarls following me out the door. I grabbed a *Gazette* on my way out so that I would have something to hide behind if necessary. By this time my quarry had a five-minute head start, but since I knew where they were going I didn't have to actually shadow them.

The Patisserie Belge is a great little place on the corner of Milton and Park Avenue. When I'm heading that way I usually spend a minute or two looking in the window of the Word Bookshop, a second-hand bookstore at the corner of Milton and Durocher, to see which books have staying power. The owners, Lucy and Adrian King-Edward, change the window display on a daily basis. I didn't have time to stop, but I did take a rapid glance as I hurried by: today it was various titles by Nietzsche.

When I arrived at the patisserie the professors were already seated in a corner behind a large plant. I was pleased they hadn't decided to sit out on the terrace; they'd obviously chosen the corner for privacy. I took a table on the other side of the large plant and sat with my back to them so that I wouldn't be spotted. The better to hear you, my dears, I thought. I ordered a latte and croissant in a barely audible whisper. The waitress must have thought I was loony or recovering from a throat operation, but I was afraid the profs might notice me if they heard my voice.

Sally Howard still seemed to be in the dark and I assumed from the conversation that she was a new member of the department. Carla Schwartz, on the other hand, didn't seem to know the meaning of the word *indecisive*. She was clearly in control of the conversation.

"We were right not to tell that cop too much," she said. "But I can tell you that I'm surprised that Ron didn't kill him at lunch the other day." She must have been referring to Ron Michaels, another one of the group we interviewed at the faculty club.

"Why would Ron want to kill him?" asked Sally.

"Because Hal was about to publish a shitty review of Ron's book," Mac answered.

"You don't kill someone over a bad review," Sally protested.

"I'm only saying Ron might have wanted to kill him. I'm not saying he did. Ron doesn't have tenure and he was depending on his book to get it for him. A bad review is bad enough; coming from a member of your own department it's the kiss of death at tenure review." Carla sounded angry. "Frankly, I felt like killing Hal myself I felt so terrible for Ron. He's a nice guy and a decent historian. Hal should never have agreed to write that review, let alone say what he really thinks."

"It hasn't been submitted yet," Mac said. "The version we saw was a draft. He was going to polish and submit this week. I think he was killed before he got the chance to send it along. And I hear that his computer is missing so the review is probably missing as well. Lucky break for Ron."

"Lucky?" exclaimed Sally. "I hardly think that someone getting killed is lucky."

The conversation continued in that vein for a while. Carla and Mac managed to convince Sally that it would be best not to volunteer any information to the cops about one of their colleagues benefiting from the murder. After all, Mac insisted, he hadn't actually committed the crime. How can you be so sure? I silently asked him. From what I remembered of my own university days tenure was the brass ring on the academic merry-go-round. I was pretty sure that most of the academics I knew would kill to get tenure, or at least seriously contemplate it, if they thought that they could get away with it. Sally didn't sound totally convinced that silence was the best policy but she agreed to go along with her two senior colleagues. They agreed that as they had informal conversations with department members they would try to get the point across, without actually being explicit, that *omertà* was the best policy—for now anyway.

I let them leave the restaurant ahead of me. I dawdled over my latte, croissant, and *Gazette*, paid my bill and left.

I thought it best to avoid McGill on my way back to the store so I walked down to Sherbrooke and flagged a cab.

I got back to the store to find Jen being confronted by a poet I knew all too well, a tall, undernourished-looking guy with oily blond hair and a stringy Ho Chi Minh goatee. He was trying to talk her into carrying his slim book of poems. Normally I would hide if I saw him come in, but I decided to rescue Jen this time to get on her good side.

"Ah," she said gratefully as she saw me approach. "Here's my partner. You know Sam, don't you? He's actually in charge of poetry. I'll leave you to him. Sam, Simon has a new book of poetry that he's sure will sell." Giving me gleeful smile, she turned and scurried away.

Simon Lucas sensed that there was a subtext that he didn't fully understand but he seemed happy enough, if happy is a term that can be applied to a poet, to tell me about his slim volume. He had a peculiarly loud singsong voice, like a man who's used to not being listened to. "This is my best book ever. Some really fine poems. People will buy it, people who love poetry, good poetry, that is, not this commercial crap." He lifted a volume by a "best-selling" (read: five copies a year) poet an inch off the shelf and then let it drop back, saying "Peh."

I have never understood why poets can't talk for ten seconds without getting a dig in at other poets.

All bookstores carry poetry. It's not a real bookstore without it. But the sad fact is that supply far outstrips demand. Not only do we carry the classics and "commercial crap," but we are approached by at least three poets a week who have self-published their poems and want us to carry their books. Simon Lucas was one of a series. Normally, I hand these guys off to Jennifer. She is the buyer after all, but this time I had allowed myself to be trapped. So I capitulated: I agreed to take a few copies of his book on a consignment basis for a couple of months. However, I stipulated that he was to come back in sixty days to pick up any unsold copies. He seemed pleased by this prospect and asked when he would get paid. He didn't mind taking the money now if that worked out for me. I sighed inwardly and explained that "consignment" meant that he got paid only if and when his books sold. That was why he was to check back. He seemed disappointed at not becoming a paid poet on the spot, but agreed to my terms. I gave him a receipt for his books.

"I have one more question," he said. "Do you know if other stores will carry my book?" He was a nicer person now that he was off his high poetry horse. Montreal booksellers are a pretty collegial lot and I didn't mind recommending other stores for him to call on. I told him to try the Double Hook.

Judy Mappin, the store's charming owner and the doyenne of Canadian bookselling, feels pretty much as I do about consignment books of poetry, though we both consider it an important contribution to the community to carry these books. Unlike me she doesn't try to evade the responsibility; she is very welcoming to the poets of Montreal and arranges readings for them in her store, which is devoted exclusively to Canadian literature in English. I find it somewhat ironic that the only Canadian city that is still willing and able to support such a bookstore is Montreal.

Simon left happily to call on the wonderful group of women who staff the Double Hook. I went to find Jennifer. I found her in the fiction section checking titles. We have a computer that keeps track of what sells, what is on order, and what should be returned to the publisher. Like all good buyers Jen uses the computer as a tool and check the books in the sections to ensure that we have the right balance and mix of titles.

"So?" she asked. "How did you make out with the people's poet?"

"Just great. I'm sure we'll sell tons of his stuff."

"Great," she said. There followed a long tense silence and I waited. I knew she was angry with me and I didn't want to run off and leave any bad feelings unexpressed. Finally she spoke. "Sam, you can't just vanish on the spur of the moment and leave me to do everything. It's not right."

I put my hand on her shoulder, looked her sympathetically in the eyes and said, "I know, Jen, and I'm sorry. But it's kind of like living out a fantasy. Every young boy plays detective and I'm getting a chance to do it in real life."

"Well, I have a fantasy, too. A fantasy that I'm actually going to make a living running a bookstore, and I can't do it alone. I need you. And if not you I need you to make sure that there is enough staff so that I can get the things I think are important done. Understand?"

"You're right. I want to stick with this case for as long as I can but I'll make sure that you're not left in the lurch. OK?"

"Fine," she said. There was another silence and I waited to see if there was more anger to come. There wasn't. She smiled at me and gave me a light punch on the shoulder, our private signal that whatever disagreement we were having was over. For the moment anyway. I returned the punch and went to work. The first thing I did was get on the phone to bring in extra staff so that Jen would not have to worry if I took off again. I then worked on receiving — ensuring that the invoices that come with the shipments of books and the contents of the shipment match.

I worked steadily until just after one-thirty when Jennifer stuck her head around my office door and said excitedly, "He's here!" And and looked at me expectantly, waggling her neat eyebrows.

"Who's here?" Jennifer is not impressed by famous writers. She is as able to estimate the potential success of a new Margaret Atwood as impartially as the work of a first-time novelist. But she is in awe of the writers whose work she likes, so I thought one of the few she venerates must have dropped by unexpectedly to sign a few copies of his or her new book. They all do that, big or small.

"The cop. The murder guy you're involved with. What's his name, Lemieux."

"Gaston Lemieux is here to see me?"

"Yeah. Is it really true? Are you actually involved in a murder? It must be true, if he's here."

"I told you," I replied testily. "Why do you believe me now?"

"Because he said so."

"What did he say?"

"He said that he had to see you about a little matter you were helping him out on. God, it's so exciting — 'a little matter'!"

"Jennifer, you surprise me. I've never seen you this hyper about something that didn't involve good writing."

"Well, it's fascinating. More interesting than books, that's for sure."

"You're right. It is. And I'm enjoying it. That's horrible, isn't it? To enjoy something associated with the death of someone?"

"You're only human. Why shouldn't you enjoy it? You didn't kill the guy."

"Thanks, Jen," I said. I stood up to go to meet Lemieux. "You always know the right thing to say to cheer me up. Come on." I took my *Collected Works of Shakespeare* with me.

I expected to find Gaston calmly browsing in fiction. Instead I found him pacing in the open area around the service desk, deep in thought.

"Gaston," I said walking over to him. "You remember my partner, Jennifer Riccofia, don't you?"

He took her extended hand and made a slight bow over it. For a moment I thought he was going to raise it to his lips. Apparently Jennifer did too, because I noticed that she was blushing.

"I apologize for taking Sam away from his duties. I hope I am not causing you too much inconvenience, but he is becoming a big help to me," he told her.

"Oh, thank you for being so considerate. I'm sure I'll be able to do without him for a while." God bless you, Jen, I thought to myself. I owe you one.

"Now I must impose again," said Gaston. "I gave Sam an assignment and I want to see if he completed it. Can I take him away for a few moments? I need to hear his report."

From Gaston's manner, you would think I had solved the case. All I had done was give up a few hours of sleep to read Shakespeare. I was apprehensive as we walked over to the Café Paillon. I hoped that what I had read really would be some help to him.

As soon as our lattes were placed before us I began to tell Lemieux what I had read in *Hamlet*. "This is one hell of a play. There's enough violence, anxiety, revenge, scandal and general moodiness for an entire season of television. Hamlet is pretty depressed in act three scene one. In fact he's pretty depressed throughout the play, but in that scene he gives the famous soliloquy, 'To be or not to be: that is the question,' and later on in that same speech there's the line about, 'in that sleep of death, what dreams may come, when we have shuffled off this mortal coil ...'"

Gaston didn't say anything, just nodded thoughtfully.

So I rambled on. "Does that mean that Hilliard was melancholy or depressed? It could. Hamlet's love life is going nowhere with Ophelia and he's angry with his mother. So does that mean that Hilliard made a note of that scene because it describes how he felt? But what could that have to do with his murder? Unless he was tricked into a duel and killed with a poison-tipped sword like Hamlet it's not much help to us. It's not exactly a message with a direction 'To be opened in the event of my death.'"

Gaston said, more to himself than to me, "Well, it could have been kind of accusation. There is no question he was murdered. And the note was found in one place and the body in another. It must have some other significance. *Hamlet* meant something to Hilliard that we don't understand yet."

We were both silent for a few moments. As usual Jake and Jackie were snapping at each other in Romansh or Serbo-Croat or whatever their native language is. There was a guy sitting at a table beside the window who was writing something in a black notebook. He was dressed all in black and hadn't shaved or combed his hair in at least a week. Another poet, obviously. It wouldn't be long before he self-published his poetry and tried to force Jen and me to take the book on consignment. It seemed a long time since this morning, when I'd followed Mac Edwards and Sally Howard and listened in on their conversation with Carla Schwartz.

I realized I hadn't yet told Gaston about all that. "This morning I—"

At which point Arlene Ford materialized at our table. She just stood there looking belligerent. Gaston, ever polite, rose. "Ms. Ford. How are you? Would you join us for a coffee?"

I wanted to get up too, but she was standing so close to me that I would have knocked her over if I'd tried. So I half rose and indicated the empty chair at our table. "Yes, please sit down."

"OK," she said, and sat abruptly.

I groped in my mind for something to say, but came up with nothing.

Jackie came over and without waiting for her to speak, Arlene said, "Cappuccino." Then she turned to Lemieux and asked, "Have you found the murderer yet?"

"Alas, no. But Sam and I have just been discussing it. Do you happen to know whether Professor Hilliard liked Shakespeare particularly? Did he ever talk about *Hamlet*?"

"Shakespeare? Shakespeare? What has Shakespeare got to do with murder?" Arlene asked. "I never heard him mention Shakespeare. He went to the theatre from time to time and to Stratford every couple of years. But I don't think he had a particular passion for Shakespeare or anything like that. Why do you ask?"

"We found a reference to *Hamlet* on one of those yellow sticky notes in his study. It was hidden. It looked like it was a reminder of something but we don't know what."

"You were at his apartment?" Arlene seemed unpleasantly surprised by this. "Already?"

"We searched it yesterday," Gaston informed her. I wondered why she was so taken aback, when she had given us Hilliard's address herself. Did she think the police would not visit the apartment of a murder victim? Or that we just knocked and, getting no answer, went away again?

"So, what did you find?" she asked, trying and failing to make the question appear conversational.

The expression on Gaston's face, though it was studiously neutral, told me that he too had sensed that Arlene Ford was nervous about something. He gave me a look that told me to keep quiet so that he could try to get Arlene to open up.

"Well, the place was very tidy. It was easy for us to go through his belongings to see if anything appeared to be out of place. And the lab crew is probably there right now, checking for fingerprints and other physical evidence."

"Yes, he was unbelievably neat," Arlene said in a very soft voice. She looked a bit panicked. "So if there was something there that didn't belong to Harold you would have found it?"

"Yes, of course. But we don't broadcast that kind of thing. We save it so that we can use the information at the appropriate time."

We were quiet. Arlene wasn't very good at hiding what she was thinking. It was clear from her guilty look that she was worried about what we might have found. Something of hers? I could almost read her thoughts. Gaston and I had both guessed that she was keeping a secret of some kind, and it looked as if we were getting too close for comfort. She was frightened that we had evidence that might point to her and she was wondering whether she should open up to us now or wait to see what we knew.

Gaston, without telling her anything, had made her believe there had been something there that shouldn't have been and she was worried about that. Very clever. Gaston was able to deceive her without lying; you have to admire that in a person.

Of course, we hadn't actually found anything that we associated with her.

Or perhaps we had, I thought, suddenly remembering the perfume that had lingered in the air.

Gaston and I sipped at our coffee and said nothing as Arlene twisted her coffee spoon in her hand and continued to think. Finally she convinced herself that she had better talk now or things might be even worse later.

"I may have left something there," she said in a low nervous voice.

"Tell me about it," Gaston said encouragingly.

"Something personal," she continued. Her skin had turned a greenish white colour and I could see beads of perspiration at her hairline and on her upper lip. She looked as if she might faint or throw up. She pulled her large leather handbag up onto the table and started to fish around in it for something, sniffling and on the verge of tears, looking for a tissue, I assumed. The bag was large and she had to dig through a lot of stuff. I could hear the click of the things inside her bag banging into each other as rummaged around.

And then the most amazing thing happened. She froze. The sniffling stopped, colour returned to her face and cheeks. Whatever she had feared, whatever precipice she had been hesitating on, seemed to have vanished. Her expression changed to one of secretive satisfaction. She was not going to tell us what she came so close to confessing.

Sighing with relief, she took out a Kleenex and snapped her handbag shut. "It's something personal," she said again, in a louder, more self-confident voice. "I did some extra work for him at his place and I left a pen and pencil set there. It was an expensive gift, a Mont Blanc, from someone very dear to me and I really don't want to lose it. It has great sentimental value."

She gave a fake little sniff and dabbed at nonexistent tears in the corners of her dry eyes. This was meant to convince us that she was telling the truth about some object that was so meaningful that she was overcome at the thought of having lost it. It was a good save, almost, but she was not much of a liar. We saw right through her. Still, what could we do?

"What kind of work did you do for him at his place?" Gaston asked suspiciously.

"Proofreading. I proofed his manuscripts for him. The university doesn't let us do that as part of our jobs as it would take too much time and it's unfair anyway because not all the professors need proofreaders. So I picked up a bit of extra money moonlighting as an editor. I did a lot of work for Hal and I must have left my pen at his place. Is that what you found? Please tell me it is."

She looked Gaston straight in his eyes and covered his hand with hers to convince him of her sincerity, I suppose. Luckily she didn't see me raise my eyebrows when she referred to our victim as Hal. Somehow, the nickname seemed too informal. To me he was Professor Hilliard, the historian.

Gaston wasn't buying it. "I'm sorry. There was no pen and pencil set there. If we find it I'll let you know."

"Oh, thank you so much," Arlene said, getting up to leave. "I'm so worried about my writing set. I'm glad

I ran into you, because at least I know now that I didn't leave it there."

"Please. Just one moment before you leave. There's something I'd like you to do for me. Sit down for just one more minute." Gaston, too, had stood up and was now holding the back of Arlene's chair inviting her to sit down again.

She resumed her chair and was beginning to get that trapped-animal look in her eyes again.

"There are some people in the history department that I must see. I'd like you to set up appointments for me and my colleague to meet with them tomorrow morning." Gaston reached into an inside pocket of his blazer and pulled out his notebook and flipped through it. "I need to see, ah, yes, here they are — Sarah Bloch, Jane Miller-More and Allan Gutmacher. I'd like to see one of them at ten o'clock and the others at eleven and noon. Can you arrange it? I'll use the conference room if no one minds."

"Well, I don't know if I can summon people just like that. And what if the conference room is in use?"

"Just tell them that you are co-operating with the homicide investigation. I'm sure that the university wants to help in any way that it can." Gaston gave her a hard look to convince her that he was in no mood for any more prevaricating from her; not after her earlier performance about the lost Mont Blanc pen and pencil.

"I'll do what I can," Arlene said as she got up to leave. Again, Gaston was on his feet a split second after her.

"Thank you. I appreciate your co-operation," he said, meaning that he expected her co-operation.

Arlene Ford turned and walked away without thanking us for the coffee.

"Did you believe any of that?" I asked after she was safely out of the café.

"Not really."

"Then you think she did it?"

"That's not what I said. But she is not telling us everything she knows. She could be the guilty person or she could be afraid that she will look guilty if we find whatever thing I almost convinced her we had found."

"So you don't think she did it?"

"I don't know. She is a suspect, that's for sure. Whether she's one of many suspects or the prime suspect we'll know only after we interview some more people. She obviously thought she had left something at Hilliard's place, something small enough to fit in her bag and personal enough that we could identify it as hers. And it was that specific thing. She didn't mind telling us she'd been there and had left her nonexistent pen there. But then she found it in her bag, whatever it was, and regained her composure. Do you have any idea what it might be?"

"It could be anything from a wallet to cosmetics to birth control. Her bag was large enough to hold all that plus a change of clothing."

"I hadn't thought of that. It could be an article of clothing as well as one of those other things."

"We're not getting very far, are we?" I asked.

"Don't be impatient. It's very early in the case. Unless the perpetrator is found at the scene with some incriminating evidence these things take time. Remember, the murderer is in no rush to be found. It will take a couple of days just to sort out the details and determine who the suspects are."

"Speaking of suspects," I said. "I was going to tell you before Ms. Ford came in that I've found another one."

Gaston looked both surprised and amused, but as I told him the story of the small and impromptu meeting of the historians the hard-eyed, analytical-detective look returned.

"... and that may explain the connection to Hamlet," I concluded. "Maybe Hilliard was telling us that if he was ever found murdered it would be due to revenge or trickery and the murderer would be a member of his court — his department — I mean."

Gaston could barely suppress a smile as he listened to my conclusion. He relaxed into his chair and said, "I don't know if *Hamlet* points the finger at Professor Michaels but you certainly do. I will definitely have a talk with him. You have done good work, Sam, but please be careful about doing things that are best left to the police. I'll solve this crime. Don't worry."

Didn't he know me well enough yet to realize I wouldn't give up? I was still puzzling over the two objects we were looking for: a laptop computer and something of Arlene Ford's. In one case we knew what the object was but not where it was, and the other we knew where the object was — in Arlene Ford's bag — but not what it was. It was a devilish riddle. I loved it.

Gaston got up and pulled some money out of his pocket to pay for our coffee. "I suppose you'll want to join me for the interviews tomorrow morning," he said casually.

"I'd like that, yes," I said, delighted and at the same time feeling guilty about dumping all my real work on Jennifer. But I was hooked. I intended to see this thing through.

"OK. Meet me at the history department at ten. Actually, I'd like you to get there early. Maybe the reluctant Ms. Ford will open up to you if I'm not there."

Back at the store I found Jennifer trying to bring order out of chaos. We had just received a very large delivery of books and the boxes were spread all over the place.

Jennifer was directing two of the staff members, Nicole and Rob, on the order in which she wanted to boxes stacked. Our stockroom wasn't very large and the overflow of boxes would have to remain in the store until the books were received into inventory.

When people find out I work in a bookstore they get all dreamy-eyed and talk about all the books I must get to read. I tell them about the tonnage of books I get to carry around. People think books walk into the store and float up onto the shelves, but alas they have to be heaved, and believe me, boxes of books are heavy. It takes brawn as much as a love of reading to work in a bookstore.

After the boxes were stacked Jennifer said, "Nicole, you and Rob will have to handle things for a while. Sam and I have some very important things to discuss. If things get busy call me but I think you'll be OK. Anyway, Bill and Jim will be in in about an hour so you can take your breaks. Sylvia is working in the back but I'll send her out to help. Your office or mine, Sam?" she said, directing her attention to me.

This was a joke we never got tired of telling each other. We shared an office that was barely large enough to accommodate the two of us, with no room for a visitor. When Jen had an appointment with a sales rep I stayed out of the office so they could both sit down.

"Mine," I said. "I just had a wet bar installed."

On the way through the stock room to our office I got a couple of Snapples from the fridge in the corner while Jen sent Sylvia out to help in the store and we settled down to our important meeting.

"OK," Jen said, popping the top on her Snapple. "Spill. I want to know everything that happened between you and your cop."

I told Jen what happened at the Café Paillon in as much detail as I could remember. And that's a lot of detail as I have a good memory.

"She's up to something," Jennifer snorted when I finished my story. "She didn't lose a pen and pencil set."

"We figured that out ourselves. Neither Gaston nor I are all that sure what women carry around in their purses. Help us. If we could peek into Arlene Ford's bag what would we find?"

"You guessed most of the stuff. There might be a cheque book and an agenda as well. And certainly an extra pair of pantyhose if she wears them at all," she told me.

"All right. Of that stuff, what is she likely to panic over if it were discovered at the scene of a crime?"

"Not the make-up, that's for sure, unless the make-up case was special. Engraved or something. Women leave make-up all over the place. We just replace it. It could be a piece of jewellery that would be pretty easy to identify as belonging to her, especially if it was engraved. If she left birth control pills or a diaphragm around somewhere that could be embarrassing, especially if you could trace it to her somehow. Any other medication could be easily identified as hers as would a chequebook or an agenda. It might be harder to determine who belonged to a stray piece of clothing, or worse, intimate apparel, but if you could figure it out no woman would want to have to explain how or why she managed to leave a man's apartment without that article, especially if it's something like underwear or a bra."

Jennifer confirmed what I had been thinking but it didn't bring me any closer to a solution. I was dying to know what Arlene Ford had discovered safe and sound in her bag.

"Not to change the subject," Jennifer said. "But as I told you while you're off playing detective I'm going to need some extra help around here. Have you arranged for it?"

"Yeah. It's not a problem. Sylvia wants some extra hours and so do a few of the others."

"Can the bank balance stand the extra expense?" the ever worried Jennifer asked.

"No problem," I told her. And if there was a problem I would solve it later.

We had a late appointment with the sales rep from Murray & Kerr, Jen's former employers, to discuss an author tour. Jennifer and I chatted about business and books for a while longer while we waited for Mary-Anne Dolan, the M&K rep to show up.

She arrived promptly at four-thirty and as was her habit wasted very little time with chit-chat and got right down to business. Mary-Anne wanted to arrange for Allison Fitzgerald to have a reading and autographing at our store some time in early November. Jennifer thought it would be a good idea and since I look after this kind of thing she set up a meeting for the three of us to make plans. Arranging for an author visit is not as simple as it may seem. First the sales rep proposes an author and works out a potential date, then the bookseller and someone from the promotion department of the publisher make the final plans, including advertising and the division of expenses. The publisher normally pays for up to half the advertising according to a complicated formula that it works out for each bookstore. I don't really understand the formula or the need for it and I've never met a bookseller who does understand it but so long as I get the amount of money I'm owed I really don't care how the formula works. We concluded our business at about five and Jennifer and I each spent an hour or so finishing up paperwork, order processing and bookkeeping — all the stuff that keeps a small business running.

Just after six I turned off my computer, stretched and asked Jen if she wanted to go out to dinner. "Don't you have to go out with young Susan?" she asked with a bit of a snippy tone in her voice.

"Not tonight. Too busy with her homework."

"OK, then. Where do you want to go?"

We agreed on Philinos, a family-owned Greek restaurant on Park Avenue. The food is great, the atmosphere warm and friendly, and the staff all family members. One of the great things about the place was that they didn't mind if two people shared one order — and the portions were large enough that Jen and I could easily do that and both have plenty to eat. Over beers, while we waited for our brochettes and salad, Jen again asked me about Susan. Although Jen was never judgemental about my girlfriends I don't think she entirely approved of Susan. We had got past our sexual feelings about each other, more or less, but we didn't accomplish this at the same time — nor was the solution permanent. There were times when I felt a strong attraction to Jen and I was almost certain she sometimes felt the same way about me. The problem was, we had never felt the same way about each other at the same time, and we had taken to referring to our ill-timed crushes on each other as a big joke. I certainly didn't want to ruin our friendship, not to mention an excellent business partnership, by getting serious about the "joke." Besides, what if I was wrong?

We sat out on the small terrace of Philinos enjoying an after dinner Cointreau talking about nothing in particular, books we had read, movies we'd seen, and industry gossip. The night was warm, and the moon sailed above the city street full and bright. We were sitting side by side and Jenny leaned her head on my shoulder and sighed. I put my arm around her and sighed back. My feelings for her at that moment were totally fraternal. In spite of her boyfriend of the moment I'm not sure that her feelings toward me at that moment were equally platonic. We left the restaurant arm in arm. She lived a couple of blocks east and north of me on Jeanne-Mance so I walked her to her door. After a chaste hug and kiss good night I walked back to my place to an early night of dreamless and much-needed sleep.

chapter twelve

I woke up early feeling refreshed and energetic and I treated myself to a run on the mountain as the sun came up over Montreal. There is no better start to the day than a run up Mont Royal in the early morning. My preferred route takes me up the east side of the mountain and affords me a glorious view of the Montreal skyline as I pant up to Beaver Lake. If I'm feeling really energetic I push on to the top of the mountain to the cross that dominates the city below. The only sounds are the rustle of the wind in the trees, the rhythmic thump of running shoes on the hard-packed earth of the path, and huffing and puffing — mine and that of the other runners. It was great preparation for my next detecting assignment: a return visit to the history department at McGill University.

Lemieux's message to me was clear: I was to use the informality of my unofficial status and as much charm as I could muster to get Arlene to take me into her confidence. I wasn't all that optimistic that I — or anyone — had enough charm for that, but I was prepared to give it a try.

I thought it would be a good idea to bring a small bribe and so I stopped in at the Café Paillon on my way to pick up a couple of cappuccinos to take with me. Something more tangible might have worked better but a well-made cappuccino has helped me to smooth relations with members of the opposite sex on more than one occasion.

I retraced my steps along Sherbrooke Street to the McGill campus and into the Elwitt Building to the history department. Before I opened the door to the department I put on my best smile and a warm look in my green eyes. I don't know why I bothered.

"You're early," Arlene Ford snapped at me as I walked through the door. "No one is here yet. Especially not the cop."

Without losing the smile or the friendly look in my eyes I got my shoulder under the rock and started pushing it up the hill. "Yes, I am a bit early. I'm sorry. I hope I'm not disturbing you. I brought you a cappuccino." I carefully opened the bag and placed a cardboard cup of cappuccino on her desk.

Arlene Ford looked at it as if it was something a low-flying bird had dropped on her desk. "Thank you," she said coolly but made no move to touch it. "You can wait over there," she said, pointing to a chair.

I sat down. There are people in the world, I reflected, that you like the moment you lay eyes on them. People who are immediately attractive in some way. Jennifer is such a person and Gaston's sister is another. Susan, too, despite her prickliness. I sighed inwardly, thinking of Susan. I can think of many more. And then there are people who instantly repel rather than attract you on first meeting, and then things go downhill. When it's mutual — as it certainly was with Arlene Ford and me — there's no way you're ever going to hit it off. I suppose the fact that I suspected her of murder didn't add to my appeal. But if I was going to get anything out of her, it wouldn't be with charm. I'd have to scare her. This would be a new endeavour for me. I don't think I've ever scared anyone in my life.

I sipped at my coffee and tried staring at her for a while. I was really just trying to figure out a good opening line, but my unblinking attention did the trick all by itself.

"What are you staring at?" she snarled.

I jumped right in with the first thing that popped into my head. "I'm trying to figure out how someone as smart as you are thinks they can get away with the stunt you pulled yesterday."

"What are you talking about?"

"What am I talking about?" I repeated softly with, I hoped, just a touch of sarcasm. "You were terrified over what you thought we found in Hilliard's condo. But then you realized that whatever it was that you thought you left there was actually in the bottom of your bag. You did your best to talk your way out of it. But it didn't work."

"It didn't work?" Her throat was so constricted with fear that she could barely squeak out the question.

"Not even close. It was obvious that all that stuff about the Mont Blanc pen set was just a ruse. You'd have been much better off crying and telling us all about how you used to go to Hilliard's apartment to work on his manuscripts, and he tried to come on to you sexually and you barely got out with your virtue intact and in the struggle some intimate possession of yours got left behind. See, that would have been convincing — because you could have told that story and maintained the confessional mood you had established." I couldn't believe that I was teaching her how to lie. "We probably would have believed you. We might even have been sympathetic."

Arlene Ford looked at me through squinty eyes for a moment and then suddenly got up and ran into the conference room. I was so taken aback by this that I didn't know what to do. It took me a minute to notice that she left the door open and I took this as an invitation to join her.

She was in the far corner of the conference room. She had flung herself down at the table with her head on her arms. The top of her dyed blonde head moved up and down as she sobbed and gasped for air. I took a minute to get the Kleenex and all-important coffee from her desk and, closing the door behind me, I went over and sat down beside her. In the most fatherly voice I could manage I asked, "Is there anything I can do?"

"It's true," she moaned between sobs.

"What's true?" I asked.

"What you said." She lifted her head and took the Kleenex I was holding out to her. "I went over to his place to do some extra work and he came on to me. Just like you said."

It sounded like she was beginning to hyperventilate and I was getting more worried about her. "I resisted and finally he promised to leave me alone. I told him I would stop proofing his manuscripts if he didn't leave me alone," she continued, still crying. "But he didn't mean it. I was fooled because he would never bother me here. Oh no, at the office it was all Ms. Ford this and Ms. Ford that. He never even called me Arlene, never mind the things he used to call me at his place. So I believed him and kept going back and I went back one too many times. He just about raped me. He was tearing at my clothes. I played along hoping to distract him so I could escape. And I did. But I had my clothes off and all I could throw on was my jeans and a shirt. And I took off leaving my other stuff behind. I was too scared to hang around."

I said nothing. It wasn't true, of course. If she'd actually left her underwear it was pretty unlikely she'd forget she had eventually got it back. I also doubted she would have forgotten it and left it in her bag for — I wondered when she would claim it had happened.

"When was this?" I asked sympathetically.

"About three weeks ago. I never went back and I did my best to avoid him around here. Although around here Dr. Hilliard was Dr. Jekyll. You'd never know what he was like off campus."

And with that she put her head back down on her arms and cried some more.

Time to switch tactics.

"I'm impressed," I said. I got up and took a step away, then turned and examined her coldly. "That was quite a performance. If you had done that when we were at the café it would have been really convincing. But not now."

Arlene sat bolt upright. Apparently I had thrown the stop-crying switch. She glared at me with pure narrow-eyed hatred. I had never experienced the venomous stare of a murderer before but at that moment I was convinced that I had found the killer.

Without taking her eyes off me she stood up and slapped me hard across the face.

At that moment, Lemieux appeared. "What's going on?" he asked, surprised.

"Arrest that woman," I said angrily, gently stroking my burning cheek. "That woman" packed quite a wallop.

"For what?" He asked. "Slapping a bookseller? That's hardly a serious crime."

"No," I growled. "For murder. For killing Professor Hilliard."

"Has she confessed?"

"Not in so many words," I answered.

"Then do you have any evidence?"

"Not really," I said sheepishly.

Turning to Arlene, Lemieux asked, "Did you murder Professor Hilliard, madam?"

"Don't be ridiculous!" she responded angrily and stalked out of the room. Following Arlene Ford from room to room could become a time-consuming endeavour. I was half out of my chair but Lemieux held out his arm in the universal signal for stop. "Sit down, my friend."

He walked over to the door, closed it and sat down. "Tell me what happened to earn you such emotion."

"She's a liar. Everything she told us was a fabrication. We can't just let her walk out of here."

"I'm sure she's just going into the next room to cool off. I'm not concerned about her at this moment. I want to hear your story."

I recounted what had led up to the slap. When I had finished, Gaston just looked off into space and stroked his moustache. By now I knew not to interrupt him when he was thinking; not that he would have heard me anyway.

Finally his eyes came back into focus and he said to me in a bemused tone, "Well, well, Sam you seem to be getting the hang of police work. Pretty soon you'll be considering a career change." Then he turned serious again. "We still don't know what she left in that apartment but her theatrics have given us more confirmation that it was something important and probably incriminating. She's still on our list of suspects. Let's see if anyone else makes it onto that list."

Lemieux went into the reception area to see which of the people he wanted to see had arrived. I liked his attitude. He had asked Arlene to have three people available and he never doubted that they would be there.

I could hear Arlene introducing him to someone and sure enough he returned a moment later with a pretty blonde woman — a natural blonde — about the same age as Susan but with less fire in her eyes. She was dressed in the uniform of the nineties student: Gap jeans, a Roots sweatshirt, uncomfortable-looking black boots and an Eastpak backpack which she let slide to the floor as she sat. She was pretty, I suppose, in a conventional sort of way, and she carried herself with assurance. She showed no nervousness at being questioned in a murder investigation.

"May I present my colleague, Miss Bloch, this is Sam Wiseman. He is assisting me in the investigation."

I rose and nodded a courteous bow to Miss Bloch. I was too far away to shake her hand.

"I know you," she said. "You work in the bookstore." She sat down and laced the fingers of her hands together on the table in front of her. Gaston sat on the same side of the conference table, and I took chair at the end. I had them both in profile. Sitting like that she made me think of the star pupil in a grade eight class waiting for the teacher to begin, not wanting to miss a word. I straightened up to look as attentive as she did.

Lemieux began in a very formal way. "Thank you for coming to meet with me, us I mean, Miss Bloch. I appreciate it. As you know there has been a murder and we must talk to all those who may have information concerning the murder."

"I don't know anything about the murder." Sarah looked alarmed.

"We shall see," intoned Lemieux. "What was your relationship to Dr. Hilliard?"

"He was my thesis adviser. And I was his teaching assistant."

"What I meant was, how did you get along with Professor Hilliard? Were you close?"

"I wouldn't say *close*. We had a formal relationship. I always called him Professor and he tended to call me Ms. Bloch in public. I respected him as a thesis adviser and my teacher. No more than that."

"I see," Lemieux said. "Did you work closely with him?"

"During my first year here, no. More during my second year and a lot more over the summer as I was preparing for my exams and trying to work out a thesis topic."

"So you spent a lot of time with him this last summer?"

"Yes. My field is the Revolution of 1848 in France and there is already so much written on that period that I needed help finding a topic that would be suitable for a doctoral dissertation. I had a lot of ideas but Professor Hilliard thought that they were too broad or lacked focus. He helped me find a topic that was narrow enough to be manageable and broad enough to be a PhD thesis."

"And you found such a topic?"

"Yes. I'll be working on the role of Parisian merchants during the revolution."

"And you spent a lot of time with Dr. Hilliard to work on this topic?"

"Why do you ask me that? What's it got to do with anything?" Sarah was beginning to lose her cool and become a bit exasperated with Lemieux's questions.

"I've been hearing rumours that Dr. Hilliard was not always so correct in his relationships with his students. I was wondering if you had any experiences with him. Did he ever try to initiate a more personal relationship with you?"

Gaston was so roundabout in the way he led up to and asked the question that I almost didn't realize where he was going. There were pads and pencils on the table and I reached for one of each to be ready to take notes should anyone say anything noteworthy.

Sarah looked at Gaston and repeated, "Personal? Do you mean did he try to cross the line between student and teacher? Is that what you mean?" Sarah acted as if this was the craziest idea she had ever heard. "If he wasn't dead, it would be almost funny. Where on earth did you hear this so-called rumour?"

Gaston tilted his head toward the wall that divided the conference room from the secretary's office. Sarah understood what he meant and said, "Well, you have to consider the source, don't you?"

"What do you mean?"

"There have been lots of rumours about Professor H. since Jane broke up with him. I'm sure that some of them have been based on truth. But the only person I know of who actually had an extracurricular, shall we say, connection with him is your source." This time Sarah tilted her head toward the wall between the room we were in and the secretary's office.

I didn't get these two. Why didn't someone just say Arlene Ford? Why all this circumspection? Did they expect her to be listening through the wall? Then again, maybe she was.

"And how can you be so certain?" asked Gaston.

"They were pretty discreet. But there were times when I'd see her stand a little too close to him when going over something, making body contact, if you know what I mean."

"Really?" I blurted. "The cold and angry —" I was

about to say Arlene's name but in keeping with recently established practice I finished the sentence by inclining my head toward the wall.

"Yes. Appearances can be deceiving. Sometimes she would leave her hand on his after she handed him something. There were small gestures. Maybe they thought nobody would notice, but I did. After the first few I saw how many of them there were. Once when I had to drop something off at his house I smelled her perfume."

Of course. I remembered that perfume, too. It had nagged at me like a song, the title of which I could not remember, running through my head. I knew I recognized the scent put for some reason I did not connect it with Arlene. I guess the perfume gave off a different scent on the air of Hilliard's condo than it did on the person of Arlene Ford.

"So you saw her there?"

"No, that's the point. She was obviously there but not in the living room or the study which was where I was with Professor Hilliard. We spent about fifteen minutes together going over some marking I had done and then I took home another set of papers to grade."

"When was this?"

"Last spring. At the end of the semester. I was doing the final grading. And if she wasn't in the living room or the study that only left one other room."

"I guess you don't mean the kitchen," I said.

"I don't mean the kitchen, believe me."

I was certain, now that Sarah jogged my memory, that Ms. Ford had been in Hilliard's apartment just before our visit. I wondered why Gaston hadn't noticed the perfume. I almost laughed out loud at the thought that he was the professional detective but I had the nose of a bloodhound.

"Did the professor seem different in some way that night?" Gaston inquired. "Did he give any indication that he had a visitor?"

"He was somewhat more impatient than usual. And it looked like he got dressed in a hurry. Jeans, his shirt hanging out, no shoes or socks. And I was so sure that she was there that I got out as quickly as I could. I felt embarrassed at disturbing them. And here's the really funny thing; I'm sure that I recognized her perfume, but I didn't know what it was. It certainly wasn't the stuff they spray on you when you're in the Bay. I imagined that it was pretty expensive and I was right. One day I happened to be in Holt-Renfrew and I discovered what it was that she wears: Jade. It costs about a million dollars an ounce."

"Hmm, I guess we'll have to have another chat with our friend." Gaston was silent for a minute or two while he digested what Sarah had told him. He got up and began pacing back and forth in front of the windows, pausing every once in a while to look out at the campus. Finally he bent forward, placing both hands on the table and looked Sarah straight in the face, locking his eyes on hers. "Ms. Bloch," he said sternly, "I don't for a minute doubt what you have told me but you avoided my original question. I wanted to know if Professor Hilliard ever tried to have more than a student-teacher relationship with you. You told me that you never had anything but a professional relationship with the professor and that he probably had an affair with someone," he nodded his head at the wall, the sign for Arlene, "but what I want to know is did Professor Hilliard ever try to cross the line? Did he try to initiate a personal relationship with you?"

Lemieux did not take his eyes off Sarah. She blushed and turned away from him and said, "Yes," so softly I could barely hear her.

"I beg your pardon?" Lemieux asked. From where he stood he probably heard a timid squeak more than the word yes.

"Yes, he tried," Sarah said, louder than her previous attempt to talk but not by much.

"Tell me about it," Lemieux prompted.

"Yes, he tried," Sarah said again, more confidently this time. "In my first year he would call me late at night every once in a while and ask me to meet him for coffee or a drink. He seemed so lonely he scared me. I always made up some reason not to go but I was very nervous that he would try something during the day, around here, when I couldn't just make an excuse and hang up."

"Did he?" Gaston asked. "Did he try anything here or in class?"

"No. Not then. In fact after a few phone calls he gave up all together. I was so relieved. He stopped calling me and I got over my fear of him and actually got to like him."

"You said 'not then' a moment ago. Does that mean that he approached you again?"

Sarah inhaled and expelled her breath in a long sigh. "A year later. I guess he got restless in the fall. But he was different this time and so was I. He asked me out on real dates, not just last-minute calls. We'd go to dinner or long coffee breaks. At first it was all business. But it turned into more, or rather it *began* to turn into more than business. I was more flattered than frightened that time around. I was more sure of myself and I was pleased by the fact that he took me seriously as a historian. You have no idea how close I came to crossing the line and having an affair with him. He was very romantic. He would send me notes and letters telling me how much he enjoyed my company and how much he enjoyed talking to me and how much he valued my opinion. I was very flattered by his attention. I wrote to him, too, and told him more personal stuff than I probably should have, about my feelings, things like that.

I came within a breath of falling into his bed. But I didn't. Fall, I mean. Instead I went to the country for a week with a girlfriend, to regain my centre, to break his spell. You didn't know him. He could be so charming and considerate. I had to put some distance between us to stop myself from doing something I knew I would regret. It worked. A week in the country with a friend and some books and I was my old self. Thank God."

"How did he take it?" I asked.

"Well. Better than I thought he would. I was worried that it would affect our student-teacher relationship. It didn't. I guess he didn't really care for me as much as he said. He just turned his attentions elsewhere."

Sarah fell silent, and we waited for her to continue. But after a moment it was clear she had said all she wanted to say about her almost-affair with her teacher. She looked down at her hands, and said nothing.

"What happened to the letters?" asked Gaston.

"I don't know what happened to the ones I sent him. I burned the ones he sent me. When I was out in the country with my friend ... she helped me. We had a kind of ceremony."

"So for all you know he still had your letters?"

"Yes."

"Weren't you afraid that they could embarrass you at some point?"

"Yes, I was. But I was more afraid of stirring things up by asking for them back. I trusted that Hal, Professor Hilliard, would be a gentleman. I hoped that the past would be forgotten."

Heck of an attitude for a historian, I thought.

"I'm sorry, but I'll need to confirm your story. I don't disbelieve you. It's just part of the process. Please write the name, address, and phone number of your friend down for me so I can contact her." Gaston slid a pad and pencil across the table to Sarah. She wrote the information he requested.

"Thank you," he said. "Now, let's return to the present. What time did you come into the history department yesterday?"

"Allan, my boyfriend, and I usually start the day with a coffee in here at about eight-thirty and then head off to class."

"Did you see or hear anything out of the ordinary?"

"No. It was quiet, as usual."

"Well, did anyone see you? Other than your boyfriend, that is?"

"I passed Jane Miller in the hallway. But the staff doesn't get in till nine so things are pretty deserted until then. If any of the professors are in that early they're usually in their offices."

"Jane Miller? Is this the same person as Jane Miller-More?" Lemieux asked.

"That's right. She added the More after she married but I never got into the habit of calling her by her married name. To me she'll always be Jane Miller, I guess."

I noticed, and I am sure that Lemieux did too, that without actually lying Sarah gave the impression that she and Allan arrived together. She told the literal truth but I was sure she was trying to deceive us. I was hoping that Gaston would wrap up his conversation — I would hardly call it an interrogation — so that we could take another crack at the divine Ms. F. But just then the conference-room door flew open and a very dishevelled young man barged in.

chapter thirteen

I jumped to my feet.

"Allan!" Sarah exclaimed.

"I'm sorry I'm late," he said, out of breath and breathing hard. "My last class ran overtime and I ran across campus to get here. Let me catch my breath and we can begin." He dropped his six-foot frame into a chair.

This, obviously, was the boyfriend, Allan Gutmacher. He was dressed in the student style but instead of adopting the fashion of the nineties he dressed as if it were the late fifties, in a pair of grey trousers with a yellow shirt, a bit worn at the collar and cuffs, and a red, yellow, and blue striped tie. He wore a pair of heavy black lace-up shoes, the kind my father wears to bar mitzvahs. A blue two-button blazer, also a little worn, completed the outfit. Sure enough he was carrying the editorial section of the *National Post*, folded so that the sketch of David Frum peeked at us out of his blazer pocket. I don't know why he thought that we were waiting for him. I thought Lemieux had made it clear he wanted to see people one at a time — not in groups.

"We're almost finished interviewing Ms. Bloch. We'll be delighted to talk to you next. Why don't you wait outside?" Lemieux said, very politely. I sat down.

"Outside? Finished? Why didn't you wait for me? You had no right to talk to Sarah without me."

Sarah cringed. She cast him a quick look that plainly asked him if he had just arrived from some other planet, then said quickly, "Please forgive Allan. He's being gallant or overprotective, or both, and both are totally inappropriate and unnecessary." She pronounced the last three words very slowly and distinctly so that Allan would get a message.

"Unnecessary?" Allan sputtered. "Sarah, what did you tell them?" He noticed me across the table and demanded, "Who are you? You're no cop."

"But I am," interjected Lemieux. "Please let me introduce my colleague, Sam Wiseman." I stood up to shake Allan's hand but he ignored me and I pulled back my arm and sat down again. I was beginning to feel about as useful and as bright as a jack-in-the-box. Lemieux turned to Sarah. "Thank you, Ms. Bloch. If there are any more questions we'll be in touch."

"Sarah, stay here. What did she say?" Allan demanded. "Did she tell you that Hilliard tried to molest her and should have been brought up on charges? Did she?"

"Allan," Sarah said, with a warning tone to her voice. "I've told you, it wasn't like that. Nothing of the sort happened. It was all a big misunderstanding."

"Misunderstanding." Allan literally spat the word. He had to use his hand to wipe spittle off his chin. "He was a moral idiot and should have been thrown out of the university. He was an animal. He had the values of a jackal." For emphasis he whacked the table with the sketch of David Frum.

It was clear Allan could not take a calm view of Sarah's brush with a professorial fling, even now that the man he despised was dead.

Gaston tried to restore order. "Please compose yourself, Mr. Gutmacher. Ms. Bloch already told us what happened."

"I'll tell you what happened," Allan stormed, flinging himself violently back in his chair. "Sarah may want to make excuses for the guy, but —"

"That's enough." Gaston smacked the table. Obviously he was finding Gutmacher as much of a pain as I was. And I was beginning to wonder if he had been listening at the keyhole. He seemed to know what Sarah had said and he was prepared to contradict her. His breathless I-dashed-across-campus entrance could have been a fake.

Allan subsided a little under the force of Gaston's anger.

"You'll get your chance soon. If you can't be quiet you'll be asked to leave." Gaston glared at Allan for a minute to make sure he got the point.

Sarah turned to Allan and said in sharp voice, "I told them the whole story. It was nothing, nothing happened and it's in the past anyway. Let's just drop it, OK?"

"Do you not believe her, Mr. Gutmacher?" Gaston asked Allan.

"I believe that Sarah told him where to get off. I'm not sure he didn't try again. He had a reputation for always being on the make. I swear if he had tried anything with Sarah again I'd have ..." Allan realized what he was about to say and shut up.

"You'd have ... what?" Gaston asked.

"I don't know. But something." Allan shrugged, slouched even farther into his chair and, unable to meet Gaston's eye, turned his head away and glared at me instead.

Well, well, I thought to myself. We now have suspects two and three. This was a very productive morning.

Sarah got to her feet. "Should I leave now?" she asked Gaston, pointedly ignoring Allan.

"No, please stay a moment longer," said Gaston, in a neutral but still very courteous tone. She sat down again. I wondered why he was letting her remain; it wasn't his usual practice. Maybe he wanted to observe see more of her interaction with her boyfriend. It was certainly interesting. "Tell me, Mr. Gutmacher, what time did you arrive here yesterday?"

"Yesterday? The usual, I guess. About eight-thirty. Sarah and I met at the subway, walked over to campus together and had a coffee here before getting down to work. Just like every other morning."

That was an outright lie. We already knew that they had arrived separately. Allan was a lot less subtle than Sarah; she had prevaricated, carefully not saying anything untruthful. Her evasion and his lie told me that they had agreed to tell us that they arrived together as usual. But we knew he had got there first, and had had enough time to kill Hilliard before she arrived. I wondered whether Sarah was protecting Allan because he was the murderer, or because she thought he was the murderer, or because she thought he was a lunatic who would get himself in trouble for a crime he didn't commit.

"And did you see anybody else or hear anything out of the ordinary?"

"No, we didn't see a soul. Except Jane More, that is. She passed us in the hallway."

"Fine." Gaston smiled warmly, as if he was very pleased with them. "Thank you both. I needn't detain you any longer. Here's my card. Please call me if you remember anything and please give your addresses and phone numbers to my colleague so that I can get in touch with you if necessary."

They both looked relieved that it was over.

They were almost out the door when Gaston stopped them. "There is one more thing. You were both here early on the day of the murder. Did either of you see Professor Hilliard's computer, the one he carried around, anywhere? In the secretary's office, in his office, in here, anywhere at all?"

Allan and Sarah looked at each other and then at Lemieux. "His computer?" Sarah asked. "Is it missing?"

"It is missing and I was wondering if either of you saw it."

"No, we didn't," Allan said, speaking for both of them.

Sarah gave him a look and said, "I'm sorry. I haven't seen it."

Sarah and Allan would have been the perfect nineties couple — if Allan could get himself out of the 1890s and into the 1990s. They left quietly together and I had a feeling he was going to get some tutoring on how to treat a 1990s woman.

As the door closed behind them Lemieux looked over at me with a sigh of relief and a slight roll of the eyes. "Did you get the information?"

"Yes, I got it. And I put two more names on our suspect list," I responded.

I tore the page with the Allan's and Sarah's addresses and phone numbers from the notepad, and passed it to Lemieux along with the page on which Sarah had written her girlfriend's name and address.

"I'm not sure Sarah belongs on the list," Gaston looked pensive. "She seems very self-possessed and I think she can handle herself. She just isn't the kind that commits murder. Allan is another story. If he thought that Hilliard was harassing Sarah, and especially if he thought Sarah was still attracted to him, he might have tried to confront him. Things could have got out of hand. A jealous rage: it's banal, but it happens all the time. We know that Hilliard was murdered but not that the murder was premeditated."

"If Allan did it in a moment of passion why would he take the laptop?"

"To make it look like a robbery maybe? I don't know. It seems that every time we try to narrow our list of suspects we expand it. Do you think Ms. Ford thought that she left her perfume at Hilliard's?"

"Could be. Especially if she thought she left a bottle of the distinctive brand that could easily be traced to her. She must have known that Sarah recognized her perfume and so knew that Sarah knew she was in Hilliard's bedroom. This is beginning to sound like the Watergate hearings: Who knew what and when did they know it?"

"Exactly. We'll have to question Ford again, but first let's see if Professor Miller-More is waiting for us."

It turned out that Professor Jane Miller-More had declined to come to meet us. Arlene, looking annoyed, told us the professor had asked us to see her in her own office. She directed us to go out the door, turn left, the third door on the left; but if we got to the main entrance to the Elwitt Building we'd missed it, and we should retrace our steps. This time her office would be the fourth door on the right.

As we walked out I asked Gaston if he'd got that.

"Got it."

"Good," I muttered. I just hoped her name was on her office door.

It wasn't actually that hard to find. It was only a

few steps down the hall. The door was ajar. Lemieux knocked and then walked in without waiting to be invited. I was right behind him.

Startled, she looked up from her work. "May I help you?"

"I'm Detective Sergeant Gaston Lemieux, and this is my colleague, Sam Wiseman."

We all shook hands and as we sat down she said to me, "You're not from the police. I know you from the bookstore. You're always extremely helpful." She smiled as she said this in a deep voice with a bit of a rasp to it. Her eyes were the colour of dark brown corduroy.

"Yes, I'm discovering that I'm quite well known. I didn't realize that I had so many friends."

"Mr. Wiseman is assisting me in certain matters relating to the case — to the murder of Harold Hilliard," said Gaston.

I was finding it difficult to pull my eyes away from Jane More. She was a small woman, five feet four inches or less, and perfectly proportioned. She wore her brown hair short, with bangs that came to her eyebrows. She wasn't conventionally pretty but there was something very warm and attractive about her. I must confess that if I was in one of her classes I might find myself concentrating more on the teacher than on what was being taught.

"Isn't it horrible?" she said, with real, deep sadness in her voice. "Harold murdered. God, I haven't adjusted yet. I can't believe he's gone." I realized that this was the first time I had heard anyone express any genuine feeling for the departed professor. Yet it didn't seem personal. There was sorrow in her words, regret about the end of a life, but I could not detect any personal grief.

"Were you close?" Lemieux asked.

She paused a moment, looking carefully at both of

us before she spoke. "At one time, we were very close. We even talked about marriage. But we drifted apart and I don't think that Hal was really the marrying kind. He was a little obsessive about his privacy and independence." I coud believe that, having seen his apartment. "He wasn't good at sharing, either his space or himself. But there was a bond between us even after our relationship ended, and I remained fond of him. We saw each other regularly of course, here at work. I still expect him to come into my office with a coffee and some ideas to discuss. We both did French history. I guess I have to get used to talking about him in the past tense."

She paused again, either because she had nothing more to say or because she didn't want to say anything more, and stared at us.

I considered it rude to stare back so I looked around her office. It was smaller than Hilliard's, her academic status being much lower. There was just room for the three of us. Gaston was sitting facing her and I was to her left at the corner of her desk. If a fourth person wanted to join our conversation he would have had to stand outside in the hall with the door open. Her desk was centred against the back wall and pushed forward so that there was just enough room for her chair. She could only back up so far before she hit the wall. The desk itself was standard-issue grey metal. There was a mass of papers spread over it along with a pencil cup, a telephone and a bottle of Naya water. To her right, our left, was a window that started about halfway up the wall. The window ledge served as a table; there were more papers and books stacked on it and in the corner, where the window ledge met the wall, a printer and laptop computer. Hers, I assumed and I almost blurted out something about the computer but I held my tongue as I figured that Gaston would ask about it at the appropriate time. Other than the window and the door all available wall space was taken up by bookshelves, and they were crowded with books and papers. Miller-More's office was almost as messy as the murder scene — and she was still alive. I wondered what kind of household she and Hilliard would have had if they had married. She was as compulsively messy as he was compulsively neat. On the floor next to her desk on her left — our right — and directly in front of me was an old leather briefcase. It was open at the top and I tried to get a peek inside but all I saw was more papers.

If she meant the silence to be intimidating it didn't work. Gaston seemed lost in thought during the break in the conversation. Finally he said, "We don't meant to intrude, but there are questions we have to ask if we are to catch the murderer."

Jane took a drink from her water bottle, regarded us neutrally and said, "Please ask your questions." I gathered from her tone that she wanted to add, "and then get out of here and leave me alone," but didn't. Maybe I misjudged her but she seemed to have gotten over her earlier emotional reaction to Hilliard's death. Whatever she was feeling when we first started talking to her was well under control now.

"You said you and Professor Hilliard were considering marriage at one time?"

"That's right. But it didn't work out. And then I met Fred —"

"Fred is Fred More, the dean?" I interjected so that Gaston would know who the players were.

Jane nodded and continued "... and we got married two years ago. It was two years in July."

"But you remained on good terms with Professor Hilliard?" Gaston continued.

"Yes, of course. Hal and I were almost better friends than lovers even when we were together. He was a hard man to get close to emotionally but he was a wonderful friend and colleague." She took a deep breath. "There was no animosity over our break-up. I guess we wanted different things out of life."

"So you saw him frequently?"

"Oh, yes. At least three times a week. We would talk here in the department or we would have coffee together. Once in a rare while we would have lunch or dinner."

"So you only saw him on campus, never at his apartment?"

"I don't think I've been to his place since we stopped seeing each other, if you know what I mean. I didn't think it would be right somehow."

"When was the last time you saw him?"

"Friday, certainly. We had coffee and discussed a book on French capitalism we had both read. He was writing a review of it for the *French Historical Quarterly*. I saw him briefly on Monday, just to say hello but not more than that."

"You didn't see him on Monday, the day he ..." Gaston let the sentence hang to see how Professor Miller-More reacted.

"... died," she finished the sentence for him.

She shook her head, then again stopped and stared, waiting for Gaston to continue. Most people are intimidated by silence and will say almost anything to keep a conversation going. I knew that Gaston liked to use silences to get suspects and witnesses to talk. The tactic didn't work with Miller-More; she didn't mind the pauses in conversation at all.

"That's strange," Gaston said. "Several people saw you walking out of the secretary's office early on Monday morning. I was also told that you had lunch together the Friday before he was murdered."

"Not together. We were at the faculty club at about the same time but I wasn't with Hal. I was having lunch with my husband. It's possible that I saw him in the morning when I went to the reception area to get a cup of coffee. That's where the departmental coffee pot is kept, near to the offices of the tenured professors."

"I see," Gaston commented, but I wasn't sure what it was that he saw. "I just have a few more questions. We have not been able to locate Professor Hilliard's computer, his laptop. It may have been stolen. I was told it was small — about the size of that one." He indicated the computer on the table under the window.

Miller-More turned her head to look at the computer and said, "Yes, his is almost identical to mine, but his was white." Hers was black.

"So you know what it looked like?"

"Yes, of course. We live and die by our computers these days. Everything is on them. Our research notes, articles, even books and dissertations. And of course we all communicate by e-mail."

"You mean you communicate with someone in the next office by e-mail?" Gaston was incredulous. Apparently he could not understand the virtues of technology. He would probably just go to the next office and talk to the person.

"Well, yes, sometimes, but not only the next office; all scholars from everywhere communicate with each other on the Internet. I correspond with historians all over the world; so did Hal."

"Interesting. But you are telling me that you don't know where Professor Hilliard's computer would be, correct?"

"That's right. I haven't seen it."

Gaston stood up and so did I. "Thank you very much for your time. I'm sure none of this has been pleasant for you. Can you tell me how to reach your husband? I have a few questions for him as well."

"Fred? Why?" She looked doubtful. "I don't think Fred will be able to help you. He and Hal didn't have much contact, really, and his office isn't in this building."

"I understand that your husband is a dean. He may be able to help us with some of the practical aspects of Professor Hilliard's life here. An overview, so to speak."

"Well, if you say so. I'll call him."

She picked up her phone and dialled a four-digit number. "Hi darling, it's me. I'm with a police detective. He's investigating Harold's death and he wants to talk to you, about departmental politics, I think, or ... I don't know what, really. I'll get his number and you can call him back later. See you at home."

While she was speaking into the phone I took another look around the room. I had a better view of things standing than I did sitting at the corner of her desk. Like Hilliard she had a lot of books crammed into her office. Unlike Hilliard, she didn't seem to keep her collection in any particular order. A fat volume on the table against the wall looked familiar.

She hung up and looked sheepishly at us and said, "Voice mail." We needed no further explanation. Gaston took out a business card and gave it to her, after writing his cellphone number on the back.

"Do you have the complete *Cambridge History of England*?" I had wandered over to have a look, and immediately my eye had lighted on a single volume of that interesting series. I picked up the book and showed it to her.

Jane Miller-More turned and held out her hand for it, almost peremptorily, as if I had no right to touch it. I gave it to her and she folded her arms over it, holding it to her chest as if it was precious. "No, I don't, " she replied.

"That's a coincidence. There is a volume in that series missing from Professor Hilliard's office."

Jane relaxed and smiled very slightly. "Who are you? The book police?"

"This is no laughing matter, madame," Gaston informed her. "Anything and everything associated with the victim is important until the murderer is apprehended."

"Yes. Of course. Well, you've found the missing book. This is Hal's, or I should it was Hal's. It's mine now, because I spilled coffee on it. He wouldn't take it back so I had to buy him a new one. He was fastidious about his books. He barely cracked the bindings when he read them. In fact I ordered it at your store," she said looking at me.

"Oh," I said noncommittally. I didn't want to let on that we already knew that she had ordered the book from Dickens & Company.

"Isn't it a little out of your field?" Gaston asked. "I thought your speciality was French history?"

"It is. I've been assigned to teach the freshman survey course next year, you know, history from the primeval slime to the present time, and I need to brush up on all the areas which are not my speciality. That includes sixteenth-century England."

"That would include Henry VIII, wouldn't it?" Gaston asked. He was slipping into his book-loving persona.

"It sure would. The students always love that period. They're used to movies and mini-series and they'll really enjoy Henry and his wives and his Lord Chancellor, sort of a sixteenth-century *Dallas*."

"Ah yes, conscience versus expediency. Things haven't changed much, have they?" I could see that Gaston was ready to sit down and have a discussion about British history.

Jane Miller-More looked at her watch. Gaston might have been warming up to a good chat about the past but she obviously had things to do.

We thanked Professor Miller-More again, expressed sympathy for her loss and left her office. I almost added that I hoped that she would be spared future sorrow but I wasn't sure that was appropriate.

Between her office and the front entrance of the Elwitt Building there was an alcove with two chairs in it and a narrow window. I stopped and sat down in one of the chairs and asked, "Did you come too the same conclusion I did?"

"And that conclusion would be ...?" Gaston inquired, taking the vacant chair.

"That she killed Hilliard."

"Are you certain?" he asked, teasing me.

"Well, look at the evidence. Hilliard is bashed on the head. He realizes he's dying and in the second or so he has left of consciousness he grabs the special order form knowing that the book named on it will be found in the murderer's office. It's like pointing a finger right at her," I explained.

"Well, it's certainly suggestive, but inconclusive. We need a lot more evidence to convict someone of murder. But you're right, it does point a finger at her. But, as you know, I've learned not to form to conclusions until I've interviewed all the suspects and all the witnesses and gathered as much evidence as I can. We haven't done that yet. And I still think the secretary is holding out on us. She seems a lot more suspicious than Professor Miller-More. We may have reason to suspect the professor but we know that the Ford woman is lying to us about something. Believe me, witnesses who lie make me a lot more suspicious than those who spill coffee on books."

Hah! I thought. You just like the professor because she's read as many books as you. I also knew that Gaston was the expert and, of course, I respected his judgement.

"Let's take one step at a time," he said, getting up, and as we walked down the hall to the entrance area Gaston's pocket began to ring. There was a time when I would have considered a ringing pocket to be odd, but not now. So many people carry cell phones around that once-quiet places such as restaurants and bookstores are now a cacophony of ringing pockets, brief cases and purses. Gaston answered his phone and listened, restoring the hallway of the Elwitt building to its academic quiet.

I could only hear his end of the conversation in French but after an interminable string of *oui-non-oui-non-c'est possible* he told someone to have someone else available at the deceased's apartment at ten the following morning.

"We've found the cleaning woman, Betty Smith," he said to me, folding his cellphone and repocketing it. "I want to interview her tomorrow morning at the Professor's apartment. An idea just occurred to me. Let's have a final word with Madame Ford."

We turned and walked back to the history department. We found Ms. Ford at her desk.

"What do you want now?" she asked in exasperation.

"A final request before we leave. Because you were on the scene of the murder, you are extremely important to the investigation. I'm sorry to impose on you further," Gaston was being elaborately courteous and anyone but Arlene would have been glad to help such a gracious person. She, however, continued to look frosty. "But would it be possible for you to meet us at Professor Hilliard's apartment tomorrow morning? I hope that would not be inconvenient."

"Of course it's inconvenient. I have a job. I can't just go waltzing off whenever I feel like it, can I?"

"I understand. But I still have some questions for you and have to do a last survey of the apartment before we release it to the deceased's family and it will be easier for me if I can meet with you as I finish up there. I can speak to your boss and explain that I am causing you to be absent from work due to a police investigation and that we appreciate your co-operation."

"Don't bother. I'll take care of it myself. When do I have to be there again?"

"Ten-thirty would be fine. Do you have the address?"

"Of course I have it. I gave it to you, remember?"

"Yes, of course," Gaston said. "I'd like to see Professor Michaels on my way out. Please tell me where his office is." She gave us directions and we followed them to Michaels's office. Luckily he was in. His office was, if anything, even smaller than Miller-More's. If what I had heard was correct Michaels would soon be moving, but out rather than up.

He didn't appear to be very happy about our visit. But you can't say no to a cop so he invited us in. "Arlene mentioned that you might be coming back to haunt us. I have a class in half an hour but I'm all yours until then. But I don't think I can tell you any more than I told you the other day."

"There is one more thing," Gaston said. "I've come to understand that Hilliard wrote an unfavourable review of a book you wrote and that this could hurt your career."

"Who the hell told you that?" Michaels exclaimed, almost shouting.

"I ask the questions," Gaston informed him. "It doesn't matter who. Is it true or not?"

"I don't know. I've heard rumours to that effect but I haven't seen the review. You have to understand something. Most of my colleagues hate me. They think I'm too ambitious and not respectful enough so they take every opportunity they can to chip away at me, especially the older ones."

"So you're saying that there was no negative review — that it's just that your colleagues don't like you? Is that correct?" asked Gaston.

"What I'm saying," Michaels spoke slowly, barely able to restrain his anger, "is that I don't know if Hilliard wrote a negative review or not. It wouldn't matter anyway because I can show dozens of good reviews to counter his bad review — assuming it exists. He'd end up looking foolish, not me."

"But surely a bad review coming from you own department is bad for your career."

"I'm telling you that there is no reason to assume that even if he wrote such a thing, and there is no guarantee that it would be published. Maybe he wrote a critique and showed it around the department but couldn't find a journal to publish it. You've got to understand universities. People rarely attack you directly. Everybody tries to pretend that they're your friend. But then they damn you with faint praise. Things like 'let's help poor so-and-so with his writing or his research or his teaching or whatever.' It looks like they're being supportive but what they're really saying is that you are incompetent. And that's how they treat me. But it's not going to work. My reputation outside this department is too good for them to destroy."

"I see," said Gaston noncommittally.

"I hope you do," said Michaels. "Now if you'll excuse me." He stood up and we preceded him out of his office.

"I may want to see you again," Gaston called after Michaels, who was already stamping off to his class. To me he said, "What was your impression of his colleagues? Were they damning him with faint praise as he suggests?" We talked as we walked to the door of the building.

"Not Sally Howard. She seemed genuinely surprised by what Schwartz and Edwards said. But those two did seem kind of patronizing. Appearing to want to help when they really didn't."

"Hmm," Gaston agreed. "This place seems to be quite a nest of vipers, no?" and with that we left the building.

We paused at the Roddick Gates, the Sherbrooke Street entrance to the McGill campus, before going our separate ways.

"What's your plan for tomorrow morning?" I asked.

"You'll see tomorrow. Meet me at the professor's apartment at nine-thirty."

I had no idea what was going to happen except that it involved the cleaning woman and Arlene Ford. I wondered if I was going to witness the unmasking of a murderess. My voyeuristic side was excited by the prospect. I did not like Arlene Ford and I was looking forward to seeing her get what she deserved.

chapter fourteen

I walked into the store to find a happy buzz of activity. I love it when the store is full of customers and staff talking about and selling books. In charge of all the activity was, of course, Jennifer. She too loved the energy of a busy bookstore and she was glowing.

"Hi," I said catching her eye as she finished serving a customer. "You look happy."

"I am. I've been having a really great morning and business is booming. How about you?"

"You know what it's like solving crimes. Busy, busy, busy."

"No kidding, you solved it?"

"Not exactly. But it feels like we're getting close. Gaston is setting a trap for one of the suspects and he's going to spring it tomorrow. Someone may find themselves in a lot of trouble."

"Try not to enjoy it so much! Don't forget, murder is a tragedy for the victim and the murderer. Oh, my

God," Jennifer shrieked, covering her mouth with her hand, embarrassed by the volume of her voice. "That reminds me. Susan is waiting for you. Because you said someone would be in trouble," she explained.

"Where is she?" I said, looking around. I had totally forgotten that she expected me to meet her for lunch today, I'd become so involved with Gaston and the murder. I hadn't checked my machine or left a message. I felt really guilty — even if the days of our relationship were numbered, I didn't want to be dumped for being inconsiderate.

"She went over to the café. She hung around for a while but decided to wait for you there."

"Did she seem angry?" I asked tentatively.

"Actually, no. She seemed in a great mood. Maybe we're all having good bio-rhythms today. Go, I've got things under control here and I have extra staff coming in tomorrow so you can go see your murderer get arrested."

"You're the best," I said giving Jennifer a hug and a kiss on the cheek.

I walked around the corner to the Café Paillon. The place was packed with the lunchtime crowd. The Paillons, as usual, were arguing about something. This time they were speaking English; it seemed that Jake had either not done something he was supposed to do or done something he shouldn't have. Whatever the case, it was really Jackie's fault because she had forgotten to remind him to do something or she prevented him from doing something for some reason. If I didn't know how devoted they were to each other I might have been worried that the café might be closing soon.

Susan was at a table in the back having a cappuccino and she gave me a big smile as I hurried over to the table, then jumped up and hugged me hello, which was,

I admit, unusual for her. And she certainly didn't appear to be mad at me.

She started in telling me all about what she'd been doing, and from the sounds of it, she'd been so overloaded with work she hadn't had time to notice that I'd been wrapped up in a mystery and hadn't called. However, I did the manly thing and blamed myself for not calling. "I'm sorry," I said, "but I haven't been able to tear myself away from the investigation. Every time I think Lemieux is going to blow me off for being a pest I find some way to stay involved."

"I'm sure you're not in the way," she said cheerfully. "Anyway, the victim wouldn't be any less dead if you weren't around. And Gaston usually enjoys your company when you two talk about books and stuff so why not enjoy the chance to experience his world? If he minded I'm sure he'd tell you."

Why was she being so sunny and approving? It wasn't like her. What was she up to? "What do you want to do tonight?" I asked.

"A movie. I want to lose myself in someone else's life."

"What movie?"

"*The Piano*."

"Let's go to an early show and eat afterwards, OK?" I suggested.

"I'll meet you at the store at six so we can make the six-thirty show."

After lunch Susan went back to her lab. I spent the rest of the day at the bookstore helping customers and gossiping with Jennifer.

Susan and I met as planned and got to the movie theatre just as the lights were dimming. We settled into the dark and I lost myself completely to the story of a mute woman who expressed herself through her music. Of a man who seemed rough on the surface but was sensitive to music and also to the culture of the Maori, among whom he lived. Of another man who seemed civilized but was in fact a philistine, and of a child who was as complex, mature, and insightful as any of the adults. I loved the movie and to my surprise, so did Susan. Since we hardly ever agree on anything I assumed she must be hating the movie.

Afterwards we went out for Chinese food. My restaurant of choice is, and always has been, the Yen King. It's one of the few restaurants that remain from the good old days of Chinatown in the fifties and sixties, when there were lots of underdecorated restaurants that served unadulterated Chinese food. My motto has always been, the more Formica in the decor the better the menu, but most of the restaurants I used to love have been forced out of business by a series of mayors and city councils that practised a form of urban ethnic cleansing. Instead of rifles they used bulldozers. The Yen King catered to a mixed crowd of students, artists, and writers from the area around the Main, and also a more bourgeois crowd, former students and artists and writers, who trekked in from the western suburbs. When it was available I always preferred a table in an alcove cut off from the rest of the dining room by a folding screen painted with bright fire-breathing dragons. I'd taken Susan there at the beginning of our acquaintance, which was now verging on three months.

"Wasn't that the best movie you've ever seen?" she enthused over a dish of spicy shrimp and black bean sauce. "It is so great to see a story told intelligently from a woman's point of view. For a while it seemed like there was nothing out there except *Die Hard* and similar crap.

The Dieharderator," she said in a low pitched, sing-songy sarcastic voice. "I swear I thought I'd have to give up movies altogether. But this film was wonderful. There wasn't a false note in it. The characters were all well developed with complete personalities and finally sex that's actually erotic instead of a wrestling match between a bimbo and a bozo. Did you like it as much as I did?"

"Yes, but my favourite part wasn't the sex — it was the scene where the colonists put on that awful play which the Maori take literally and try to defend the poor actors who they thought were going to be harmed. It was such a lovely statement about people without even a scintilla of sensitivity who try to impose a European bourgeois culture on an aboriginal one. The colonists were too far from Europe to be able to sensibly express its culture and the Maori were too wise in their own ways to even have a clue what the white folk were trying to say in their silly little play. Didn't you just love the total lack of civility of those who thought of themselves as the bearers of civilization? It was so funny."

We had moved on to the General Tao chicken and vegetables with spicy noodles and the conversation moved on to other things as well. We seemed to be communicating rather well for a change. It was very pleasant. I brought Susan up to date on where we stood in our efforts to solve the murder of Harold Hilliard, and she told me about her progress in school. But there seemed to be something else on her mind. In fact her happy mood seemed to be darkening, and there were frequent pauses in the conversation. I had no idea what the problem could be, so I just went on eating and hoping for the best.

During one of these lulls I heard a lovely contralto voice from the table on the other side of the screen say, "Did you see the police all over the campus yesterday and the day before?"

"Yeah. What was that all about?" asked her female companion. The companion's voice had a nasal twang that made me think of the American mid-west.

"A professor died. Murdered," Contralto said in a matter-of-fact tone, as if she was used to keeping her friends up to date on the various deaths in and around McGill University.

"Murdered? Some one was murdered right on campus? That's awful!" Twangy-voice exclaimed. "Who was it?"

Susan was telling me something about her feelings of insecurity and I realized that she would consider it an unforgivable lapse if I didn't listen attentively, but I couldn't help myself: I gazed soulfully at Susan, but my attention was fixed on the gossiping of my unseen neighbours. I tried to divide my mind into two tracks, but it wasn't really working.

"...a history professor," Contralto was saying. "I never had him but a friend of mine is in his course and she told me all about it."

"Do they know who did it? This is so frightening. I swear I'll never feel safe on campus again," said Twangy-voice.

"Why not?" asked Contraltro. "The murder has nothing to do with you."

Susan's voice suddenly got louder. "... run over by a herd of stampeding elephants," she was yelling at me.

"What?" I asked, startled, switching my attention from the gossip behind the screen to Susan.

"You're not listening to a word I'm saying." She looked sulky. "And if you lean back any farther you'll fall off your chair."

I leaned forward and whispered to Susan what the women at the next table had said.

She wasn't impressed. "Listen, Fenton Hardy, gossip,

even in a Chinese restaurant, is only gossip. Unless one of those women is the murderer, it doesn't mean much."

"Well, it means that people are talking about it," I said defensively.

"Of course people are talking about it. You talk about it incessantly. Can't we put it out of our minds for one evening?"

I put on a contrite expression, but took advantage of a her momentary silence to pick up the words Twangy-voice was saying now: "... well, I'm sure the professor thought that he was pretty safe too and now he's dead, isn't he?"

"Yes," Contralto said. "But my friend told me that her TA was having an affair with him and then her boyfriend killed him."

I was leaning back in my chair again. Susan rolled her eyes and began tapping her long pink fingernails on the tabletop.

"My God, this place is becoming worse than home," said Twangy. "People are being sexually harassed and murdered right in the middle of the university. I could have stayed in Dubuque for this."

"But I heard something else, and this is even stranger," said Contralto.

At that same moment, Susan said in a warning voice, "Sam, are you with me or are you with —"

"Shush!" I said to her loudly, and instantly realized that I had done a very, very wrong thing. "Susan, I'm sorry," I apologized desperately.

Stony-faced, Susan was gathering up her bag and her jacket.

Contralto's voice droned on. "Then I heard that some people are saying that a bookseller killed him because of a bad review, but that it was a book written by the bookseller's wife, and ..."

Abandoning any attempt to listen I trailed after Susan, pausing only to pay our bill. When I got out into the street she was gone.

I went home and phoned her. There was no answer. I left a long, penitent message on her voicemail. It occurred to me that I might never hear back from her.

Maybe, I thought, that would be for the best.

chapter fifteen

Next morning, fearing that Susan might call and forgive me, I left my apartment at seven-thirty and went directly to the store. I didn't want Susan *and* Jennifer mad at me, and I knew I was going to be out of the store for hours later in the day, so I did my penance in advance. I got right down to some paperwork that I normally put off as long as possible — opening the mail which had arrived late the day before, filing, and writing up the daily cheque deposit. We do a large volume of institutional business and a big part of our cash flow comes in the mail in the form of cheques. Most retailers dread the mail as it brings more bills than money. In our case it was different. On a typical day we received about as much in the way of cheques as we did of bills. It helped keep income and outgo in balance.

Jennifer was coming in just as I was leaving.

"Leaving so soon?"

"I have detecting chores to attend to, I'm afraid."

"Not again," she said, but she was smiling. Good old Jennifer.

"I've done the paperwork and I'll be back at about noon — I hope," I threw back over my shoulder as I left the store.

"Go get those bad guys!" Jennifer called after me.

I was tired of having to scrounge for paper to take notes on. This time I took the precaution of bringing a pad and pen along in one of those dull red legal-size file folders, the kind that close with an attached covered elastic band. I hoped it made me look more official.

When I got to Hilliard's building, Gaston was already there. There was a patrol car parked in front of the building, and my friend was in the lobby, deep in conversation with the concierge, Grant, and the uniformed cops. They were just finished talking when I walked in. Grant went back into his office, and Gaston told the cops that he would call them when he needed them to come back. They went back out to their car and drove off.

"I'm not late, am I?" I asked.

"Not at all. I came a bit early to enlist the aid of the concierge. He's going to play doorman and keep track of the comings and goings of our, what shall I call them? Invitées? Guests? Let's go up to the apartment and I'll fill you in,"

"Great," I said following him into the elevator.

Even though I knew what to expect I was still taken aback by the blackness of the foyer, now decorated with yellow barrage-de-police banners. Gaston removed them and used the key that M. Grant had given him to enter the apartment.

As we waited for our interviewees I told Gaston what I had heard the previous night at the Yen King.

"Vraiment," he said consigning my news to the garbage heap of unreason. "Two people talking nonsense

on a subject about which they know nothing." I wished I
had not said anything about the conversation I had overheard. Not that his dismissive attitude changed my mind;
Allan and Arlene were my top two candidates for murder.
Who better than a jealous boyfriend or a rejected mistress?

"My plan is this," Gaston explained. "I'm going to
ask Mrs. Smith if anything seems out of place and if she
has or had any knowledge of any visitors Professor
Hilliard may have had while she worked here. I want to
know if she saw any of the women he is rumoured to
have invited up here. I'm hoping that she will be able to
help us in that regard. I also intend for Ms. Ford to
arrive without either of them knowing that the other is
coming to see their reactions. If one of them gives any
suggestion that she recognizes the other we'll know that
Ms. Ford is lying and I'll be able to pressure her into
telling us the truth."

I complimented Gaston on his plan. It seemed to me
like pretty straightforward detective work — keep the ele-
ment of surprise on your side and don't tip your hand.
Where I learned all this I don't know. Books, maybe. And
even though it was obvious it seemed like a solid idea that
might well force a confession out of Arlene Ford.

"I also want to see if Mrs. Smith can give us any
clue as to the whereabouts of Professor Hilliard's computer," Gaston added as an afterthought.

Just before nine-thirty the buzzer sounded and we
heard the elevator start up. Apparently Gaston had
arranged with Grant to give us a signal when Betty
Smith arrived. Gaston went to the door to let her in
and I stood far back in the room so as not to give the
impression that we were going to attack her. She
stopped at the threshold, not sure what to do. Part of
her wanted to march right into the apartment as she
was probably used to doing but another part of her

wanted to respect police protocol but she wasn't exactly sure what that was.

Gaston, ever the gallant, immediately put her at her ease. "Mrs. Smith?" he inquired politely. "How do you do? I'm Gaston Lemieux of the Montreal police and this is my colleague, Mr. Wiseman. Please come in." He gently took her elbow and escorted her into the apartment. "Won't you sit down?"

Betty Smith was a short woman of an age somewhere between fifty and sixty-five. She had short hair which was once brown but was now mostly grey. She was one of those women who look chubby even though they are actually quite slim, but are top-heavy with a very large bosom and a short waist. She had an energetic down-to-earth look about her and she was scrubbed clean and wore almost no make-up. She sat in one of the chairs and looked suspiciously at the torn bag and empty cardboard coffee cups on the coffee table.

"I only have a few questions at the moment but I may have more later. First, would you mind walking through the apartment with us to see if anything is missing or not in its usual place?"

"Not at all," she said standing up and heading for the study. We followed her from the study to the dining room and kitchen to the bathroom and the bedroom. She moved quickly and spent only the amount of time she needed to give each room a complete once-over. In the kitchen and bathroom she opened and closed cupboards and the medicine chests to satisfy herself that everything was as it should be. Back in the living room and seated she stated, "Everything's been moved."

"What do you mean?" asked Gaston.

"Nothing is exactly where I left it and there are bits of white powder everywhere."

"That must be because I had a team up here dusting for fingerprints. But are you saying that things are generally as you left them when you were last here?"

"Yes. Things are close to where they should be. But really, can't you people be a little more careful about how you handle things?"

It is very unlikely that a police investigation will ever satisfy the demands of a professional cleaning woman. Gaston ignored the rebuke and moved on to his next question.

"Did you notice where he left his laptop computer?"

"He always took it with him, to his office. The only times I ever saw it was during the summer when he didn't go to the university every day."

"Did you know the professor for a long time?"

"Yes, I guess I did. I started working for him just over ten years ago. Before he moved here. He had another place. And when he bought this one I followed along."

"Did you see him much?"

"No. Well, at first I did. But we developed a routine and I was able to do my job without too much interference from him."

"What exactly were your duties?"

"Well, housekeeping, really. I cleaned and tidied but he made a point of not allowing me to move anything. So I kept things as he left them. I did some laundry, the sheets and towels and things he didn't send out. And I cooked. I prepared three meals and I left them in the freezer. He bought prepared foods or ate out the rest of the time."

"How did he pay you if you hardly saw him?"

"He left a cheque."

"And how often would you say that you saw him in a month?"

"About once."

"Once a month?" Gaston couldn't believe how tightly organized the good professor was.

"That's right."

"Do you know if he entertained at all?"

"Entertained? I don't think so. I know that he had people over, mostly women from what I could tell, but, I don't think he went in much for entertaining."

Gaston perked up like a hunting dog at the whiff of a prey. "Mostly women? Did you ever see any of his guests?"

"Not hardly. But women leave things behind. Make-up and things like that. I stored it all in the second medicine chest in the bathroom if I found any. And other things. Perfume. I could tell by the scent if a woman had been here. I could tell when he got a new girlfriend. The smell of the place changed," she said with a smile.

"When was the last time you noticed such a change?"

"Boy, that's a tough one. It's been the same scent for quite a while, but ... I've got to think." She closed her eyes and sat back in her chair and was obviously lost in thought. Her head nodded slightly and her lips pushed in and out as she tried to recall the various scents of the perfumes that passed through Professor Hilliard's home. I thought that we were lucky that smells are stored in long-term memory otherwise Mrs. Smith would never be able to answer the question.

Finally she sat upright and opened her eyes. "A couple of years ago," she said. "There was a definite change. I started to notice a really nice scent. I didn't know what it was called but it sure smelled nice. I wanted to buy it but I could never find it at the places I shopped. Then whoever she was left a bottle of it in the bathroom. Jade it was called. No idea where she got it but I'd sure love a bottle of it."

"Jade?"

"Yes, the cologne. It's probably expensive and hard to get."

"I see," said Gaston. "Jade. And what is there about this perfume that makes it so different from its predecessors?"

"Not perfume; cologne. Well, one of the things that is different is that there was someone wearing cologne at all. Before that it was all soaps and lotion but nothing fancy and certainly no perfume or cologne. Do you see what I mean? For the first time in a long time there was some one here who treated herself to some of the finer things."

"So, before the arrival of the Jade lady the visitors, so far as you could tell, were less luxurious in their tastes." Gaston summarized.

"Exactly. Now may I ask you a question?" Mrs. Smith inquired of Gaston.

"Certainly, madam. What is it?"

"Has any one seen to funeral arrangements for the poor professor?"

This was the first time any one had expressed any practical concern for the deceased. Jane Miller-More was unquestionably sad at Hilliard's passing but her grief seemed more self-centred than altruistic. Arlene Ford seemed to be more angry at the professor than sad. Neither Sarah nor Allan seemed particularly upset at the death of Professor Hilliard; in fact Allan seemed almost pleased that Hilliard was out of the way. Mrs. Smith who only saw Professor Hilliard once a month had a personal interest in the man.

"It's thoughtful of you to ask. But we've had the body at the morgue for the last few days so that we could do an autopsy. These things take time."

"Yes, but sooner or later a family member will want to arrange for a proper burial won't they?"

"I suppose. But so far we haven't been able to locate any family."

"He wasn't from here. I think he was American originally, from Ohio or one of those places."

"We'll make some efforts to find his family after we finish the autopsy. If you hear from them please have them get in touch with me." He handed Mrs. Smith one of his cards.

The buzzer from the lobby sounded again and I checked my watch. Ten o'clock exactly. "We have another guest coming," Gaston explained. "Please tell me if you recognize her."

We waited for the knock at the door and Gaston answered it. "Please come in, Ms. Ford. Thank you for being so punctual." He stood back to allow Arlene to enter and we heard the tap of her high heels as she walked into the room.

Arlene stopped short when she noticed Betty Smith sitting in the chair with the window's light behind her.

"You know my colleague, Mr. Wiseman. Permit me to present Professor Hilliard's housekeeper, Mrs. Smith. Mrs. Smith, this is Ms. Ford from the University. She worked for Professor Hilliard. I don't think you've met." Gaston was standing behind Arlene and she couldn't see him.

"No. I haven't but there is something very familiar about you," Betty said, getting to her feet. We were quiet as we watched Betty Smith extend her hand to Arlene Ford.

"I know!" Betty said suddenly. "You're Jade!"

Arlene Ford froze. But only for a second. She dropped Betty Smith's hand as if it were suddenly aflame and turned quickly. I think she was in the "flight" part of fight-or-flight but Gaston stood between her and the door. She froze again and I could see her facial muscles tighten with fear and anger. She whipped her head around and saw me standing in the alcove archway. It was clear to her that neither flight nor fight was a possibility. She turned her tight, frightened face back to Gaston and I noticed that large tears formed in the corners of her eyes and rolled down her cheeks. For the first time I believed that her tears were sincere and that she had something to cry about.

"There, there, dear," Mrs. Smith said and put a maternal arm around Arlene's shoulder.

Gaston caught Betty's eye and indicated with a tiny gesture and a step forward that he would take over now. "Thank you very much, Mrs. Smith, you have been extremely helpful. I'll get in touch with you if I need to speak to you again. Will you be able to get home all right? Shall I call for a taxi? Would you like me to have a police car drive you home?"

"Lord, no. It's a nice day and I'll take the bus. Thank you." She dropped her arm from Arlene's shoulder but not before giving her a comforting squeeze. "Goodbye, now. Please let me know if there are any funeral arrangements, or if you locate the family."

"I certainly shall, madam. Thank you again."

And with that Betty Smith walked out of the condo.

We turned our attention to Arlene Ford, who was standing white-faced and as still as death.

chapter sixteen

Arlene collapsed onto the chair recently vacated by Betty Smith. She looked awful. Tears had streaked her make-up. Fear and anger were fighting for control of her face. After the surprise Gaston had prepared it was difficult for her to retain her cool, in-your-face persona.

We gave her a few more moments to bring herself to the point where she could talk. I sat on the other of the two chairs, beside Arlene, with my pad and pen poised to take notes. Gaston sat opposite her.

After a pause, he leaned forward, looked her straight in the face and said very, very sternly, like a school principal talking to a badly behaved youngster, "Ms. Ford, you must pull yourself together. I shall not be offering you any sympathy even though I know that you've had a terrible shock. You've lied to me on more than one occasion. I must insist on the truth now. I'm prepared to talk to you here, but if you do not co-operate we'll have to continue our conversation at the police station. If that is your preference I strongly recommend that you have a lawyer present. At the very least you will be charged with interfering with a police investigation and at the very worst you will be charged with murder. Do I make myself clear?"

Arlene looked at Gaston. It was clear from her stricken face that she finally understood that she was in real trouble and that lying was no longer an option. "Yes." Her voice was barely a whisper.

"Do you intend to co-operate?"

"Yes."

"Do you intend to tell me the truth?"

"Yes." Another whispery croak.

"Do you understand what will happen if you continue to lie to me?"

"Yes." This time there was a touch of asperity that made her sound more like herself.

"When was the last time, before today, that you were in this apartment?"

"A week ago."

"What was the purpose of your last visit?"

"To collect my things — the few things that I left here that Hal allowed me to leave here, or that I plain forgot."

"Am I to understand from what you are saying that you and Professor Hilliard were having an affair?"

"Yes."

Arlene had regained much of her composure but she was much less hostile than during our previous meetings. Maybe the fact that she was resigned to telling the truth helped her to relax. It could not have been easy for her to lie so elaborately. Unless she was pathological it would have been difficult for her to remember all the details of the lies. She didn't seem happy but she did seem to have come to terms with her predicament.

"Would you like a glass of water?"

"Yes, oh, yes please." For the first time since I met her I saw Arlene Ford smile. She was grateful for even this small consideration.

"I'll get it," I said jumping to my feet, anxious to be helpful. "Would you like one, as well, Gaston?"

"Yes," he said and smiled.

I went to the kitchen and returned with three large tumblers of water. None of us wanted to put the glasses on the polished coffee table so Gaston and Ford held onto their glasses and I set mine on the floor so I could continue to take notes.

"Please tell me about your relationship with the professor," said Gaston.

"The whole story?" Arlene asked.

"From the beginning, if you please."

"From the beginning," she said softly, almost to herself. She sighed and started talking in a louder, clearer voice. "I already told you that I've known Hal for twelve years; since I started at the department. For most of that time our relationship was strictly professional. And since I worked for all the staff in the department I can't say that I had that much to do with him. Even at the annual staff Christmas party he was kind of aloof, distant. He didn't mix much. At least not with non-academic staff. So time passed and not much changed."

"We've heard rumours that he had relations with some of his female students. Do you know if there is any truth to the rumours?" Gaston interjected.

"Maybe. I can't be sure. He was incredibly discreet — believe me, I know — so I don't know for absolute certain, but I heard all the rumours and I'm pretty sure that some of them are true. But not all. He was lonely and susceptible but he wasn't crazy. He never did anything in his office, like some I could name, so I never actually caught him at anything. And I'm also pretty sure that he never tried anything with undergraduates. But he paid a lot of attention to graduate students and new faculty, like Jane Miller." She pronounced Jane Miller's name with some of that old Arlene Ford sharpness. I wasn't sure if Gaston noticed the change in tone, but I made a note of it — just in case we had some final questions about her relationship with Professor Miller-More.

Gaston, too, seemed to be storing the information away, though without a pencil and paper in his case. Arlene was silent for a moment, then said, "Shall I continue?"

"One more question first. I have to be quite sure about what you are saying. You do believe, then, that Professor Hilliard had affairs with his graduate students, correct?"

"In essence, yes," she responded.

"Is it possible that he was having an affair with Sarah Bloch?"

"Possible? Yes, it's possible, but I doubt it."

"So her boyfriend, Allan, is overreacting if he thinks something took place between Sarah and Hilliard?"

"Overreacting? I'll say. Allan is the jealous type. You know the kind I mean. Every time he sees Sarah talking to a man, he thinks she's making a date to meet him at a hotel. Allan is capable of believing almost anything. And he has a temper. Sarah is a lovely person and Allan is going to ruin the relationship with his possessiveness. You'll see. I've known men like him. They're only happy when they're making some woman miserable."

Gaston pulled Arlene back to her story. "I understand," he said soothingly. "Please continue telling us about your relationship with Professor Hilliard."

"At first I knew him in a kind of distant way. He was one of the professors in the department and I did some work for him. He was always polite but not much more than that. When Jane Miller came to the department as a teacher he took up with her. For a long time he kept the relationship pretty quiet. Usual behaviour for him. But slowly he and Jane became more open about things. I guess you could say that what started out as an affair turned into a real romance. It did him a lot of good, if you ask me. Made him more relaxed and approachable. While he was with her he would actually say more than hello and goodbye to me. We would sometimes have an actual conversation about whatever, politics, the weather, anything. I was pretty sure that this was the real thing and that they would get married or at least move in together. Everybody believed that and everybody was pleased at how positively the relationship changed Harold. Then the rumours about her doctoral dissertation began."

"What kind of rumours?" I asked. I knew enough to know that the integrity of a doctoral dissertation is sacrosanct and that even the hint of a problem could destroy a career.

"Just that there were some irregularities. I don't really know what. There was never more than that. She spent a term back at the university where she got her PhD, the University of Toronto, and that was that. By the time she got back the rumours had faded away. So I guess that there was nothing to them. But it was around that time that she suddenly dropped Hal and started seeing Fred More, whom she later married.

"The breakup just about destroyed him. One day he was happily in love and the next he was back to his old withdrawn self. Well, almost back to his old self. The difference was that somehow I happened to catch him in one of his few talkative moods. One day we were leaving at the same time and he suggested we go for a drink and dinner. The poor soul poured his heart out to me. I

was so surprised I didn't have much to say but I listened
and I guess we both had too much wine with dinner. The
wine loosened his tongue and my defences and we ended
up here, in bed. The next morning I was furious with
myself for slipping into bed with someone from work
and having a one-night stand. I was determined to go
back to our old relationship of hello, goodbye, politeness and nothing more. I wasn't going to be one of his
conquests. I fully intended to put that night behind me
and out of my mind. It didn't work out that way.

"I'm not sure why but we each found something that
the other needed at that time. He needed a shoulder to cry
on and then to have his fragile male ego restored. And I
was tired of being alone. I may not have had an ideal relationship with Hal but it for a while it was better than
nothing. And nothing is what I had before I took up with
him. We're the same in that we are both very private people and, all in all, live better without too many demands
on us. So the one night stand became an arrangement that
seemed to work. It lasted two years and it made me
happy, and I thought he was happy too."

"I gather from the way you're talking that it wasn't
you who chose to end it," Gaston said sympathetically.

"Oh, my God," she said, reliving a bad memory.
"No, it was Hal. Just like that, he told me that he was
seeing someone else and that it was a serious, permanent
relationship. I couldn't believe it. I just went berserk. I
cried and screamed and berated him and it did no good.
He said his mind was made up and that he was sorry but
it was over. I couldn't believe it. I was being dumped and
he was sorry? You can bet I told him what I thought of
him. But it didn't do any good. He listened until I ran
out of steam and he even agreed with my assessment of
him. He didn't change his mind. It was over. Looking
back on it I suppose that I have to admit that at least he

was honest with me. He didn't try to string me along or take the passive-aggressive route out — you know, slowly pulling away from me and engineering a break up by forcing me to confront him. It was quick, clean break, but it was incredibly hurtful. Apparently there was never any chance that I could have been a 'serious, permanent' lover. I was being dumped and insulted in the bargain. He just told me it would be best if I cleaned my stuff out of here and that we go back to being secretary and professor. I told him that two years had passed and that it wasn't that simple. He said it would have to be. So I got my things together and left and spent a weekend at home in tears and tried my best to deal with it, with him, in some way so that I could restore my pride."

"You said that you got your things out of here. What exactly did you mean by that? Did you have a lot of things over here?"

"Hardly. It's not like we lived together or anything. There were just some odds and ends around, things I had forgotten, a sweater, cosmetics, things like that."

"And it was one of those things you thought we found that day in the café?" Gaston inquired.

"That's right. I suddenly thought I might have left a small jewellery case. I couldn't remember seeing it at home. But when I looked in my bag I realized I'd put it inside a zipper compartment and forgotten to take it out. So I knew you didn't find anything of mine."

"Were you angry with Professor Hilliard?"

"Angry? I was furious. I felt used and discarded like old clothes. I was hurt and angry and I just hated the son-of-a-bitch. I wanted to hurt him right back. I was trying to think of a way to make him suffer the way I was suffering. But before I could do that he *died*." Arlene began to cry, as if she had just this moment heard about his death.

Gaston gave her a handkerchief and some sympathy. "I understand. You were hurt and you had no one to talk to. Take your time. I'm sure you'll feel better now that it's all out."

There was the little matter of murder but I was sure that Gaston would get to it in his own sweet time.

We waited for Arlene to regain control of herself and then he asked her, "How long ago did this take place?"

"Not long, a couple of weeks ago," she said between her sniffles and her tears.

"And do you know who he was seeing, with whom he had developed a 'permanent relationship'?"

"That's the really strange thing. At first I thought it was Jane Miller-More again. It's nuts, I know, but after he dumped me I started to think really hard about things he did around the department. And I began to suspect that there was something going on between them. They didn't spend any more time together than they ever had, but I imagined there was something conspiratorial between them. They would talk in this kind of strange way so that no one could be sure what they were talking about but they understood each other. It was almost a code. But they were always close friends, even after she married Dean More. Then I thought maybe he'd told her about his new relationship — confided in her as a friend — and that they were referring to some conversation they'd had about it, but you couldn't be sure when this other conversation took place. And I have no idea who the other woman could have been. It sounds crazy, I know, but that's the best way I can describe it. And I'm sure Jane knows more than she's letting on."

"I see," Gaston muttered. "How do you feel about Professor Hilliard now?"

"I miss him. And I know it's an awful thing to say about the dead but I wanted to tell him how he made me feel. I wanted to get it out of my system and get on with my life. Now I can't." Arlene had her emotions under control. She gave her eyes a final dab with Gaston's handkerchief and twisted it through her fingers like linen worry beads as he spoke.

"But you hated him and you were angry and you felt betrayed by him. You know, these are the feelings that sometimes lead to murder. And then we regret what we did and try to hide it. But it never works out. The crime is based on anger and passion and too many mistakes are made and we always catch the murderer." Gaston had leaned forward and was looking straight into Arlene's wet eyes as he said this. He spoke softly almost hypnotically and she sat still, apparently mesmerized by what he was saying.

She was silent for a long moment and then she said, calmly, "I didn't kill him. It's not that I didn't think about it. I wanted revenge. But I could only kill him once. You know what it's like. You're mad at someone and you wish they were dead but you don't really — it's just anger talking. That's how I felt. And I know how it must look. But if I had killed him it would have been a crime of passion and I would have made mistakes in trying to hide it, wouldn't I? And you're smart enough, you would have found out by now. But you haven't found one single clue that ties me to his death, have you?"

I had to admit that she had us there. What made us suspect her turned out to be things that tied her to his life, not his death. Gaston sat back on the sofa and regarded Arlene thoughtfully. I could see that he had developed some respect for her brain power and that he had no answer for her question. As things stood now his own logic proved that she didn't do it. We'd need physical evidence to tie her to the crime and we didn't have any.

"You are quite right, madame. But until we find the

murderer I must suspect everybody and that includes you. My suspicions will only be lifted when I find the guilty party."

And that goes double for me, I wanted to say, but didn't. I, too, agreed with her logic, but I was still was not completely convinced of her innocence.

"I understand," she said, getting to her feet. "So you had better get on with finding the guilty person. And I'd like to get back to work, if you're finished with me." She marched off in the direction of the bathroom and I could hear the water running. She returned looking refreshed and in control of herself. "You know where to find me if you need me and I'm assuming that our conversation today was private." She gave me a hostile look.

Gaston spoke for both of us. "You can depend on our discretion. If you're innocent we have no desire to harm you and nothing you've told us will leave this room. If you're guilty, this conversation will be evidence in court."

"It won't be," she said, then turned and walked out of the apartment.

Gaston and I looked at each other.

"That was quite a performance," I opined.

"It was that, but I think that she's telling the truth now, for the first time since this whole sorry mess began. I'm not ready to take her off the list of suspects yet but she's not my first choice for guilty either. We'll have to keep looking. She's right about one thing. The physical evidence is inconclusive.

"Inconclusive, how?" I asked.

"Well, it is not yet clear to the medical examiner if Hilliard was killed by someone about his own size who struck him from behind while he was standing, or by a shorter person who got him while he was seated or perhaps bending over. One of my first cases had to do with a woman who was barely five feet tall, but still managed to kill her biker boyfriend. She did it by tossing him his pack of cigarettes so that they landed on the floor behind him. When he bent over to pick it up she clobbered him with a brick. It looked like he was murdered by someone bigger than he was — and he was big,"

"Wouldn't strength have something to do with it? Wouldn't the murderer have to be pretty strong to hit Hilliard hard enough to kill him?"

"Strength isn't really the important thing here. It's force. If the murderer was able to get a good swing the speed with which the fatal blow was delivered would be enough to kill. Size and strength don't really matter if there is no resistance on the part of the victim. Remember, we concluded that Hilliard's office was messed up as a result of a sloppy search not as the result of a struggle. He probably never knew what hit him."

We both thought about that for a moment. I looked at my watch and realized that it was one o'clock. "Can I make a quick phone call?" I asked.

"Use the study," he responded.

I checked my answering machine. There were no messages from Susan. That was a relief. But then I felt guilty about feeling relieved. And then for a brief moment I felt guilty about being so rude to her last night. And then I thought the hell with it and put her right out of my mind. I was free! I called the store to tell them not to expect me for a while and I rejoined Gaston.

At that moment I realized I was hungry, and apparently Gaston did, too, because he said, "Let's get something to eat and review and plan our next steps." As we were getting ready to leave, the buzzer from downstairs started ringing furiously and we heard the sound of the elevator.

"What's this?" I exclaimed.

"Uninvited visitors. Follow me." Gaston answered and quickly gathered up the empty coffee cups and the bag, turned off the lights, and made for the dining room. I was right on his heels and I made sure that the door stopped swinging the moment we were safely on the other side of it.

Gaston sat down at the head of the table and motioned me to station myself in the corner near the door so that if the intruder came into the dining room I could get between him and the door, blocking the only escape route.

We could hear a key turning in the lock. Our visitor, not expecting the door to be unlocked, inadvertently locked the door. He or she then shoved against the door and tried the key again. I was afraid that the intruder would realize that if the door was unlocked there must be someone inside the condo. Luckily this didn't seem to occur to him. The key was turned again and then, with much knob-twisting and door-banging the visitor entered the apartment. There was silence for a moment. Then heavy footsteps (from their sound I concluded it was a man) moved through the living room and turned right. He went into the bedroom and slammed the door, making a lot of noise as he moved around the condo — obviously we were not dealing with an experienced thief. There was no sound from behind the closed bedroom door. Suddenly he emerged and clomped down the hall, past the dining room door. The study door opened, then slammed shut. This time we could hear him inside, yanking open the drawers of the file cabinet and the desk. He spent a little longer in the study than in the bedroom, but not much. A moment later he barged into the dining room and stopped cold, with a deer-caught-in-the-headlights look on his face, at the sight of Gaston sitting at the dining room table.

"Won't you sit down, Mr. Gutmacher? Allan, isn't it?"

Allan responded by hyperventilating and when he found his voice he let out a shriek of fear and surprise. "What, what?" He sputtered. "What the hell?" He looked around wildly and turned to run out the way he had rushed in. But I had placed myself in front of the door, blocking his exit. He took a step toward me and I gently shoved him backwards. He stumbled and almost fell.

"I believe you've been asked to sit down. So sit!" I commanded like a movie tough guy. I moved in on him and he had no choice but to flop into a chair.

His breathing was getting into the normal range and I realized that on both occasions I had run into this guy he was charging around out of breath. I wondered if he ever entered a room in the normally accepted fashion.

He was wearing almost the same clothing as he had the day he had insisted on joining our interview with Sarah Bloch, the same or similar grey trousers and the same heavy black shoes — which accounted for the racket he made stomping around Hilliard's apartment. His shirt was blue and he was wearing a red tie with a faded blue pattern of some sort, little crowns which had weakened into polka dots, I think. He had exchanged his blue blazer for a beige windbreaker — a concession to the more relaxed standards of breaking and entering. As before, he carried a folded section of the *National Post*. Again, the sketch of David Frum peered at me from Gutmacher's windbreaker pocket.

"What are you doing here?" Gaston asked.

"None of your fuckin' business," Allan responded belligerently.

"Actually it is my business," Gaston told him. "It's my business to catch murderers and I think I may have caught one. What do you think, Sam?"

"You may very well have. I think I know what our friend is doing here, what he is looking for."

"Who the hell do you think you are? Dick Tracy?" Allan asked sarcastically.

I sat down on the side of the table between him and Gaston and said, "I think I'm helping Detective Sergeant Lemieux solve a murder. I think we found the murderer: a hot-headed guy who goes charging into places in a jealous rage. You probably bashed Hilliard on the head because you thought he was interested in your girlfriend. I also think that you tore Hilliard's office apart looking for something and when you didn't find it you came up here to search his apartment. What are you looking for? Something to do with Sarah?"

He clutched the newspaper in his right hand and jabbed it at me, the picture of David Frum the tip of his paper sword. "I don't have to tell you anything," he spat.

"But you do have to tell me," Gaston said in a calm voice that seemed to further infuriate Allan Gutmacher, who began to shake his head and laugh sardonically, presumably to indicate that we were way off base. "Listen to me. We know you lied to us earlier. Mr. Wiseman checked your story. You and Sarah may have met at the metro station and walked to school together on most mornings but you didn't do it the morning Hilliard was murdered. You got into the department first. You saw Hilliard was in his office and that there was nobody else around. You were angry at him for making a pass at Sarah and in a fit of jealous anger you killed him. Or maybe you had some other reason to hate the professor. Believe me, whatever it is, we'll find out. We'll investigate everything you've done in the last ten years if we have to in order to prove that you killed the man. Now what have you got to say for yourself?"

"You can't prove a damn thing!" he said.

"Oh yeah?" I pointed out. "Then how did a key that was missing from the dead man's pocket get into your hands? Isn't that what you just used to open the door of this apartment?"

Allan's eyes darted wildly. The he sat down heavily on the sofa and covered his face with his hands, apparently realizing that he might be looking at a murder charge. At the very least he was caught breaking into the deceased's home and searching for something. He sat up straight and placed both hands palms down on the table.

"I didn't kill him," he stated. "I found the body. But I didn't kill him."

"Tell us what happened," Gaston prompted.

"It was like you said. I waited for Sarah but she didn't show up. It happens sometimes and I didn't think much of it. Sometimes she gets there ahead of me and instead of waiting she goes on ahead and I meet up with her at the history department. So I bought coffee and walked to campus. When I got to the department I put the coffee in the common room and I noticed that Hilliard's door was ajar so I went down to see if she was there. But I didn't really think she was because I didn't hear any voices. Normally if there is someone around they make noise, you hear typing or someone talking on the phone or pacing around or something. But the place was so quiet I wondered if something was going on. I walked down the hall to Hilliard's office and looked in. And there he was lying on the floor in a pool of blood."

"So you returned to the common room and calmly had a coffee with Sarah?" I asked.

"No, not calmly," he said, looking at me resentfully. "When I got to the common room Sarah was just coming in. I told her what I had found and we decided to let someone else find the body. We didn't want to have anything to do with it."

"What did Hilliard's office look like?" Gaston asked.

"You saw it. You know what it looked like. It was a mess."

"I saw it after you left. I want to know what it looked like when you found the body."

"I didn't touch anything. It was a mess, I'm telling you."

"Listen to me," Gaston said sternly. "How you answer my questions will determine whether or not I arrest you for murder right here and now. Do you understand?"

Allan nodded and said, "His office was like it always was. Neat. The guy was a bloody fanatic. Except that this time he was dead on the floor and there was blood everywhere."

"And you say you touched nothing."

"That's right."

"That's a lie, and a pointless one. Whatever you touched will have your fingerprints on it. You tore the office apart looking for something, yes?" Gaston reached under his jacket and pulled a pair of handcuffs from his belt. He placed them on the table as a reminder of what Allan could expect if he was not totally honest.

Allan's head sagged forward, and he said, almost inaudibly, "Yes."

"What were you looking for? I'm asking you for the last time."

"Anything that would inadvertently tie me or Sarah to a murder we didn't commit. That's the truth."

"Why would there be anything in the office that would tie you to the murder, if you didn't commit the crime?" I burst in. "Anything that tied you to the murder would hardly be inadvertent, would it? You weren't studying with Professor Hilliard. But Sarah was ... you were afraid that she might have got to the history department ahead of you. Am I right? And that Hilliard made another pass at her and she bashed him on the head to defend herself?"

"Yes, goddamn you. But Sarah didn't do it. She got to the department after me."

"But you couldn't know that at the time you were in Hilliard's office. So you pulled Hilliard's office apart looking for anything that might incriminate Sarah and stole his keys, right?" Gaston asked.

"It was easy to identify the keys I needed. Once when Sarah was working with Hilliard she was supposed to meet me but she phoned and said she had to go over to his office with him to borrow some historical journals. I was over in two minutes to make sure I went with them. Sarah was mad at me but she knew what I thought of the guy so she just let me go along. He seemed kind of pissed off, of course, but I didn't care. I noticed that fancy key he had when he opened the door. After that I checked from time to time to see if a key to his apartment ever showed up with Sarah's keys. It was a good thing for him that never happened. Anyway, I knew which ones they were. I figured that if I only took the keys to this building and left his key ring no one would notice."

"So, I can expect that your fingerprints will be all over the office? How were you planning to explain that?"

"That wouldn't prove anything. I've been in and out of Hilliard's office a thousand times. So has almost every other graduate student in the history department not to mention the faculty."

"Perhaps, perhaps," Gaston said. "We'll see when I get a report from the crime scene unit."

"What would you have done if you had found something that pointed to Sarah?" I asked.

"Destroyed it," Allan answered bluntly. "I love her and I want to protect her."

"So you do believe she might have killed Hilliard?" Gaston looked at him curiously. "You love her enough to try to cover up a murder you think she committed? Bizarre form of love, if you ask me. It seems more likely that you killed Hilliard on the impulse of the moment, because you feared that Sarah was getting more interested in him than in you. You're not much of a planner. You act impulsively. You come barrelling into Hilliard's condo without checking to see if it's empty or under surveillance; for all I know you went charging into his office with the same disregard for consequences and killed him. For all we know you trashed his office covering up the traces of your own crime rather than trying to protect Sarah."

"Yeah? Well, bullshit. If that was the case why would I bother to come here at all? There's no reason for me to check out his apartment if I killed him. I only risked coming here to protect Sarah. Just in case. I've been waiting three days for your cops to go away so I could get in."

We were quiet as we thought about Allan's last point. I had to admit that it was a good one. At that time we had no hard evidence that he had done anything except act like a fool and that was not against the law.

"I don't fully believe you," Gaston told him. "But I don't have enough to hold you so I'm going to let you go for the moment. Do not get in the way of the investigation again. Go about your business and be sure to keep out of my way. If I find you poking around again I promise you that I'll arrest you for something — tampering with evidence, interfering with an investigation

— something. You may only have to spend a day or two in jail but believe me when I tell you that it won't be an experience you'll enjoy. Do you understand me?"

"Yeah," Allan answered sullenly. Allan did not seem to appreciate the break he was getting. I was hoping that Gaston would arrest him and throw his arrogant, sullen ass in jail.

"Now give me the keys and clear out of here," Gaston told him, "and don't let me catch you interfering in this investigation again."

Without a word Allan slid the keys to Gaston, got up and left the apartment. I followed him into the living room to make sure he left and did not make a detour into the bedroom to hide until we left.

Gaston followed me into the living room and said, "Well, that was unpleasant, wasn't it? You don't really get to see people at their best during a murder investigation."

My stomach growled reminding me how hungry I was. "Lunch," I reminded Gaston.

"Right. But let's go somewhere decent for a change."

We left the apartment, taking our garbage with us, and headed off to find a good restaurant. Good thinking has to be supported by fine cuisine.

chapter seventeen

The closest good restaurant was a place called Cellini on McGill College Avenue. It was a cavernous, split-level affair situated under one of the high-rise office towers that had taken over that street. The place was filled with what looked to be lawyers and stock-brokers, all wearing their business blues. I felt decidedly underdressed as I wasn't wearing a tie or a jacket.

After we ordered, spaghetti *alla putanesca* for me and fettucine with pesto for Gaston and a bottle of the house red to help put the events of the morning into a warm glow, Gaston pulled his notebook out of his pocket and began to flip through it. Not to be outdone I opened my file folder and pulled out my notes and began reviewing them.

"OK, my friend, let's see who we have as suspects. Arlene Ford remains on our list even though she went a long way to convince me of her innocence this morning. Allan Gutmacher is a candidate, as well. He's a loose cannon. He may have believed that the professor was interested in his girlfriend. If he barged into Hilliard's office to protect her honour or something he may have got into a fight and killed him. Michaels is definitely on our list. I don't know about opportunity but it certainly seems that he had a motive. We also have Professor Miller-More, the former love interest. She seemed the most genuinely upset of the people we interviewed but, who knows, maybe he left her and she was angry. I don't see more than that as a motive for her yet but we may as well keep her on the list of suspects until she is definitively disqualified. Finally, there is her husband. Hilliard was a rival for his wife's affection at one time."

"But we haven't interviewed him. We haven't even met the man. How is he a suspect?"

"It's *because* we haven't met with him. Remember, his wife left a message on his voice mail and he was to call me. So far he hasn't called. If you had a message to call the police what would you do?"

"Me? I'd be terrified. I'd call them as soon as I could; unless I had something to hide — then I might put it off for as long as possible. I get it," I exclaimed, finally realizing why Gaston had Fred More on his suspect list. "What makes him interesting to us is that he hasn't called."

"Exactly. I think we'll drop in on Mr. More as soon as we finish our lunch. Is there anyone else on our list?"

"I think we can safely exclude the cleaning woman, Mrs. Smith, and even Sarah Bloch. Neither of them appears to have had a motive. Regardless of what her boyfriend thinks I think Sarah handled herself intelligently and she appears to have been more or almost honest with us. Certainly as regards her relationship with Hilliard. I'd love to know what she and Allan talked about when they found each other in the history department. Maybe she thought he killed Hilliard and she was protecting him by not telling us exactly what happened that morning. Who knows? There may be others, random love interests and/or their boyfriends. But at the moment we have five solid suspects: Arlene Ford, Allan Gutmacher, Ron Michaels, Jane Miller-More, and Fred More. The evidence does not point directly to any one of them."

"And so our next move will be ... what?"

"For now, just to keep an open mind should be enough. The secret to solving crimes is to keep plugging away, gathering the facts to ensure that we see and understand all the possibilities, and jumping to no conclusions."

There seemed little more to say about the case for the moment, and Gaston sat back and relaxed. We finished our meal, and had just been served coffee. "The last time I was in this restaurant I was with my father," he remarked, looking around at the elegant, comfortable room. "This place is one of his favourite haunts. He is the senior partner at Lemieux, Clark, Beaubien and Stein. You can see that the legal profession is very well represented here. And he looks the part: a very judicial-looking, elderly gentleman, very formal in his behaviour, even with me ... or especially with me. He has always considered that relations between a father and son should be very formal."

I said nothing, thinking that I now understood from whom Gaston had inherited his cool demeanor.

"We see each other rarely," Gaston continued. "There has been a certain coldness between us for years over my choice of profession. My sister" — I was instantly on the alert at this mention of the beautiful Gisèle— "thinks that the rift is much more serious than it is and is always trying to bring us back together, and she manoeuvred us into having lunch together here a few weeks ago. We ran out of conversation after each of us had asked about the other's health and well-being and ended up in an embarrassing silence."

Again Gaston paused, and I wondered if now was the moment to ask whether Gisèle was married or in love.

"Then suddenly," Gaston went on, "he asked me a surprising question: if I still 'worked for the police'. I thought it was a strange way of asking the question, as if the police were a competing law firm rather than a public institution. I was also surprised that he thought I might have changed careers without his knowing. But it was just his way of letting me know what he thinks of my job. Since I'm not a lawyer, not even a notary, I have not chosen a career worthy of the name Lemieux."

"He sounds formidable. The forbidding patriarch. Perhaps a bit —" I searched for a diplomatic term — "rigid." I visualized myself approaching the austere figure my imagination had conjured up and asking for his daughter's hand in marriage. The very thought was terrifying.

"Perhaps a little rigid, yes. My father," Gaston said, laughing, "would consider your profession to be a very bohemian one. Possibly not quite as bad as the police department, but still unacceptable."

Not son-in-law material then. I heaved an inward sigh.

Gaston called for our bill and we prepared to leave the restaurant. I was beginning to see why Gaston had befriended me. As the scion of an haut-bourgeois Quebec family, he was out of place on the police force, though he loved the work. He saw in me a contemporary who was not of his world but with whom he could share some of his interests. Someone whose life conspicuously lacked the kind of social pressures and demands his family background had exerted on him. I could see why his colleagues on the force thought he was a stuck-up snob. I could also see that he was nothing of the kind.

As we walked to the campus in silence I thought about the last time, the previous Friday, I had a meal with my parents and how different it was from Gaston's experience.

My parents like to have my brother, my sister, me, and all of my nephews and nieces come over for dinner on Friday nights — a sort of shabbas for the assimilated. I try to leave work by six o'clock on Fridays so as not to be too late. My parents live on Randall Avenue, in a duplex that they bought in the fifties when prices were cheap and this part of NDG was considered practically in the country.

Last Friday was no different from any other Friday. I was, as usual, the last to arrive. My parents, my brother Ben, his wife Sandra, my sister Naomi, and her husband Max were all in the overfurnished living room sipping on soft drinks. The children were in the basement watching TV. I went downstairs to see them. Playing with them on Friday nights made me long for a family of my own. However, by Saturday morning the longing had passed, so I remained single and childless.

Shabbas in my family is a long way from a religious event. My father, a cab driver, comes from a working-class background and is a proud, lifelong socialist. He considers religion a way to keep the masses in their place and so there is no religious practice in his house; I know my mother, an elementary schoolteacher, would like to be a little more observant but only goes so far as to light the candles at sundown. But they have never given up their religion's vocabulary of reverence for the family. Friday night is shabbas and the night the whole family should be together for a home-cooked meal. My siblings and I rarely miss one of these family get-togethers. We are too important to each other to go more than a week without some kind of physical contact.

"Sammy, come and sit with us. I'll get you a coke," my mother called when I came up from the basement. My brother and sister and I hugged and my father tousled my hair as if I were still a child. "So what's new in the literary world?" he asked. "Ben and Naomi were just bringing us up to date on the financial world. I tell you, I could have made a fortune if I had a fortune to invest."

Ben is an accountant and Naomi is a stockbroker. They are both very successful. My father, given his socialist beliefs, doesn't quite understand how they can devote their lives to the pursuit of profit — surplus labour value to him — with such pleasure, but he is proud of their success. (Ben and Naomi are investing money for my parents so that they will have a comfortable old age — I contribute too but not as much as they do, given my bookseller's income — and be able to retire to Florida. So it's quite possible that my father did make a fortune that day thanks to my older siblings.) As the baby of the family I am the most indulged, spoiled, some might say, but not so much that youthful sibling rivalries carried into our adult relationships.

Dinner, in fact any meal with my family, is a noisy adults-only affair. The kids are happier eating in the basement rec room — away from their boisterous, embarrassing elders. There's always lots of food, a more or less traditional meal of matzoh ball soup, chicken, kugel and that awful sweet wine. The meal, shorn of religious content, is full of jokes, familial teasing, and banter. There are also times when we have political debates that are real table-banging events. Anyone who doesn't know us but overheard the arguments would probably think that we're getting ready to kill one another. It's easy to beat my father in an argument based on logic, impossible to win based on volume. My mother, the one with the more common sense, tends to stay out of these fights until we run ourselves down and then she usually ends discussion with a sharp, insightful remark. That doesn't exactly stop us but it does get us to change the topic or the tone of our discussions.

I love these evenings with my family. I wondered, as Gaston and I walked to McGill, a murder very much on our minds, how he would react if he ever attended one of our family meals. Would he be shocked by the differences between my family and his? Or would he be jealous?

We walked to the campus in silence.

chapter eighteen

We stopped at the main entrance to the campus and asked where Dean More's office was. We were directed to an administration building in the most out-of-the-way corner of the university campus. It was a nondescript box of about nine stories, the only structure in sight that was in any way modern. The bottom three floors were brick and the rest black siding. The building directory told us that More's office was on the top floor. We took the one working elevator. Just inside a glass door inscribed with Dean of Graduate Studies, we found a secretary whose desk name plate identified her as Donna Nichols. She was typing away on a computer at a speed to be envied and didn't notice us for a moment. She had coal-black hair cut short, in a kind of 1920s bob. What I could see of her face in profile was pretty, with regular features and a smooth complexion, but she wore too much make-up. She was wearing a denim shirt with an appliqué flower design across the back and a red kerchief around her neck. As I had her in profile I could see the beginnings of a black lacy bra at the opening of her shirt. A discreet clearing of Gaston's throat finally got her attention and she turned to us and asked officiously, "May I help you?"

"We'd like to see Dean More," Gaston responded.

"Certainly. Today is out of the question, in fact the rest of the week is booked. Perhaps next week some-time?" she said, referring to a large agenda.

"I beg your pardon," Gaston said with exaggerated politeness. "I didn't mention who I am. Gaston Lemieux, detective, of the Montreal police department. This is my colleague Mr. Wiseman." He showed her his badge and identification. "Perhaps Dean More could find room in his busy schedule. Would you be good enough to tell that we'd like to see him now? If it's not inconvenient. I'm afraid this is a matter that can't wait."

Ms. Nichols got up, and looking at him warily, said, "I'll tell him you're here." She walked into Dean More's office after the most perfunctory of knocks.

After a couple of minutes she was back, holding the door open for us. "Dean More will see you now," she recited as if reading from a cue card.

Fred More rose from his chair and came out from behind his desk to greet us. He was a tall man, over six feet, with the build of an athlete. His shoulders were broad and his waist was trim. He had straight dark brown hair and a matching wispy moustache. He looked more like a football coach than an academic. We intro-duced ourselves and shook hands all around. His grip was, of course, vice-like; I tried to hide the wince of pain I felt. At least he was dressed like a dean, in a tan and brown Harris tweed jacket, dark brown slacks, and loafers. His yellow oxford cotton shirt was a button-down, with a monogram at the cuff. He wore a striped tie and looked collegial as hell and I half expected him to start smoking a pipe. He didn't.

"I expected you to call me," Gaston explained. "Your wife left a message on your voice mail giving you my phone numbers."

"Yes, I've been meaning to call. But as you see, I'm extremely busy and haven't had time to call." I couldn't see that he was busy at all. His office was neat and tidy and looked more like a showroom for office furniture than a place where actual work got done. His desk was clear except for a cup of sharpened pencils and pens and a yellow legal pad. On the credenza behind his desk was a telephone, some pictures of himself and Jane in various rustic and vacation settings and the omnipresent computer. A regular desktop computer with screen and key board. This one was beige.

"But I'm sure you're very concerned about the murder of one of your faculty members," said Gaston neutrally.

"Oh, yes, terribly concerned." He sounded terribly unconcerned as he motioned for us to take chairs. We did so. He returned to his power position, seated at his vast, shiny desk. I began to see why he hadn't returned Gaston's call; he probably never returned anybody's call. He was smooth, self-centred and oblivious. "I've ordered a full-scale inquiry into our security measures," he was saying, sounding extremely pleased with his own efficiency. "I've asked all department chairs to review their procedures. I've solicited quotes for combination security locks on all doors that open onto public area and hallways. And I've sent out a number of memos outlining steps to be taken in the event that a suspicious person or persons are seen wandering about the buildings. I expect to be able to bring some specific proposals to the deans' meeting at the beginning of next month. I have been very concerned. I don't ever want anything like this to happen again."

He had been busy. All those memos and reports in four days. The man must be a memo-writing machine.

"Now, what can I do to help your investigation? Of course I'll do whatever I can." He said this with an earnest look as if he'd been eager to help all along, but had not been asked.

"Did you know Professor Hilliard well?" Gaston asked, taking out a notebook.

"In a professional way, yes. We were never close, but we had a cordial relationship. When I was in the history department I saw a bit more of him than I have recently. Of course you know that my wife was engaged to him at one time. But that was in the past. Her feelings about him changed, though she continued to regard him as a friend. As did I. Their previous acquaintance didn't affect our ability to treat each other with respect, genuine respect. He was also an admirable scholar. A fine historian."

So that was how he wanted to play it. Oh so civilized. But then he'd ended up with the girl, hadn't he? So he could afford to be smug.

"We heard that her decision to break off her relationship with him and marry you was rather sudden."

"Sudden? no, I wouldn't say it was that. We both knew Jane as our star undergraduate, top of her class, on the honour roll from her first year to her last and she won the history prize and a scholarship to the University of Toronto to do graduate work. So I've known her at least as long as Harold did. When she wanted to return here to teach I was delighted. And although we normally prefer not to hire our undergraduates or graduates for their first jobs, in Jane's case I was able to convince the history department to make an exception. I was chairman of the department at that time so my recommendation carried quite a bit of weight."

"I had heard that Professor Hilliard was instrumental in getting Professor Miller-More her job here."

"Harold was in favour of it, certainly. But I hired her."

"But she was romantically involved with him at the time, I think."

"Yes, for a short time. She was young, after all, and Harold was quite a lady's man. But Jane is a serious person and Hal wasn't one for commitment. Jane and I got to know each other over the years of working together and our relationship is built on a very firm foundation of love and respect."

What about passion? I wondered. The dean looked every inch the bluff, hearty he-man, but he spoke like a pompous dry stick of an academic. Why a woman would prefer him to the dashing Harold Hilliard was beyond me. But women like stability and solidity. Or so I'm told.

"I see," said Gaston. "So there is no truth to the rumours that your wife was contemplating returning to Harold Hilliard?"

"I haven't heard any such rumour," he said, unperturbed. "But of course no one would mention any such nonsense to me. Universities are incredible rumour mills, as I'm sure you've discovered in the course of making your inquiries. No, no, there's no truth to it at all. Jane and I are devoted to each other."

"I'm sure it's just the gossip of the bored, trying to make a story where there is none," Gaston said. "When was the last time you saw Professor Hilliard?"

"I think I saw him at the faculty club last week."

"And on the morning of the murder, your wife left home at her usual time?"

"Yes, it was a very ordinary morning, until we heard the news of the murder. My wife was very shocked, as I'm sure you understand."

Gaston's cell phone chose that moment to ring, and he said, "Excuse me, please," taking the phone out of his inside jacket pocket. He spoke to someone in French, in low tones, then hung up. To Dean More, he said, "Do you know someone named Steve Mandopolous?"

"Steve? Why, certainly. He's part of our security team."

"Well, it seems that your chief of security, Mr. Alexander, assigned him and a couple of other fellows in his department to search for Hilliard's computer, which as you may have heard, was missing from his office. And they've apparently found it."

"Hilliard's laptop?" I asked, excited.

Ignoring my question, he asked me, "Do you know where the McIntyre Science Centre is?"

"Yes," I replied. "It's the round building up on Docteur Penfield Boulevard."

"The computer they found may be Hilliard's. They can't be sure until they've done some checks. Tell me, Mr. More, is there someone on campus who looks after computer installations, programming, that type of thing?"

"Well," A strange look passed across More's face, as if he was trying to do an intensely difficult bit of mental arithmetic, much too fast. "There's Barbara Young downstairs. She's in charge of our campus network and the Internet hookups and that kind of thing. I suppose that she's our resident computer expert."

"Please call her and ask her if we could drop by her office later. Tell her we'll be bringing a computer with us. After the crime unit has had a chance to try to get prints from it, I'd like her to help me find out what's in the files."

Fred More looked a little put out at receiving a direct order from a police detective, but he picked up his phone, pressed a button and said, "Donna, get me

Barbara Young down in ..." he turned his head and looked at me and then at Gaston, apparently realizing that the two of us, who were not used to university protocol, might be surprised that he was unable to make a simple phone call without help.

He cleared his throat and said, "Never mind, I'll do it myself. Just get me her local."

He hung up.

Gaston walked over to the window of Dean More's office and looked out at the McGill ghetto. Once it was an area of inexpensive greystone buildings, rooming houses, and apartments, but it's been yuppified over the last few years, and converted back into single-family dwellings and condominiums. There are some high rises that accommodate students, but the urban poor who used to share this neighbourhood with them are gone.

About ten seconds later, Donna came in and placed a sheet of paper in front of him him. "Will that be all, sir?"

"No, wait here, Donna. These gentlemen will be *leaving* in a minute," he said with a distinct emphasis and a significant look in our direction, "and then we can go over the, the ..." he glanced wildly around his bare desk.

"The registration spread sheets, sir?" asked Donna solicitously.

Neat save, I thought.

"Yes, yes."

Donna said in soothing voice. "I do have some questions about them."

"Of course," the dean said, pride intact, and called Barbara Young all by himself.

"Hello, Barbara?" he said. "It's Fred More calling." There was a pause while he listened to her and he continued, "Fine thanks. Listen, I've got a policeman with me and he needs your help with a computer. He needs to know what's in it. He's investigating the Hilliard murder. He wants to know if you'll be available to meet with him."

He covered the mouthpiece and asked Gaston, "When to you want to see her?"

Gaston looked at his watch and mumbled, to himself as much as to anyone else, "It's two now and the fingerprint tests will take about an hour plus travel time for the CSU so let's say between three-thirty and four."

"Between three-thirty and four." Dean More repeated into the phone. "Thanks, Barbara, I'll tell him." He hung up and looked at Gaston. "That will be fine. She won't leave until she sees you."

"Thank you. May I use your phone?" Not waiting for Fred More's agreement, Gaston got up and walked over to the credenza and dialed his office. He told whoever he spoke to where the crime scene team was to go. The person on the other end of the line apparently thought that they had all the time in the world to do this; Gaston, with a commanding edge in his voice, said he wanted the unit there *immédiatement* or faster, if possible. He gave directions, hung up, and turned to Dean More. "Thank you for taking the time to see us."

"Not at all," said More, stiffly. "I'm glad I could help."

As we left More's office I glanced back and observed that he appeared to be a lot more interested in his secretary than he was in the registration statistics.

"How far is it to the McIntyre building?" Gaston asked.

"About a five-or ten-minute walk. Just up the hill on Docteur Penfield."

We crossed the campus. At McTavish Street we turned and went up past the student union building.

As we walked I made conversation about the missing, now found computer. "It's good luck that the computer was found," I said.

"Humpf," Gaston responded. He obviously didn't like the idea of having to rely on luck and wanted to reserve judgement until he saw the computer and learned how it was found. He puts a lot of meaning into a "humpf." We passed the rest of the walk in silence.

In the lobby of the McIntyre building a man of about my age, wearing the uniform of the campus police, was waiting for us. He had neatly combed black hair and eyes as black as printer's ink. He was standing next to a table on which there was a green plastic garbage holding what I took to be the computer.

"Mr. Mandopolous?" Gaston said, extending his hand.

"Inspector Lemieux?" Steve Mandopolous said, shaking the extended hand.

"This is Sam Wiseman," Gaston said, introducing me. Steve and I shook hands.

"Is that the computer?" Gaston asked.

"Yes. I put it in a garbage bag so as not to ruin any prints."

"Where did you find it?"

"I didn't. The elevator repair people found it. It was on top of one of the elevators. They were inspecting the car and when they went onto the top to check the cabling they noticed it."

"Let's take a look at it. Put it down on the table."

Mandopolous did as he was told. Gaston pulled a set of surgical gloves from his pocket, slipped them on and carefully slid the computer out of the plastic bag. It was stained with black grease but it didn't look damaged, at least not from the outside. There were no obvious dents or banged corners.

"Where exactly was it found?"

"On top of the elevator. We were in luck — the elevators were out of service. It's their annual inspection," Steve told Gaston. "Someone must have shoved it down the elevator shaft to get rid of it. Their bad luck that the elevator was stopped between floors."

"And our good luck," I put in.

"Quite," agreed Gaston. "The crime lab will have to take a close look at it but I really think that the most important thing about this computer is what's in it, not what's on the case. Steve, tell me how you think the computer ended up on top of an elevator car."

"Sure." Steve straightened his back and stood at attention as if he were reporting to a superior officer in the army. "The elevators are inspected once a year. There are a lot of elevators in the university when you consider how many buildings there are so the inspection crew is here pretty much all the time. We're pretty used to at least one elevator being out of service somewhere on campus and we know the repair men pretty well, almost as if they worked for the university, too.

"They were in this building testing the doors and the braking mechanism on each floor. The elevator doors can be open between floors while they do their tests. There are danger signs and barriers at each open door to prevent accidents. But it doesn't prevent someone from tossing something down the elevator shaft. The thing is, it's really dark in there and you can't tell if the elevator car is above or below the door you are tossing something through. I believe that the person who tossed this was in a hurry and didn't realize that the car was just below the level of the open door. So the computer didn't fall very far. If the car had been above the open door we never would have found this thing. The only place they never inspect is the bottom of the elevator shaft."

"Do you know from which floor the computer was thrown into the shaft?"

"It's very difficult to say. The last thing they do is crawl out onto the top of the car to check it out. But the repair guys can't tell when or from where the computer was tossed in. They'd been working on that car for at least two days around the time of the murder so there was a lot of opportunity to use the elevator shaft to dispose of unwanted items, whether it was murder evidence or not."

"Mr. Mandopolous," Gaston said warmly, "your kind of reporting makes my job so much easier." He must really have loved Mandopolous's summation because he stopped and shook his hand.

Just then one of the CSU team came over and took Gaston aside. They went into a huddle; Steve Mandopoulos and I stretched our ears trying to eavesdrop on their conversation. Gaston noticed our interest and said, "If you don't mind, I'd prefer that you wait for me in the foyer."

What he meant was the lobby we'd passed through on our way to the scene. There were chairs and a coffee-and-soft-drink machine. It was full of students, most of them wearing white lab coats, hanging out between classes. Steve Mandopolous and I looked at each other, then we left. Reluctantly. We went to get a cup of vending-machine coffee in the snack bar on the main floor. Frankly, I thought we deserved better.

I didn't understand why we could not be present when Gaston and his team took fingerprints from a computer and examined the corridor and elevator shaft. But I was sure he had his reasons. I thought it would be a good idea to see what Mandopolous knew in the way of campus gossip. Fingerprints of a different sort, you could say.

"Do you spend a lot of time with the academic staff?" I asked him. I mentioned specifically the dean and his assistant, but I hoped he would have some comments to make about the rest of the campus at the same time.

Steve understood that my question was motivated by more than just idle curiosity. "Too much time. Like those two, the dean and his assistant. That guy is such a mook it's not funny."

"What do you mean?"

"What do I mean? The guy can't do anything. He looks good for the university but he sits on his hands and wonders why he can't find his ass. Look. Instead of doing something or taking a coffee break he has to look important and she knows how to make him feel like a big shot. If he didn't have a lot of people to cover for him he wouldn't have a job. He was no big deal as a teacher and I can't see that he's any better as an administrator. He's constantly ogling his assistant, and she lets him get away with it."

"You mean they're ...?" I raised my eyebrows but did not finish the question.

"Who knows for sure. I see things, that's all. Maybe I have a suspicious nature."

"But he's married to Professor Miller-More. She seems so nice. Or does it turn out that she's some kind of controlling bitch? I mean, sometimes people seem nice, but ..."

"No way, everybody likes her. I don't mean she's everybody's friend, she's rather a reserved person, but she's nice to everybody. But that's what I mean. First she was going with the dead guy, Hilliard, and everybody says they're just right for each other and then, all of a sudden she dumps him and marries More and everyone says *they're* the perfect couple. So who knows? Get what I'm saying?"

He seemed to be saying he didn't know anything. I decided to take one final shot at uncovering some more information. "What about Hilliard? I hear that he was something with the ladies."

"Yeah, he seemed to get around. Lots of juicy stories there but no one ever actually caught him at anything. So, either it's all just talk, or he's a real careful guy. I know he wouldn't try anything like More does, with his secretary. Too obvious. I guess it's the quiet ones who get away with murder." Then, remembering that Hilliard actually didn't get away with anything, he paused and finished his thought, "Or get murdered, anyway."

"So you think his murder had something to do with a woman?" I asked.

"What else? No one ever got killed over a class assignment, did they?"

"I guess not," I answered.

We sat in silence as I thought over what Steve had told me; it wasn't much, but it did tend to confirm some of our suspicions about Hilliard's love life. Still, he told me nothing that would narrow the list of suspects. Arlene Ford was still a suspect. Nothing I had learned eliminated her. There was still the possibility of jealousy over another woman. Jane Miller-More might have had a fight with Hilliard because he wanted her to leave her husband. A fight that could have ended badly. Dean More had once had a motive for jealousy, when he was trying to get Jane away from Hilliard, but he'd succeeded, and apparently was more interested in Donna than his wife anyway, if Steve was right. Allan Gutmacher could have done it in a fit of possessiveness over his girlfriend. It didn't seem that anything actually developed between Sarah Bloch and Hilliard but one never knew, did one? And there didn't have to be anything between them. Allan only had to believe that there was something going on to become enraged and try to have it out with Hilliard. That kind of thing can end violently even if nobody intends it to.

At this point Gaston reappeared, carrying the computer in the plastic bag.

"We're finished," he announced. "Thanks for waiting. Mr. Mandopolous, would you be so kind as to accompany us to Ms. Young's office? I'd like you to be there in case she has any questions about where and under what circumstances you found the computer."

The three of us trooped off back to the administration building.

chapter nineteen

We knocked at Barbara Young's office door. There was a sound of conversation behind the door and then it was opened by Fred More, who invited us in. I wondered what had happened to the important registration work he and Donna had been so keen to get to. But his office was only two floors up, and why shouldn't he be here? It seemed a little funny, though.

Barbara Young must be a pretty important person, I thought, because she had a large office. There were stacks of computer printouts everywhere. The pages of the ones I could see were in some kind of computer hieroglyphics. She also had three computers on a long table behind her desk. Two of them were flashing screen savers and she was working on the third. When she got tired of looking at her computer she could turn her head a quarter turn and look out one of her three windows onto lower campus.

Ms. Young — Dr. Young, I was to learn — was sitting with her back to us at her desk typing away at top speed on a computer on the table. Without stopping or looking up she said, "Hi. Be with you in a moment. I just want to get this code down before I forget it."

While we waited I took another look at the colourful screen savers on the computers next to where she was working. After staring at them for a few seconds I realized that I was looking at something a little more complex than the usual whirling lines of a screen saver. One of the computers was constructing a very colourful design. As new pieces to the computer jigsaw were added the puzzle became larger. I noticed that a small part of the design would become magnified, changing the screen completely and new pieces would be added to the abstract for a while until it magnified a small section and changed again. I then observed that as the design on one computer got larger the design on the other computer became correspondingly smaller. Pieces of the colour puzzle moved from one computer to the other. As one design was broken down the other constructed itself with the imported pieces. I realized that I was looking at the construction and deconstruction of a fractal; that one computer was importing pieces of the fractal from the other. At a certain point, as one of the computers finished its design and the other was left with a blank screen, the process reversed and the computer with the blank screen began importing fractal data from the other computer to construct its own design. I didn't understand how all this worked but I was impressed.

Barabara Young finished typing, got up and walked over to where we were standing, snapping me out of my reverie. "I see you like my artwork," she said to me as I was still transfixed by her computers.

"It's very pretty," I responded. "What is it? Some kind of fractal art?"

"Sort of. It's an experiment I'm doing in net-

works. One computer is sending information to the
other and back again according to a set of program-
ing rules I wrote. I'm trying to find the most efficient
way of transferring data. The computers could just as
easily be in different cities or countries as next to
each other."

"Why use fractals?" I asked.

"Why not? I wanted to see how complicated sets of
information can be transferred. Fractals are nicer to
look at than screens full of code, don't you think?"

I didn't get a chance to answer as Dean More
cleared his throat in order to insert himself into the conversation. Gaston had patiently gazed around the room
during the explanation of data transfer.

"Barbara, Dr. Young, I'd like you to meet Detective
Gaston Lemieux, you know Steve, and Sol Wiseman."

"Pleased to meet you," she said to Gaston, shaking his hand. "Hi, Steve." Turning to me, she said,
"It's nice to meet you, Sol. Don't I know you from
somewhere?"

"It's Sam, Sam Wiseman," I told her, shaking her
offered hand. "Maybe you know me from the bookstore,
Dickens & Company. I work there," I added modestly.

"That's right," she said. "I know the owner, Jennifer
Rico-something."

"Riccofia," I finished for her.

"What can I do for you gentlemen?"

Barbara Young was a tall, large-boned woman. She
had long, curly reddish blond hair which she kept out of
her face by wearing her glasses on the top of her head. I
don't know how well she saw us but wearing her glasses that way helped us to see her pretty face and lovely
warm smile. She had an ample body, but because of her
height, almost six feet, she didn't look overweight, just
big. She wore a grey blazer over a blue corduroy shirt-

waist dress. She was a very attractive person and I took an instant liking to her.

"Let's sit down," she invited. We followed her over to a worktable with four chairs and sat down.

"I would like you to look at this computer and tell me if you can tell me what's on it," Gaston explained. "We have reason to believe that it belonged to Professor Hilliard and that it might contain some clues that will help us identify his murderer."

"Be glad to. Poor Harold. He could be a charmer if he wanted to. Didn't want to mostly. Still, he didn't deserve to die. He was bright and he could be funny and I'll miss him." A cloud passed over her face as she thought about our victim but her sunny disposition returned and she asked, "Do you have a warrant to show me or something? Sorry to be sticky but we care a lot about privacy laws here."

"A warrant's not necessary in this case," answered Gaston. "The computer is lost property and was turned over to the police as such. At the very least, we need to identify the owner and ascertain whether it was lost or stolen. If it turns out not to be the property of Professor Hilliard I'll turn it over to the university lost and found. But if it is, it's evidence in a murder case and it's legal for us to impound it."

Steve told Barbara how and where he had found it.

"On the top of an elevator! I see," Dr. Young said in an amused voice. "Well, let's take a look and see if it survived its fall." She fished about on her worktable and found a free cable which she plugged into the back of the laptop. She flipped open the cover and pressed the on button.

The machine just whirred and made scratching noises for a while, but finally something came up on the screen. "Well, there's no question that this belonged to

Harold," Dr. Young told us. "Look at this." She turned the machine around so we could see it. The screen had a custom designed screensaver: it was flashing the word *Clio* in large letters in the centre of the screen, and the name Harold Hilliard scrolled along the top and bottom of the screen. Kind of egotistical, I thought, but I was also excited that we had an important clue in the case.

Gaston was also pleased. "Excéllent!" he said and added, "This is an important piece of evidence. Let's be very careful with it."

"Don't worry," Barbara assured him. "It's plastic and metal and if it could survive a fall down an elevator shaft I doubt that I can harm it. Let's see if we can find out what's on it."

She hit the enter button. The screen cleared and a message popped up in the middle of the screen: *Enter password*.

"Anyone know the password?" Dr. Young asked us.

Gaston asked, "Why would we need a password?"

Where had he spent the last twenty years or so? He seemed to think that it was odd behaviour for the professor to have protected access to his computer with a password.

Barbara looked at him to see if he was kidding. Obviously, he wasn't. "Well, Hal Hilliard locked everybody, except himself, out of his computer. It is a bit paranoid to require a password right at the beginning. Most people protect various files and everybody password-protects their e-mail boxes, but Hal was one of the few to program his computer to need a password just to get into the thing. You couldn't even play the games unless you knew the password."

"Is there no way to probe the machine's memory to find the password?" Gaston looked baffled by all this. He was used to probing human nature.

"Yes and no," Barbara answered. "I don't think I can. I might be able to worm my way in by creating a network with one of my computers. It's possible I could get access to his hard drive that way. But there is no guarantee that I'll be able to find his password. A network will only get me past his first line of defence, onto his front porch but not into his house. The door will still be locked. But I might be able to look under the mat to see if there's a key, if you get my analogy. Or we can guess. A lot of people use a familiar word or phrase — their last names or street names and such. Want to try a guess?"

"Sure," I interjected. "What about Hilliard?"

Dr. Young typed Hilliard into the computer but nothing happened. We got a beep and the password prompt reappeared.

"What about HilliardH or Hhilliard?" I asked.

"Too many letters," Dr. Young responded. "The maximum is eight letters or symbols in some combination, like Hilliar1 or something like that."

"Try that," offered Gaston.

Barbara tried Hilliar1 but got nowhere.

"Did you know Professor Hilliard well enough to know if he was a sophisticated computer user?" Gaston inquired of Dr. Young.

"I knew him well enough to know that he wasn't. I taught him how to program this protection, I'm afraid. It was only a few months ago," Dr. Young replied, a little embarrassed.

"Well, what password did you use when you were teaching him to set up his program?"

"I usually use TEST1 when I do that but I advise people to change the password as soon as they can." She frowned, thinking about the problem. "And the thing of it is, I advise them to come up with something nobody will ever think of, something outlandish, even crazy. I remember telling him that. I even remember what he said. 'There's method in that madness,' he said. So we may have a serious problem here. But let's try, you never know." She typed TEST1. We were still locked out. That wasn't the key under the mat. "I'd better set up a network and see if that works."

Dr. Young quickly assembled the hardware she would need to set up her network: a second laptop and some cabling. She wired the two computers together, turned on her computer and inserted a diskette into her disk drive. She hit the enter key a few times and explained, "I'm loading a networking program I wrote into my computer in the hopes that it will give me access to his hard drive."

Dr. Young's computer began to hum and whirr and she typed in spurts and then seemed to become lost in thought for a while and then she would type furiously for a minute or two and repeat the process. No one said anything while she did that. I thought about Harold saying there was method in that madness. Somebody had said that to me recently, but who was it? For some reason a mental image of my open window at night came into my mind, with a cool breeze wafting in.

And that's when the light went on in my brain. What I remembered was reading *Hamlet* in a half-crazed state of fatigue just before dawn several nights ago. Polonius says, "Though this be madness, yet there's method in it."

"I've got it," I almost shouted. Everybody looked startled. "The password."

I turned to face Gaston and babbled in excitement: "Remember the Post-it note we found under his desk blotter? It had 'Ham III 1' on it. We thought it referred to something in the play but maybe it was the password to his computer. That's why he hid it."

"Very good," Gaston congratulated me. "Try it please, Dr. Young. It's H-A-M I-I-I and the number one."

Dr. Young typed it in as Gaston recited it to her but nothing happened.

"Try Hamlet 3 1," Gaston suggested. But that didn't work any better.

"I'm going to try poking around through the network I created," Dr. Young told us.

Had my long night of reading Shakespeare been no use? I didn't think so. I wasn't giving up so easily. Phrases from *Hamlet,* misremembered and garbled, were flashing through my head. The "slings and arrows of outrageous fortune." "Get thee to a nunnery." "To be or not to be." And then the light went on in my brain a second time. "Try this," I said barely able to suppress my excitement. "2-B-OR-NOT-2-B. Get it? That's from *Hamlet* Act three Scene one!"

"Wow, that's really clever," Dr. Young exclaimed and typed it in. "But it's one symbol too long. It's nine symbols not eight."

"Shit!" I said. I was really disappointed. It had seemed so perfect.

We were quiet for a couple of minutes as I tried to think up some other Shakespearean password.

"Wait a minute," said Dr. Young. "Let's try this. *Not,* spelled *naught,* is another word for nothing or zero. Let's replace not with zero and see what we get. So that's 2-B-OR-0-2-B," she said as she typed and — lo and behold! Hilliard's computer came to life. I was thrilled. So was everybody else. They began to applaud.

"That's brilliant," Gaston told me. "Well done."

"That's a typical Hilliard type of password," Dr. Young said. "Obvious once you see it but almost impossible to see. Way to go, Sam."

Even the irritable Dean More seemed impressed.

"Now what is it I'm looking for?" Barbara Young asked Gaston.

"Please try his e-mail, first."

"OK. I'll hook his computer up to one of my phone lines and we'll see if we can crack his mailbox." Dr. Young busied herself with unhooking the cabling that attached Hilliard's computer to hers and looked around in her spaghetti of wire for a free phone wire she could use to access Hilliard's e-mail.

While she was doing this Dean More looked at his watch and said, "Well done. I'm delighted that we've made so much progress so quickly. I hope you'll soon have enough information to have the case solved. I think you've all done a wonderful job and I'm proud to have been able to help you. But the administration's work must not stop because of these extraordinary events." On the words "work must not stop" he looked at Steve, in effect telling him to get back to his usual chores. "I am late for another appointment so I'll have to leave now. You know where to find me if you need me. Thank you again for all that you have done." He signalled his goodbye with a nod of his head in our general direction and turned and quick-marched out of the room.

What a triumph of pomposity the man was. From the way he talked you would think that he had actually done something to help in the investigation. I could just see him composing a memo taking all the credit for solving the crime — when it actually got solved!

While More was making his speech, Steve Mandopolous had gotten to his feet too. Now he said, "I guess I'd better get back to crew." He started moving toward the door.

"Please, Mr. Mandopolous, would you mind staying?" Gaston asked. "We may need your assistance."

Steve, looking pleased and relieved, returned to the work-table and resumed his seat.

"I'm ready to go," Dr. Young informed us. She typed a few commands and a menu popped onto the screen. "This is his e-mail program. I installed it for him and gave him his e-mail address but he configured the program himself. That means he set his password and set the time limits for keeping e-mail."

"You mean we have to guess at another password?" I asked. "Unless he used the same one twice we could be at this forever."

"We could be," answered Dr. Young. "But I'm betting that he used a tough password to get into his computer and easy, obvious ones to get into his various programs. If the front door to your house is triple locked and patrolled by armed guards and vicious dogs and so on you don't have to worry so much about locking the doors to the various rooms in your house. I knew how Harold thought and he is likely to have done just that. We'll soon see."

She selected the menu choice, "Check incoming messages" and when it asked for the user name she typed "hilliardh" and when it asked for a password she typed "clio".

What made you choose those names?" Gaston asked.

"His e-mail address is: hilliardh@mcgillu.edu.ca and I advise every body to use their e-mail name as the login. So that was easy. I'm guessing that he used Clio because he used it for the computer and so it was easy to remember."

The computer made dialling noises, followed by that airy whistle that modems make when they look for each other, and connected. A message popped up on the screen which said: "Sorry. Your password is incorrect. Try again. Remember passwords can contain as many as

8 symbols and should contain at least one numeric or other non-alpha symbol!"

"Goddamn software," Barbara Young exclaimed. "I know, I know. My mistake." She looked up from the computer and said to the rest of us. "Sorry, sometimes I forget my own rules. Pandora recognized the login but the password didn't match. It works kind of like your bank card. Your code has to match the one on the magnetic strip on the back. In this case the password has to match the one embedded in the software with your login." She turned back to the computer and hit the enter key and when the login prompt returned she again typed "hilliardh" and in response to the password prompt she typed "clio1".

This time she got a positive response. "Checking for new messages" appeared on the screen followed by, "You have no new mail."

"Well, we now know that Hal picked up any waiting messages before he was murdered. Let's hope that there is something in his in basket." She hit the enter key again and clicked on the in basket icon. A grid popped up with one entry on it. "I hope this is significant because it looks like he cleaned out his mail. There is only one message left. It's dated a couple of days before he was murdered and it's from millerj — that would be Jane Miller-More, Fred's wife. Shall we take a look?"

I could barely restrain myself from shouting, "Yes!" and spiking an imaginary football in an imaginary end zone. Gaston was more controlled and said merely, "Yes, please."

She double-clicked on the message line and an almost blank screen appeared. There was a series of lines at the top of the screen telling who the message was from and to and the date and time but there was nothing in the message part.

Barbara Young was as surprised as I was. "What the ..." she muttered. "Oh, damn!"

"What's the problem?" Gaston asked.

"Look," she said scrolling down the screen. "Big chunks of the message are missing. Either they never arrived or part of the hard drive was damaged in the fall."

"What do you mean — that part of the message never arrived? Isn't it like a telegram? Everything comes together."

"Not really," Professor Young told him. "It's more like flashes of information, we call them packets, arriving separately and reforming when they get to the destination computer. It looks like some of the packets didn't arrive or are in a corrupt sector of the hard drive."

"How could that happen?" Gaston asked, genuinely confused. Like most of us he didn't really understand how e-mail worked. He seemed to assume that is was like regular mail — you sent a message and it was received complete and unaffected by missing packets, whatever they were.

"The same way a telephone conversation is sometimes interrupted by a bad connection," Barbara explained. "If the line is bad or if there is interference some of the information will be lost."

"I thought there were special phone lines for this stuff," Gaston said.

"There are, but the university doesn't provide them for every office; too expensive. And we don't know if he picked up his e-mail here or at home. He could have plugged into any phone jack to pick up or send his mail."

Gaston sighed. "Let's take a closer look at what is there."

"Sure," Dr. Young said and she returned to the top of the message and scrolled down slowly, line by line so we could read what was on the screen.

There was lots of blank space and then splashes of text separated by more blank space. It almost looked like the parts that did arrive were placed in the proper order waiting for the rest of the message to take its correct place. This is what the e-mail said:

"... arefully about our conversati ..." and then a few lines farther down, "... face the consequences ..." And then some more blank space followed by, "... live a lie ..." and then a few lines farther down, "horribly unfair and I'm not happy." And finally the last word that made it through, "... understanding ..."

If the whole of the message had made it through it looked like it would have filled up the screen. The first bit was easy to understand; obviously the words were, "carefully about our conversation." But it was not clear what the conversation was about or whom she had had the conversation with. Was she referring to a discussion with Hilliard or was she telling him about a conversation she had had with someone else?

"Wow," Barbara said. "That must have been some letter. 'Face the consequences, live a lie, not happy.'"

"It seems," I said meditatively, "that the stories we heard may be true. This could mean that he was trying to get her back and using some sort of blackmail. She was telling him that she wasn't going along with it and she didn't care what the consequences were. She was not going to be bullied into living a lie that would make her unhappy. I don't know. It certainly seems to say that."

"Sam," Gaston cautioned me. Meaning that he thought that I was jumping to conclusions.

"But what do you think Hilliard was going to do?" I continued, ignoring Gaston's warning. I was thinking about the blackmail aspect of the thing. "From what we've heard about his character, I'm beginning to think he may have had a very nasty obsessive side. Doesn't it seem to you that he was trying to coerce Jane into coming back to him? And that she preferred to remain with her husband?"

"Yes, but what was he using to try to coerce her? What hold did he have over her?" Gaston asked.

His questions brought me down to earth. I had no idea what Hilliard could possibly use to make Professor Miller-More do something she didn't want to do. Especially a major life-change such as leaving her husband.

"I think ..." Dr. Young spoke slowly and regretfully, as if she really didn't want to tell us what she thought. "This is really an old rumour and I didn't believe it at the time and I'm not sure I believe it now. But it would give Hal something to hold over Jane — if it's true, that is."

"Perhaps if you told me what it is that you are thinking I can find a way to verify its truth," Gaston said.

"Well, OK. But please remember that so far as I know it's just a rumour. And also you have to remember that I haven't heard these stories for about two years. Anyway, there were rumours that she had plagiarized her doctoral dissertation."

"We heard the same story from Miss Ford when we first questioned her," I added.

"True enough," Gaston agreed. "But we never got any confirmation that the stories were anything but malicious rumours."

"There's a reason for that," Dr. Young said. "They're probably not true. That is, I could never see any reason to believe them, until now."

"And now you do?" Gaston inquired.

"No, I don't. I'm expressing myself badly. Let me

explain. In an academic environment there are times, for example when jobs are hard to come by, when some people will do almost anything to discredit those they perceive to be their competition. The absolute worst thing you can accuse some one of in a university is plagiarism. It's worse than infidelity; it's almost worse than murder. So naturally, it's one of the main things that people start rumours about. I've heard whispers of plagiarism about more of the staff than you'd think, not just Jane. In most cases, 99.9 percent of cases, it's a false vindictive accusation made worse in that it's almost impossible to prove or disprove. But because these things are never in the open, no evidence is ever produced and without evidence the charge can't be refuted. It can be very insidious. If the victim protests their innocence it looks like a case of protesting too much."

"*Hamlet*, the play within the play: 'Methinks the lady doth protest too much ...'" I muttered.

"Sam," said Gaston warningly. To Barbara, he continued, "But you said you think you might believe it now?"

"No. What I meant was that I now believe that there is something in her past that someone, apparently Hilliard, was using to get poor Jane to do something against her will and she thought that — whatever dark secret was going to be exposed — it wasn't as bad as living a lie for the rest of her life. She appeared, from her letter, to be saying she was ready to pay the price to get out from under the threat. You've met her. She's a bright, sweet person. I can't imagine what she could have done to be used as blackmail so I naturally thought of the old rumours. That's all. I still don't believe them but it is clear that there is something from her past that is haunting her."

"You said that these rumours of plagiarism were in the air about two years ago, is that right?" Gaston asked.

"Yes," Dr. Young answered.

"About the time she left Hilliard for More, yes?"

"That's right. I guess the shock of her leaving Hal and then taking up with Fred and marrying him kind of drove the other gossip out of people's minds."

"Or she stood up to the person who was spreading the rumours and they, he, stopped."

"I suppose that's possible," Barbara Young agreed.

"And maybe she had to stand up to him again," Gaston continued. "This time more forcefully."

"But if it was only a false rumour," I interjected, "it would not be something that she could be blackmailed with and the parts of her letter that we saw indicates that she was under some kind of real threat. Remember she talked about consequences and facing them."

I noticed that Steve Mandopolous was fascinated by all of this but he wasn't saying much. I guess he didn't want to call attention to himself and be asked to leave. But it was clear that he was following every word that we said. I wondered if he had an opinion. He'd known these people a lot longer than we had.

"I agree," Gaston said. "But the scenario is the same if the stories were true. At a certain point she called the bluff of the storyteller and got on with her life. Now it seems that the original blackmailer, if I can use the term, is taking a second try at her and this time she had reason to believe that he was more serious than the first time and tried to call his bluff again. But maybe it didn't work this time. Maybe this time she had to take direct action which resulted in murder."

"You can't be serious," Dr. Young said angrily. "Just look at the difference in size. Hal was a big guy and Jane is as slim as a wire." Barbara Young waved a computer cable in our faces to make her point.

"But you forget," Gaston explained, "the murderer had some help from Hegel. She was seen around the his-

tory department by two or three people that morning.
From what we have heard so far this appears to be a possible scenario: Hilliard was angry when she left him two
years ago, and in his rage threatened to expose Jane's
secret, which she had unwisely confided to him. But she
stood up to him. She married Dean More. Hilliard didn't
intend to give up. He waited for a while and then took
another crack at blackmailing her. How did he get the
information he needed? Maybe she told him, but maybe
he found out on his own. Don't forget, he was the one
who pushed to have her hired, so he was the one most
familiar with her work. He may have been the only person
other than her thesis adviser to have read her dissertation.
So maybe he found something to be suspicious about.
When she stood up to him he decided to follow his suspicions to see if they had basis in fact. We know that they
were spending time together recently and Hilliard's cur-
rent amour was pushed aside. That may have been to
make room for Jane Miller in his life again. But she had no
plans to leave her husband and she told him so.

"From what I have seen of Professor Miller-More I
wouldn't rule her out as a person capable of murder. I
think she is a person with very strong but very controlled emotions, and not likely to be accepting of anyone trying to push her around. She goes to his office to
have it out with him once and for all and things get
heated and in the heat of the moment she whacks him
with Hegel. She realizes what she's done but also that
her last message to him is probably still on his computer so she grabs it and runs. When she realizes that she
can't get into the computer she dumps it. She passes by
the McIntyre building in her way to meet her husband
and she ducks in and takes the opportunity to throw the
computer in the elevator shaft. She hopes it will never
see the light of day and also that if it is found, whoever

finds it will be unable to access the programs. Doesn't that seem like a possible scenario?"

"And the fact that Hilliard had a book order form clutched in his dead hand, an order *Jane* made and for a book we found in *her* office is more evidence: Hilliard may have been trying to indicate that she is the murderer," I added.

Steve chose this moment to add his voice to our speculations. "No way!" he exclaimed. "Dr. Miller-More a murderer? No way!"

"You have to admit that this scenario makes sense, though," I said.

"Yeah, it makes sense except for one thing," Steve said. "It didn't happen. Professor Miller-More is a really nice lady, a real sweetheart. Maybe she wanted to kill him, but believe me she couldn't have done it. Not the type."

"From what I hear, murderers come in every type. What makes you so sure?" I was ruffled by the dogmatic way he spoke. How did he know?

"I'll tell you how I know it. I come from a very tough neighbourhood. People there did grow up to be killers, some of them anyway. They'd get into fights and they'd lose control and one person ends up dead and the other in jail. This is what I learned: Some people can't kill no matter what and some can't stop themselves from killing when they lose control of themselves. The victims are the first kind. Jane is like that. She doesn't have the spark of a killer. In a situation where people got angry enough to commit murder she would be the victim not the killer, believe me."

"Arguing about it isn't going to get us any where. Why don't we go and talk to Professor Miller-More and see what she has to say?" I proposed.

"Of course," Gaston agreed. "But we all have to walk

over to her office together." He turned to Dr. Young and looked her in the eyes and said sincerely, "Please don't take this the wrong way but you obviously care for Jane Miller-More and I can't risk leaving you here to call her and warn her that we're on our way and what we're thinking. I mean no offense. I have to do my job the best way I can and I think it would be best if you accompanied us to her office. You don't have to stay with me when I talk to her; in fact it would be best that you don't. But I would really appreciate it if you understood my procedures and walked over to her office with us."

"I don't have Mr. Mandopolous's experience with the seamier side of things so I can't be certain that she didn't do it. But it does seem unlikely. Still, you're the cop and I have to believe that you know what you're doing. Anyway, I want to make sure that Jane's not in any trouble and that you don't plan to railroad her into any. I'll walk over with you."

"Thank you. I make the same request of you, Mr. Mandopolous, for the same reasons."

"I'm coming because I'm sure she's innocent," Steve stated unequivocally.

"We shall see," Gaston said getting in the last word.

He led us out of Dr. Young's office. As we walked out Dr. Young turned off the lights and locked the door.

chapter twenty

It was a couple of hours before dusk as we emerged from the administration building. It was going to be another beautiful warm autumn evening. The campus was crowded with students walking to or from somewhere. Young men and women walked arm in arm and gave the impression that it didn't matter where they were going so long as they were going there together. The air was soft and a bit moist. The earth was arcing away from the sun, which gave a lovely warm golden light to everything. The red and yellow leaves on the trees on campus added to the fiery glow of the late afternoon. I inhaled deeply and let the fall air fill my lungs. I could smell the leaves and the grass and I thought that it would be a lovely afternoon to play touch football or to stroll the autumnal streets of Montreal and experience the city as it enjoyed the last gasp of street life before everything moved indoors for the winter.

We walked silently to the Elwitt Building, lost in our own thoughts, an autumnal reverie of murder and justice.

As if by agreement we stopped at the entrance to the building and took a last sentimental look at the campus full of fall colours and happy, playful young people. Then Gaston seemed to shake off his meditative mood, and took the steps three at a time. Turning at the top, he said, "Thank you for all your help. I want to see Professor Miller-More alone now."

Barbara, Steve, and I were right at this heels. The two of them looked disappointed. They both started to speak but Barbara's tone silenced Steve. "No way," she exclaimed. "I'm not leaving Jane alone to face you. You think she killed Harold. God knows what you plan to do to her."

"I plan to question her," Gaston replied coolly. "And I'll decide what to do after that."

"But what about her rights?" Dr. Young asked angrily. "Doesn't she have the right to have a lawyer or someone to look out for her while you question her?"

"You act as if I'm about to question her with a rubber hose." Gaston was not being very diplomatic with Barbara Young. I could see that he was running out of his not very large fund of patience. I was trying to make myself invisible and to think of some way of not being dismissed along with Barbara and Steve. "That's not the way I do things," Gaston continued. "Anyway, she would only need a lawyer if she's charged with a crime and you're not a lawyer. So far as I know no one has the legal right to have a computer specialist present while being questioned by the police. So, thank you both very much for all that you have done to help. I promise you that if I need your help again I'll call on you. But for now I'll be handling things myself."

Steve, shrugging his shoulders, turned and walked away, but Barbara grabbed Gaston's arm and continued to argue forcefully for her right to go with him. I realized that approach would get her nowhere. Leaving them confronting each other, I slipped away without a word.

I walked down the hall to Miller-More's office, and knocked on her door.

When she yelled "Come in," I entered and immediately realized that I hadn't done enough forward planning. I stood there looking like a fool and wondering what to do.

"What on earth do you want?" she asked me.

What excuse could I offer? Why *was* I barging into her office? To accuse her of murder? Something told me that would be unwise. I blurted out the first thing that popped into my mind. "It's about the book you ordered." I sat down in the same chair I had occupied on my previous visit. "I'm really sorry that it's taking so long to get here. You know how it is. Publishers get lots of orders and they can't always fill them quickly so sometimes things are slow. I'm really sorry about that."

I was talking really fast and not making much sense. She looked at me as if I was deranged, not dangerous but certainly not in full control of myself.

"I'm sure you're doing your best and the book will get here soon enough. There's no rush, really, is there?" She said in a soothing tone of voice. "Now if you'll excuse me."

I was about to start babbling something about customer service when a knock came at the door. Gaston, I hoped. She sighed, took her eyes off me and said, "Come in."

Gaston walked in. "Professor Miller-More, I have some questions I'd like ..." At this point he noticed me sitting there. He half laughed, half grimaced at me and said, "I might have known."

"He came to talk to me about the book I ordered. He was just leaving. Now what do you want?"

"I have some more questions," Gaston explained.

"But I've told you everything I know."

"Since speaking with you I've interviewed your husband. My investigators have also found Professor Hilliard's computer and I've read his e-mail," Gaston said sternly

"Oh," she said softly.

"Oh, indeed," Gaston echoed.

"This sounds serious, really serious," Jane said in a kind of distracted way. As if she was stalling so that she could do some fast thinking.

"Murder usually is, Professor," Gaston responded.

"Murder?" She asked in that same distracted tone of voice. She was silent for a while as if lost in thought. She rocked back in her chair, her gaze fixed on some point on the wall above Gaston's head. After a moment or two she sat up, leaned forward with her elbows on her desk and asked in a controlled, calm voice, "You think I murdered Harold?"

I couldn't help but admiring Gaston's technique. It seemed he was going to get a confession without even having to question her. Amazing.

"I'm not ready to make a formal charge," Gaston said. "But I do have some questions about the e-mail I found on Professor Hilliard's computer. From the looks of things it appears that Hilliard discovered that you were guilty of some form of plagiarism and that he was trying to blackmail you into returning to him and that you were resisting. I want to hear what you have to say."

She stared at him. "But ... if you really found one of my letters to Harold on his computer you would have found out that ..." she paused, then, taking a deep breath, she continued, "... that I loved him and we were planning to get back together. He wasn't blackmailing me, he was helping me. That's the truth."

Gaston looked back at her with a steely stare. "The truth? Then what you told me before was lies?"

"No. I didn't tell you anything, really. I didn't think it was any of your business. The fact that Hal and I loved each other had nothing to do with his death. He was obviously killed by some crazy person or thief who was looking for something he could sell. Maybe he had picked up the bust of Hegel, thinking it was valuable, and Harold walked in on him. That's what I think happened. Why would *I* kill him? He was everything to me."

"In fact, we only found a portion of your letter. Something was wrong with the transmission — parts of the text were erased. Perhaps if I could see a complete copy of the letter it would help convince me of what you are saying."

"That's not a problem. There'll be a copy on my computer." We all turned to look at the table where Gaston and I had seen her laptop on the day of our first interview with her. It was not there now: the tabletop was bare, except for a computer-shaped line in the faint dust on its surface.

"What on earth?" she exclaimed. "It was here this morning. It's always here." She looked at us, and a blush reddened her face. Was she blushing because she was lying? Or because we might think she was? I couldn't tell. But I thought she had sounded genuinely surprised and baffled when she saw it was gone.

"Were you in your office all day?" Gaston asked.

"Of course not!" She was beginning to sound agitated, and looked as if she might cry. "I teach, I eat, I go to the bathroom, for God's sake. But I lock my door when I leave. Even if it's only for a minute."

"You're suggesting that someone broke in and stole your computer without leaving a trace?"

"What else could have happened? It's no big deal to pick these locks." A look of fear suddenly crossed her face. "Do you think it could have been the person who murdered Hal, coming back to look for more things to steal?"

"It could," Gaston dipped his head in a single nod, keeping his eyes on hers. "Or, it could be that you heard from your husband that we found Hilliard's computer and knowing it was only a matter of time until I came to see you, you destroyed some evidence. Your copy of the letter we found on Hilliard's computer."

"Oh, for heaven's sake, why would I get rid of the computer? If I wanted to do away with my letters to Hal I'd just erase them. Your accusation makes no sense."

Now it was Gaston's turn to look embarrassed. He was stumped, but I knew a little more about computers than he did and I jumped in. "Come on, Professor More, you know that when you erase something on a computer the file doesn't really go away. You just erase the information that tells the computer where it's located. You knew that an expert could probably reconstruct anything you erased."

I wasn't sure what I was saying was actually true, and I knew I was risking being thrown out, but I wanted to help Gaston make his arrest.

He seemed to appreciate my remark. "I don't know much about computers. But it seems that you might have had a strong motive to destroy your own computer, no?"

"You've got it all wrong," Jane said, anger creeping into her voice. "I didn't kill Harold. I can prove I'm innocent." Again, she paused for a long moment, inhaled deeply, exhaled and continued. "But the only way I can do that is to confess to a crime that in my profession is almost as serious as murder. Worse, maybe." She was sitting train-rail rigid in her chair, her hands folded on her desk and she looked straight at us. There was no blushing or eye averting or any of the other things I associate with guilt. I was impressed by her self-control.

Gaston matched her cool stare with one of his own. "What crime do you mean, Ms. More?"

"The rumours were right. I did plagiarize my doctoral thesis. But I'm not a murderer. Do you want to hear my story?"

"I very much want to hear your story," he told her. "But wouldn't you rather tell it to me privately?" My mind instantly began racing through all kinds of reasons why I should be allowed to stay in the room with them, but I was saved by Professor Miller-More.

Looking over at me, she said, "Actually, I think I'd like to have a witness. I would appreciate it if what I'm about to tell you never leaves this room. But I understand that you may not be able to respect my strong desire for confidentiality. If you can't do that at least I want a witness, a disinterested witness, who can corroborate my side of the story. Can I count on your discretion, Mr. Wiseman?" I guess she knew that Gaston would do what he had to do. But if she needed an ally, she might be able to turn me into one — provided I believed her story.

"Yes," I said firmly.

"OK, then," she said with a note of resignation in her voice. She looked at a spot on the wall over our heads again, as if she were looking for notes up there. After a moment she began to speak, as calmly as if she was telling us something that happened to someone else. "I was in the final stages of working on my dissertation. My research had been complete, I had written a comprehensive outline, I was well organized. All that was left was to write the thesis itself. I thought that would be the easy part. It wasn't. I had to write some of my chapters two and three times to satisfy my thesis adviser. I had a Canada Council grant, but it only had one more year to run. After that there would be no money coming in and it was beginning to look like the writing and revising was going to take another two years. I knew there was no hope of getting funding for an additional year: I had already spent every penny I could squeeze out of the grant process. I had no family I could turn to for money and my friends were just as poor as I was. I was angry, almost hysterical, at the thought of having to work outside my field for a couple of years to get enough money together to continue. I was afraid that if I gave up working on my thesis I might never get it done and even if I did finish I would miss the first round of job opportunities, and even if I did get a job I would be much older than my colleagues at the same level and my career would be held up by a couple of years."

"Not a prospect a young, ambitious, bright graduate student wants to face," I said. I was beginning to feel some sympathy for Jane. I'd been a desperately poor young graduate student once myself.

"No. Then I had a stroke of luck. While prowling the stacks of the University of Toronto Library I discovered an unpublished thesis on my topic: artisans' political organizations in France at the time of the 1848 revolutions. At first this seemed like the worst possible luck. If my work turned out to be an echo of the unpublished thesis I would have to start over to find something original to say. Bad luck turned to opportunity when I tried to check the thesis out of the library. I discovered that it was uncatalogued. I did some checking and discovered that there was no record of a thesis by Theodore Renard anywhere. I checked dissertation abstracts and the catalogues of other academic libraries. Nothing. The thesis, 'Artisans and Politics in France in 1848,' was written during the Second World War and fell through the archival cracks. I could barely find anything out about the author. What little I did discover confirmed my belief that the thesis was, in effect, lost forever. Renard was awarded his PhD in 1942 and went on to serve in the Canadian military for a couple of years and then to a career as a professor of modern history at the University of British Columbia. He published little and what he did publish had nothing to do with the revolutions of 1848. He seemed to have spent the whole of his career teaching graduates and undergraduates at a time when a good teacher could teach and not perish if he didn't publish. In fact he had died a year previously and I could not even find an obituary in any of the professional publications."

Excited and fearful, Jane slipped the thesis out of the library and read it; large parts of it, although written forty years before, came to the same conclusions as she did. She calculated the risks and decided to take a chance. "All I had to do was plug Renard's passages into my research and I had a well-written, well-researched finished product. I told myself that it was the work I would have done myself if I had had the time and the funding, and it was true. I was able to complete my thesis to my advisor's satisfaction within the year I had left."

Things got even better, she told us, when she was offered a tenure-track appointment at McGill. This was unusual, as most universities don't like to hire their former students for their first job. But both Hilliard and her future husband, Fred More, who was chair of the history department at the time, were very impressed with her work. She was so sure that she had it made that the way in which she made it began to recede from memory. She came to believe that she earned her success. Even her relationship with Hilliard was perfect for two ambitious people. It offered her plenty of professional support: access to people that she would not have on her own as a young assistant professor, enough romance to keep her happy but not so much as to make her feel trapped.

"Fred, as history chair, should have read the whole of my dissertation before I was hired, instead of skimming the first couple of chapters and relying on the abstract of the thesis and the opinions of the others on the hiring committee. It's not that Fred was lazy, he was just too busy to read it at the time. Unfortunately for me, he did get around to reading it and was sure that he recognized parts of it from his graduate student days. It was my bad luck that he had studied with the 'totally forgotten' Ted Renard. Fred was one of the last doctoral students he took on. Fred took the time to read Renard's doctoral dissertation because he so much admired his mentor."

I mentally translated that to "because he was a toady." Jane's next words confirmed my judgement of More.

"It served him well as a graduate student, making him one of Renard's favourites, and he never forgot Renard's elegant writing style. He recognized it as soon as he read it again when he finally got around to reading my thesis. I'd tried to alter Renard's style to disguise my heavy 'borrowings' but when something has been said so well it's hard to resist using the same words. And I really didn't think it would ever be discovered."

This is where the story took a turn that I hadn't anticipated. I had theorized, and I suspected that Gaston had too, that Jane had allowed herself to be blackmailed into marrying Fred to avoid exposure as a plagiarist — that to save her own skin she had left Hilliard at the altar, figuratively if not literally, and that after a couple of years Hal started to put pressure on her to leave Fred, not knowing that she had married him under psychological duress. I had further speculated that she was afraid to leave More because he had knowledge that could ruin her, and was angry with Hilliard for continuing to pursue her. I assumed, in fact, that she hated both of them, her husband and her former lover, and that it was possible she had killed Hilliard because he would not get out of her life. Maybe it was premeditated, maybe it happened spontaneously during an argument; either way, I was almost certain that she was the murderer.

The story Jane Miller-More now told us was more or less the opposite of all that. She had broken up with Hal because after years of struggle to get her career launched she wanted a secure profession, marriage, and a home, with the possibility of children somewhere in the future. Hal was ambivalent, and when pushed he became stubborn. He didn't want that kind of life, he told her. When Fred More showed an interest, Jane was grateful and flattered. Fred represented all the things Jane wanted from life — all the things that Hilliard was not prepared to commit to.

"Maybe I loved the security Fred offered more than I loved Fred himself, even then," she told us. "But he said he loved me enough for the two of us. I came to believe that my ideas were too romantic, and that Fred and I could have a good marriage. And we did. I didn't feel the passion I had felt for Hal, but in a way that was a comfort too. Hal had hurt me so much by his coldness."

Fred had only got around to reading Jane's thesis after they were married and he only read it because he was sincerely interested in Jane and her work. He recognized the plagiarized chapters almost as soon as he read them but there wasn't much he could do about it. He was truly happy married to Jane and didn't want to ruin their relationship or her career. He was well aware that he loved her more than she loved him and that made him even more cautious about rocking the marital boat. In fact he didn't even mention what he had discovered for the first year of their marriage.

Inevitably, Hal Hilliard realized what he had lost. He decided that he was ready to offer Jane the things she wanted. In typical Hilliard fashion, he didn't see the fact that Jane was married, happily married so far as any one knew, as a deterrent — just an obstacle to be overcome. He asked Jane to come back to him.

"And I realized I had never really stopped being in love with Hal," Jane told us. She looked calm but there were tears in her eyes. She dabbed at them with a tissue. "And of course Fred knew something was wrong. He knew I was in love with somebody else, but he didn't know who it was. And he made a stupid mistake."

In his hurt pride and anger, Fred told her that he knew that she had plagiarized part of her thesis and he expected her to remain married to him. If she didn't, she could guess the consequences: he would expose her. But Jane realized more quickly than Fred that covering up for a plagiarist is almost as bad as being a plagiarist. The fact that Fred hadn't exposed her before now meant that he never could; the assumption would be that he had condoned the plagiarism until she asked for a divorce. Denouncing her at that point would only make him seem spiteful and petty. He would be a laughingstock. More was a man who cared very much for his public image, his reputation, and that would be destroyed along with his career. As he was farther up the academic ladder than she his fall would be farther than hers.

"But I could never forgive him for threatening me. I knew I no longer loved him, but then I began to despise him. I was was living for the day when I could get a divorce and Hal and I could be married. Fred tried to tell me — it was the last card he had to play — that if I left him my reputation would be ruined. That was a laugh. Divorce in the academic world is grist for the gossip mill, no more than that. The faculties at some universities are so interdivorced and intermarried that they made soap operas look like nursery rhymes. Hal and I started seeing each other in secret. It was only a matter of time before I worked out a divorce agreement with Fred. He would have agreed in the end, as long as I promised not to cause what he called a scandal."

Gaston asked the obvious question: "Do you have any evidence to support your story? The only person who can confirm that you were planning to leave your husband is dead. That is, unless you already told your husband of your plans."

"No, I hadn't told him. He didn't know anything about it. He still thought we could 'get past all this and have a great marriage.' His words. I was working up my courage to tell him he was a fool. I don't know what I'm going to do now."

"The plagiarism can be checked so I tend to believe it," Gaston said, watching her closely.

"Why would I confess to plagiarism if I was also a murderess? Wouldn't it be smarter for me to keep my mouth shut and see what happened? In my profession an act of plagiarism is worse than murder. If word of this ever got out I would be finished."

"Exactly, Professor," Lemieux said. "But being exiled from the academy is a lot better than spending the next twenty-five years in jail, no?"

"Of course it is," Professor Miller-More responded.

"Then why confess to anything?" Gaston asked.

"You all but accused me of murder and I want you to understand that I am basically an honest person who made mistakes in her life but I also am at the point where I can no longer continue to live a lie. Harold and I planned to be together again and I

had to hope that my secret would remain hidden but I
was prepared to face the consequences of Fred exposed
me. Now that Harold is gone I see that I wasted too
much time — time that Hal and I could have shared.
His death, as much as his life, made me realize that I
am not going to settle for less than I want, less than I
deserve for myself. And if it means that I'll be exiled
from the academy, as you put it, at least I'll be in control of my life. I'll find other things to do. I owe at least
that much to Hal's memory and to myself." She leaned
back in her chair and looked at us without blinking,
almost daring us to challenge her statement. "Believe
me, I've told you the whole truth."

I wasn't sure what to believe. Was her story true?
Was it a red herring? The tale of her secret love affair
with Harold Hilliard was impossible to prove. Could it
be a smokescreen to disguise her motive for killing him?

Gaston stood, and looking down at Miller-More,
he said, "You've saved yourself from being arrested
while I look into your story. But you are still a suspect
in a murder investigation so I expect you to make
yourself available when I need to talk to you again. Do
you understand?"

Jane nodded.

"One more thing," Gaston added. "Where is your
computer? These damn things keep disappearing and
they're important. If you had your computer I could verify at least part of your story right here."

"I know," Jane replied. "I don't know who stole it.
Probably the murderer but it could just be a coincidence."

"I don't think so," Gaston said. "It's also possible
that you got rid of it yourself if there was something
incriminating on it. No?"

Jane said nothing but looked Gaston in the eyes
without blinking. For my mother that would have

been a sure sign of innocence, but I wondered. It could also be a sign that Miller-More was a very cool, in-control person.

Gaston looked at his watch. "It's probably too late to find your husband in his office and maybe too late to start looking for your computer. I'll be back to see you sometime tomorrow when I'll have had a chance to do a little more checking. If you locate your computer don't touch it. Call me." He handed her a card. "Call me on my cell phone. The number is on my card."

We went out into the Montreal night, and walked across the campus together not saying a word. Just as we were passing through Roddick Gates to Sherbrooke Street, Gaston turned to me and asked if I needed a lift somewhere. I wasn't sure where I wanted to go but I was sure that I didn't want to be excluded from the rest of the case.

"Do you think she's telling the truth?" I asked, avoiding his question.

"I don't know. It has the ring of truth but I'm not sure that the confession to plagiarism is proof that she didn't commit murder. It could be the other way around: a ruse to throw us off the scent. Confess to plagiarism to avoid being charged with the more serious crime. If her plagiarism becomes public the worst that can happen is that she'll lose her job. That's a lot better than going to jail for murder. I've got to find a way to check her story. And that's the damnable thing. How on earth do you check a story like that?"

"You have to find Renard's thesis and a copy of Miller-More's thesis and compare them."

"Yes, yes, of course," Gaston interrupted me. "But you can see the complications. I have to compare two dissertations, one of which may be difficult to get my hands on. I have to determine whether her husband knew about the plagiarism, as she claims. He may have allowed himself to be tricked or seduced into marriage in order to buy his silence, and so on. Not the sort of thing a guy is likely to admit to, just like that. It will take a while to check her story, believe me."

I hadn't realized until that moment how complicated and hard it would be to find evidence to prove or disprove what she told us. If she was guilty her confession would certainly buy her time and time might help her get away with murder.

But I had come this far as a sort of unofficial sounding board for Gaston and I didn't want to be left out of the action now. The last thing I wanted was to read about the case in the *Gazette*.

Gaston was saying, "You've been a big help to me, Sam. I appreciate all that you've done to help me. I'll keep in touch." He shook my hand and patted me on the shoulder with his free hand. He turned to walk down McGill College Avenue to the parking lot where he kept his car.

Not so fast, buddy, I said to myself, and dogged his footsteps. "How would it be if I made some notes on my perceptions of what we've been told and by whom? Sort of a chronology of events and notes on the conversations we had with all the suspects and witnesses." I was thinking as I was talking and I hoped that what I was proposing made sense to him.

"Sure," he said absently. "Why not? Write up your notes and I'll look at them when I can." And he strode off.

I breathed a sigh of relief. I was still part of the case.

I decided to walk back to my place. I turned back through the Roddick Gates and cut across campus heading up to the mountain and home. Walking helps

me to think and I sure had a lot to think about if I was
to be able to write a coherent synopsis of events. In the
face of no concrete evidence whatsoever to support her
story I was now inclined to believe Jane was innocent.
My two main suspects were Allan Gutmacher and
Arlene Ford.

By the time I got to the monument at the foot of
Mount Royal, at the corner of Rachel and Park, I figured I had the case solved. I was sure Gutmacher was
the murderer for the oldest of motives — jealous
rage. At least he had a motive I could understand; the
problem was that Arlene Ford had the same motive.
In fact if Arlene knew about Harold's affair with Jane
she had a motive we hadn't known about before. And
she looked much more like a murderess to me than
Jane did.

I turned east on Rachel and headed for Esplanade and
by the time I got to my place I realized that Gutmacher
wasn't the murderer at all. Now I was almost absolutely
certain it was Arlene.

I let myself into my flat and headed for the computer
with a brief stop in the kitchen for a snack. I recorded
Jane's story in as much detail as I could remember and
then wrote a chronology of events with notes on who
said what to whom. When I looked up from my computer I had written about a dozen pages and it was one
in the morning. As I reread what I had written I realized that my opinion of Professor Hilliard had changed
somewhat. I had always liked and respected the man
but Jennifer and Arlene and even the awful Allan
depicted him as a sexual predator. I realized that losing
Jane when she married Fred More had changed him.
He seemed to try to hide his feelings, which made him

a sort of tragically romantic person. I think his real character, the person I knew, would have re-emerged if he and Jane had been able to get back together. Sadly this did not happen. I printed what I had written and headed, exhausted, for bed.

chapter twenty-one

I woke up the next morning feeling groggy after only about six hours of sleep. I decided to go for a run up the mountain in order to clear my head. I pulled on my running clothes and headed out. I crossed Esplanade and jogged across Jeanne-Mance Park, across Park Avenue to the war memorial at the corner of Rachel and on up the mountain. I doubt that there's another city in the world that looks as gorgeous as Montreal does at sunrise. If I live to be a hundred and still have the energy to jog on the mountain I'll still love this view — and on a beautiful autumn morning a run gives me a chance to enjoy the colours of and the chirping of birds and the smells of nature without actually having to leave Montreal. A city boy's version of communing with nature. It also gave me a chance to think. I do my best thinking while jogging. I must modestly admit to having solved all of the world's problems, large and small, while exercising on Mount Royal. Too bad I've never had a chance to share these solutions with anyone.

The sound of another runner coming up behind me snapped me out of my reverie. A tall, slender woman jogged past me. It took me a moment to realize that was Gisèle Lemieux. She looked glorious in a deep purple running suit. I put on a burst of speed and caught up with her.

"Hi," I said as I drew even with her. She was running at a slightly faster pace than I was and I hoped she would slow down a bit so we could talk.

She glanced over at me at me with disdain, as if I were the kind of guy who tries to strike up conversations with women on the mountain. I could see from the look of in her eyes that she was about to speed up to get away from me.

"Gisèle, I'm Sam. Sam Wiseman," I panted quickly. I'm afraid I sounded desperate but I couldn't let her think I was just some creep. "A friend of your brother Gaston's. We met at the Café Paillon."

She turned her head and looked at me with relief, and broke into a smile. "Ah, Sam. I didn't recognize you. I don't wear my contact lenses when I run. How are you?"

She slowed her pace a bit so that I could keep up.

"I'm fine," I replied. "Do you run up here often?"

"As often as I can. I'm late this morning. I'm usually here before six. How about you?"

"That's why I've never seen you. I rarely get going that early."

We ran in silence for a while. I wanted to make conversation with the beautiful Gisèle but couldn't think of anything that I could talk about while puffing and gasping with the exertion of the running.

Finally I just blurted out, "Would you like to go to see a play with me some evening?"

Gisèle did not look surprised at the question. I guess that when you are as beautiful as she is you get used to being asked out by men you don't really know that well.

"That's very sweet of you, Sam, but I'm off to New York in a couple of days to work on a case and then I'm taking another couple of weeks' vacation in France."

Although she didn't exactly say "no" she did call me "sweet" which is pretty close to being blown off. But for her I was prepared to risk a little more ego damage. I gave her a minute to see if she would say something more. She didn't and I took this as a hopeful sign.

"Then how would it be if I called you in a month or so?" I asked.

"Sure. Why not? It might be fun to do something."

"Great," I said. I didn't want to push my luck so I changed the subject to the weather and how great it was to run on the mountain. By this time we reached Beaver Lake.

"I turn off here," she said. "I live on Ridgewood."

"Have a nice vacation," I said to her as she turned left and headed home.

I continued on to the lookout and then turned around myself and ran back down faster than my normal pace.

A half hour later I was back home sweaty and exhilarated.

After a quick shower and a quicker breakfast of two glasses of orange juice and two glasses of water I was off to work. I arrived just before nine-thirty, in time to help Jennifer and the staff to get the store open. After enduring Jennifer's affectionately sarcastic remarks about taking time away from crime fighting to return to the boring world of books I got down to work and did the things booksellers do. I moved the heavy boxes of books that start to arrive on Monday morning and continue all week, processed customers' orders, whined at publishers about their slow delivery times and listened to them complain about how Dickens & Company, their favourite bookstore, should try to pay faster, etc. But I did all this with only half my mind. The other half was thinking about what Gaston was doing. I just knew he was at McGill pushing his investigation forward while I was schlepping boxes.

Then Jennifer and I spent a few hours tying up various loose ends. I ensured that all the books that came in were out of their boxes and on the shelves where they could be sold. Jennifer assigned tasks to the staff to change displays and generally get the store shipshape. The last thing I did was organize a week's worth of invoices for future payment and wrote the cheques that were immediately required. Jen and I both liked everything to run smoothly but neither of us liked to spend much time on paperwork unless it was absolutely necessary. Finally I couldn't stand it any longer, and at one o'clock I left for a lunch break. I didn't eat lunch, but instead headed for McGill to see what, if anything, was going on.

I found more than I bargained for.

I heard the sirens before I got to the campus. I ran to the university just in time to see a police car join the three other blue and white squad cars and a charcoal grey morgue van parked in front of Elwitt Building.

"Shit!" I muttered. I trotted up the stairs and into the foyer. There had been another murder, and I had almost missed it, working away in the stockroom and the Dickens & Company office. If anybody deserved to know what was going on it was me. I didn't care then how morbidly curious and insensitive I was being. I ran to the history department offices, getting there a few seconds ahead of the just-arrived patrol car officers. A crowd of uniformed cops, CSU cops and Gaston were all crowded into Jane Miller-More's office.

Jane was sitting at her desk, slumped in her chair, her dead eyes bulging out at us in a lifeless stare. A bright red scarf, the cause of death, was tied tightly around her neck. Gaston was standing near the body looking grim. I heard before I saw Steve Mandopolous telling a cluster of people to stand back and give the cops some room. His orders worked pretty well for all of the crowd except one person. Barbara Young pushed her way through the mob to the door of the office, opposite me.

"My God! Is she ... is she dead?" Barbara asked.

Gaston didn't answer for a minute and I wasn't sure he had heard the question.

"Dammit, dammit, dammit," he exclaimed. "Yes she's dead. But she hasn't been dead long. Her body hasn't really cooled off much. I must have missed the murderer by minutes, maybe seconds."

"Oh, poor Jane," Barbara said softly.

I pushed my way over to where Dr. Young was standing and asked if she would like to sit down and if she wanted a drink of water, the things I thought you were supposed to say to someone who has just found out that a friend and colleague has been murdered.

She looked at me as if I was the murderer and said, "I'll be OK. Just give me some space."

"Of course," I said, and moved away from her. She turned and leaned against the wall a foot or two away from Jane Miller-More's office door. I turned too, and looked into the office again. The place was a mess. But it was a mess when we visited Professor Miller-More there the other day and it didn't seem to be any messier than it was then. I couldn't see any signs of a struggle. No papers or books were spread all over the floor. On first glance it looked like some one had snuck up behind her and stran-

gled her, before she knew what was going on. How someone could do that in that small an office was beyond me.
Another murder. It was becoming an epidemic. And one
suspect off our list. Or was she? After all, even a murderer can become a murder victim in her turn.

Gaston issued some orders to the cops and the CSU
team and elbowed his way out of the office. "Sam," he
exclaimed. "What the hell are you doing here?"

Before I could answer Barbara Young came up to us
and said, "What's going on? How could someone just
walk into her office and kill her? Who found her?"

"I found her," Gaston told us. "If it will make you
feel any better I'll tell you what happened and then I
need your help with something." Gaston told us that he
had arrived on campus looking for Fred More. He
wanted to discuss with him the things Jane had revealed
to us yesterday. When he couldn't find Fred at his office
he decided to pay another visit to Jane to see where he
could get a copy of her thesis and find out if she knew
where her husband was. Gaston walked into Jane's
office and found her dead.

"I have to ask you something, Dr. Young. I intended to come to see you after I talked with Professor
Miller-More. Is there somewhere we can talk?" Gaston
asked. He motioned to me to come with them.

Barbara led the way down one of the hallways to an
unused seminar room.

"There is something I have to know," Gaston was
saying to Barbara as we sat down at the long table. "It's
about computers. You told us that it is not necessary to
have a password to get into all the programs of a computer. Am I correct?"

"Yes."

"Is it always necessary to have a login and a password to get into the e-mail programs?"

"Yes. That's the way I wrote the e-mail software that we use on campus."

"Can you tell me more about how it works?"

"I called it Pandora. Kind of a joke, because opening your e-mail box is a bit like opening Pandora's box. You don't know what terrible things you're going to find. The program is pretty straight forward. To access the program you log in, usually with your e-mail name and then use a password of your own devising. Once in you have access to all the regular features of e-mail and the Internet. You can check your new mail, which requires that you use another password, just as an additional security precaution, compose and send e-mail, create a directory of names and e-mail addresses, check news groups and so on. Nothing exceptional except that it's tailor-made for staff at McGill. It's not a commercially available program. All you need to get the program is a computer, a modem and telephone wire, and a staff card and you're connected to the universe."

"Thank you. I just wanted to check the use of passwords. You've been very helpful," Gaston said softly to her. "I won't detain you any longer. But I must ask you not to mention anything you've seen here until I've informed her husband and any next of kin."

"I understand," Professor Young said. "But I want to ask you something. Why are you asking me about computer software at a time like this? Does it have something to do with Jane's murder?"

"Yes. I had to be certain that I understood the way your program worked. It will help me to catch a murderer."

"But," I couldn't help asking, "I thought that you had already caught a murderer, murderess I should say, and you were wrong. Are you certain that you're right this time?"

"You're right. My error may have cost that poor woman her life. But she withheld information that might have helped to find the guilty party sooner. I did think that she was the most likely suspect but if she had been more forthcoming I might have changed my opinion. At the very worst she would have been detained until she could demonstrate her innocence. But she would be alive. I'm sorry that I could not prevent her death. But I didn't kill her. The murderer did that and that person could just as easily have not killed Professor Miller-More or Professor Hilliard. I think I know who did it and why. It's a question of setting a trap. That's why I had to make sure I understood the computer program."

"You know who did it?" I blurted out. Dr. Young was about to ask the same question but I beat her to it.

"Yes, I believe so."

"Why are we sitting here?" asked Professor Young. "Go and get the wretch!"

"I intend to but first I must ensure that the evidence is properly collected at the crime scene and then I have the sad task of informing her husband. I know it seems odd but I must follow procedure. It may seem to slow things down now but it will make it easier to get a conviction later. Believe me."

"How can you be sure that the killer won't kill again?" Dr. Young asked nervously.

"I can't, of course. But I know who the potential victims are and I can protect them. Let's go and find Mr. Mandopolous and arrange for that."

Gaston got up, held Dr. Young's chair for her as she arose and we left. "Do you mean we're the potential victims?" she asked incredulously.

"I'm afraid so. Sam and I have seen all the evidence and you and Mr. Mandopolous have seen some of it. If the murderer realizes what you know you are in danger.

It's stupid because all of us know what you know and that's too many people to kill — but murderers do stupid things. Or else they wouldn't kill in the first place. So I want to arrange for some protection for you and Steve."

At Miller-More's office the CSU technicians were busy collecting evidence and the man and woman from the morgue, dressed in grey suits, were wheeling the body out to the hearse on a stretcher. She was covered from head to toe with a white sheet. Dr. Young, Gaston, and I stood silently as Jane's body was rolled past us.

"Steve," Gaston called him over to us. "I'd like you to stay with Dr. Young until I've done a few things to ensure that the murderer does not strike again. By this time the killer probably sees the hopelessness of the situation and may do something rash. If you leave the campus please stay together and I'll ask the police to take you where you want to go."

Steve could have asked a lot of questions or given us a lot of arguments. He didn't. "Is there some way I can reach you, if I need to?" Gaston asked.

"Take my beeper number." He recited it to Gaston, who wrote it down.

"I want to check the office to see if there is anything that will tell me where the Mores lived. The first thing we have to do is inform her husband of this tragedy."

Gaston walked into the office and I could see him talking to one of the CSU people. The technician went behind the desk and picked up a small black purse by inserting a pen under the strap. She placed it on the desk and with gloved hands carefully opened it and removed a wallet. She flipped through the wallet slowly so that Gaston could see if there was any identification. She stopped and held it while he copied something into the notebook he had used to record Steve's pager number.

I couldn't hear what he was saying to her. He pointed to the place on the table where the computer had been and the technician nodded. He said something else to her and she walked over to the table and used her pen to pick up an end, the end normally plugged into the computer, of a computer cable. Gaston nodded and smiled and the technician smiled back and nodded and held up two fingers. As he walked out of the office I could see the technician start to check the cable for fingerprints.

He returned to where the three of us were standing after speaking to one of the cops who was standing around waiting for instructions. "The police will seal the scene when they're done. When you want to leave, Officer Lapointe," he indicated with his head the cop he had just spoken to, "will take you where you want to go. I'll call you as soon as I can."

At that moment the young woman who was taking the fingerprints from the cable came over to Gaston and handed him the cable in a plastic evidence bag. He slipped it into his pocket and asked, "Vous avez trouvé ...?"

"Rien," she replied.

"Très intéressant, non?" Gaston turned and strode towards the main entrance to the Elwitt Building.

I caught up and as we walked out of the building together I asked, "What was all that about?"

"I asked Officer Bouchard to take a set of prints off the computer cable so I could take it with me, in case I need it. The interesting thing is that there were no prints on the cable."

"Why is that interesting? You plug in a computer and forget it."

"Exactly. So the prints, or more likely partial prints — because the wire is narrow — of the person who plugged it in should be on the cable. This cable was wiped clean by the murderer because he knew that his prints were on it when unplugging the computer to steal it."

"I see," I said, though I didn't.

We walked out of the building.

It was a beautiful sunny fall afternoon and I inhaled the fresh autumnal air deeply. I didn't realize how claustrophobic I had found the building until we left it.

"It's important that we find Dean More," Gaston said as he strode off in the direction of his office. I had to jog keep up and I was a little out of breath when we arrived at More's office. His secretary told us that More was out; in fact had been out for most of the day at meetings. She didn't know when or even if he would be back that day but she would be glad to arrange an appointment for us for the next morning. He would be free at eleven-thirty next Wednesday, she informed us.

"I think not," Gaston told her. "I want to speak to him today. If he returns or phones in please tell him to get in touch with me. Have him try my cellphone first." He handed the secretary his card and indicated which of the phone numbers was his cellphone number.

"I think we'll try to find him at home," Gaston said to me as we left the administration building. "We're headed for Westmount, ninety-two Irving Street. That's the address on his wife's driver's licence."

We hailed a cab, and Gaston gave the driver the address. I asked him if I could borrow his cellphone. He handed it to over; I called Jennifer to let her know that the boy detective was back on the case. I wanted to tell her that there had been another murder and that we were on the way to inform the victim's husband, but I didn't.

"What's the game plan?" I asked.

"Look sad and let me do the talking," answered Gaston. "This is going to be very delicate. Also, use your eyes. If you notice anything I miss, give me a sign."

I practised looking sad for the rest of the cab ride.

The More house, about two blocks up the hill in Westmount, was a renovated three-story town house. The small lawn in front was well trimmed and a flower garden shored up by rocks nestled against the house. Either someone in the household had a very green thumb or the lawn and garden were professionally attended to. Knowing how Dean More liked to delegate and then take credit I suspected the latter.

We mounted the three steps to the shiny black front door. There was a doorbell at the right and a polished brass knocker in the centre of the door. I rang the bell and we waited. I was about to try the knocker when Fred More opened the door. He was dressed pretty much the way we saw him at his office except that he had discarded his jacket and tie. He had a newspaper in his hand. I wondered what he was doing home at this time of day. Playing hooky?

"What? You two again," he said by way of a greeting. He looked as if he wanted to close the door in our faces, but Gaston strong-armed his way into the foyer with me close behind.

"I'm afraid it can't wait till tomorrow. May we come in?" Seeing as we were already in it seemed a redundant question. Dean More stood back so that we could get all the way into the house. The floor of the foyer was hard and white and flecked with silver: marble or granite, I assumed. To the left was a comfortable-looking wing-backed chair covered in a flower print upholstery. To the right of the door was a marble table and a mirror. The foyer opened onto a hallway and on the right I could see the entrance to the living room. About halfway down the hall there was a staircase leading to the upstairs rooms.

There was a trench coat on the wingback chair in the entryway and as I passed it in response to More's invitation to, "Come this way. We'll talk in the living room," I brushed against it. I hit something hard with my shin as I brushed the coat and it didn't feel like something that hard would be a part of a chair. I was last, following Gaston and More into the house. I stopped for a split second to lift up the trench coat with the pinky of my left hand and saw a laptop computer hidden under the coat. It was probably Dean More's computer but it could have been his wife's. I wanted to show it to Gaston but couldn't. He had rounded the corner into the living room. I caught up with him and although I looked solemn I was trying to think of a way to show him the computer hidden under the coat.

The living room was large, longer than it was wide. It must have covered half the house. There was a bay window looking out onto Irving Street in the front and comfortable looking furniture spread throughout the room. The walls were light grey and the carpet was Oriental. At the back of the room was a fireplace, and next to the fireplace a black leather reclining chair where More had obviously been reading his paper. There was a Manet print on the chimney and knickknacks on the mantel. More invited us to sit down on the blue-grey sofa and he took the wing chair, the twin of the one in the foyer, opposite us.

"What is it?" he asked abruptly. "I have to go out in an hour or so."

"I'm afraid what I have to tell you concerns your wife," Gaston said in a slow and serious tone.

"Jane?" Fred asked with panic in his voice. "Has something happened to Jane?"

"I'm afraid so. There's been another murder at the university."

More looked at him anxiously.

"I'm afraid that this time your wife was the victim."

The dean looked as if he had been hit in the solar plexus. He went white, broke out in a sweat, and fell back in his chair. The newspaper he had been holding fluttered to the floor. He looked at us with uncomprehending eyes for a moment, then covered his face with his hands and rocked forward so that he was bent over, his head in his hands, his elbows resting on his knees. He was making some kind of sound but I couldn't tell whether he was crying or trying to catch his breath.

"We are very sorry for your loss. I'd like to ask you a question or two and then arrange for you to make a formal identification of the body."

More rubbed his eyes with the heels of his hands and sat up straight. "I can't believe it. No one would want to kill Jane. She had no enemies, none."

"I promise you we'll track down the murderer," Gaston assured him. "Right now I'd like to know how long you've been home?"

"Me? About an hour, why?"

"I just want to get the chronology of your wife's movements straight. Did you leave home before or after her?"

"Before," said More in a hoarse voice.

"Were you at your office today? I came looking for you this morning and couldn't find you."

"I had a meeting off campus, which I discovered had been cancelled. My next appointment isn't until later this afternoon, so I came home for a break."

"I see," said Gaston. "Would that meeting be business or pleasure?"

"Another academic meeting." More sighed. "Academia runs on meetings. Of course, I won't go now. Not now that ... if you'll excuse me, I have to telephone Jane's parents ... both of our families, and tell them. When can I see her?" His voice was regaining its strength. Dean More the smooth, efficient administrator was back. The bereaved husband's appearance had been remarkably short, I thought. A suspicion suddenly began to form in my mind.

"I want to arrange for the funeral," More was saying in a huffy tone. "I'd think you'd be better off out catching the murderer than hanging around here asking pointless questions about my schedule."

"Yes. I understand." The sympathy in Gaston's voice actually sounded genuine. Could it be that he had no idea of the possibility that had so belatedly occurred to me? "We need to keep the body for a day or so in the case of a homicide. You'll have to make a formal identification. Here's the address." Gaston took out one of his cards and wrote an address on the back. "If you'd be so good as to meet me there at ten tomorrow morning." He stood up and prepared to take leave of the Dean.

I couldn't believe that we were just going to walk out. I had to find a way to show Gaston the computer concealed under More's raincoat. If it was Jane's it could be important, but I couldn't just blurt out that there was a computer hidden under a coat. We weren't there to search the place. But in a moment we'd be ushered to the door. I had to let Gaston discover it himself, but how could I? I had to give him a signal of some kind.

We went into the front hallway, me first, Gaston second and More bringing up the rear — perhaps to ensure that we actually left. As I walked by the trench coat I stepped on the corner of it that was lying on the floor and dragged my shoe along so that I pulled the coat to the floor, exposing the computer.

"Hey," Fred shouted at me. "Be careful. That's an expensive Burberry." He bent over and picked up his coat and almost petted it like a cat, reassuring it that everything was OK.

"Yes," Gaston said. "It's important to take care."

Fred thought that Gaston was chastising me for carelessness and gave me a smug little smile. I understood that Gaston was congratulating me for exposing the computer and I smiled right back.

"Whose computer is this?" Gaston asked.

"Mine," More responded, sounding just a touch belligerent.

"I'd like to try an experiment if I may," Gaston told him.

"What kind of experiment?" Fred's face was expressionless.

Without answering Gaston picked up the computer and headed back to the living room where I noticed there was a telephone on a long dark wood coffee table next to the reclining chair. Gaston set the computer on the coffee table, moving a newspaper and a book in the process, and opened the top.

"Where's the cable to plug it in?" he asked innocently.

Relief washed over More's face. "The cable?" he responded just as innocently. "I must have forgotten it at my office. I'm afraid I often do that. Why don't you meet me there tomorrow? Whatever your experiment is, we can try it then."

"That won't be necessary," Gaston told him. "I happen to have an extra with me." He reached into his coat pocket and pulled out the cable we had found in Miller-More's office and busied himself plugging the cable into the computer and into a wall socket. He then took the phone wire from the phone and plugged it into the computer. Then he pressed the power button.

I took a covert peek at More. The look of relief had been replaced by a combination of anger and fear.

The computer screen filled with the Windows icons and happily did not ask for a password. "This is what I'd like you to do. I'd like you to log in to your e-mail," Gaston told More.

"You have absolutely no right to read my mail. None whatsoever," Fred said in a dull voice.

"I don't want to read your mail. I just want you to log in to your e-mail box. Once you've done that we can turn the computer off and we'll leave."

"You know you've got your bloody nerve," More protested, but his attempt at indignation was unconvincing. The will to be irate seemed to have left him. "My wife has been murdered, and you harass me about my computer? Don't you think I deserve some sympathy, some time to mourn, to call Jane's family and mine?"

"Yes, of course," said Gaston in a soothing voice. "And if you just co-operate with this one thing, I promise you we'll leave."

Fred More looked at Gaston and looked at me and realized that he was cornered. He had a hell of a choice to make. He decided to gamble on logging in to his mailbox in the hopes that that would get rid of us.

He bent over the computer and clicked on the Internet connect icon. The machine made some noises and I heard the dial tone, dialing, whoosh and shriek of a modem reaching out to another modem. When they connected, a new screen came up: "Welcome to Pandora. Please log in."

Fred typed "moref" at the login prompt and waited. The command, "Please enter your password" appeared on the screen. He typed something very fast so I could not make out what he wrote. Neither could the computer. After a moment it put this message on the screen: "Login and password do not match. Please try again." He tried again and got the same response.

"I'm so nervous and upset that I've forgotten my password," he said peevishly.

"Let me try," said Gaston. At the login prompt he typed "millerj," and at the password prompt he typed, "Jane1." The machine did not like his choice: "Sorry, password is incorrect. Try again."

"That's interesting," Gaston commented.

"What? That you can't log into my computer with any password you care to try? I hope it's more secure than that," More stated.

"That's my point exactly," Gaston explained. "It is secure. You got a different message than I did. When you entered a login and a password the you were told that they didn't match. When I tried I was told that the password was wrong."

"What of it?" More blustered.

I was beginning to see where Gaston was heading. "I used a different login than you did," he murmured, staring intently at More. The trap was about to snap shut on its prey.

"Wha'? What?"

"You typed 'moref' and I tried 'millerj.' The software recognized the 'millerj' login as belonging to this computer. It did not recognize your login."

"Well, that explains it then. I must have picked Jane's computer up by mistake," Fred said confidently, seeing light at the end of the tunnel.

"Yes, I think you are right. But *when* did you pick up Jane's computer? That's the important question, isn't it?"

The blood drained out of Fred's face leaving him looking an unpleasant shade of greenish white. He stumbled backward and fell into his chair as if he had taken a blow to the solar plexus. The light he saw at the end of the tunnel was a train coming at him and Gaston Lemieux was the engineer.

Now all the sympathy was gone from Gaston's demeanour. In a no-bullshit cop's voice, he pronounced, "Dean More, I believe you are guilty of the murder of Harold Hilliard, your wife's lover, and of your unfortunate wife, Jane Miller-More. But that will be decided by a jury."

chapter twenty-two

Fred More's face was white, and his hands were shaking violently. But somehow he found the will to keep his voice steady.

"It's my wife's computer. It's not a crime to pick it up by mistake."

"Monsieur More, est-ce que vous me prenez pour un imbécile? You didn't pick your wife's computer up by mistake. You slipped into her office yesterday and took it. It took some daring but not much. If she had discovered you in her office you would have claimed that you were looking for her and found her office door open. But she didn't return to her office in the, what? twenty or thirty seconds it took you to sneak into her office, steal her computer and leave, did she? Yesterday I wasn't sure why her computer was taken. Today I think I know the answer. But first things first."

Gaston paused for breath. Pulling up a chair, he sat facing Fred. He also paused so that what he said could penetrate Fred's consciousness. I realized that he wanted More to understand the hopelessness of his situation. I too found a chair and pulled it over to where Gaston was sitting. I placed myself just behind him at his right elbow.

Gaston continued, "You just told us that this morning you returned to your office and then went to a meeting, which was cancelled. We'll check that. But whatever you did, you did not mistakenly pick up your wife's computer. Not yesterday, not today. As I said, at the very least you removed evidence from the scene of a crime. Am I wrong?"

"No," More's eyes were darting around now. He leaned back in his chair and crossed his arms. It was obvious that he was panicking. "I went to Jane's office to see if she had time for a coffee. Like I told you, my meeting was cancelled. I found her dead. I lost my head. I don't know why, but I did. I know I should have called you but all I could think of was her message on Hilliard's computer and I wanted to spare her memory any embarrassment so I took her computer and brought it home. I'm sorry. But I think that under the circumstances it's hardly the crime of the century. Now, if you'll excuse me, I'd like to call our families."

The dean obviously thought that tampering with evidence was a better crime to admit to than murder. Gaston was not to be put off that easily.

"Dean More," Gaston said patiently, "you left Doctor Young's office before we discovered that there was an e-mail from your wife in Professor Hilliard's mailbox. You knew that your wife was going to leave you for Harold Hilliard. No?"

"No!" More exclaimed. "She left him for me. She married *me*. Not the other way around, remember?"

"Yes. That is what I thought. And that's why I made a fatal error in judgement. An error that, as you know, cost your wife her life. I believed that she killed Hilliard because he was trying to blackmail her to return to him. I believed that when I read her message to him that we found on his computer. I even went to her office yesterday evening and virtually accused the poor woman of murder. She told me, us, a very interesting story which I wasn't sure I believed but, as it turns out, was the truth. I had the whole thing backwards. She married you, in despair and anger, because Hilliard didn't want to marry her, at least, not then. She also figured that if she married you, you wouldn't or couldn't turn her in for plagiarism. But then things changed. Hilliard wanted her back. They resumed their affair. You found out about it, killed him, and then tried to destory the evidence you knew was likely to be on his computer. Then you guessed that there might be evidence on *her* computer that incriminated you, so you beat us to her office yesterday and stole it. But you knew we had found Hilliard's laptop and it was only a matter of time before it yielded evidence that might point to you as his killer.

"This morning you realized that even with Harold gone, she was still going to leave you and that there was a pretty good chance that you would be arrested for the murder of Harold Hilliard. So you followed her to her office and killed her, out of fear and jealousy, thinking that if you did it there that you would not be found out, that her murder and the murder of Harold Hilliard would both be attributed to the same unknown person, and you would get away with it. You were losing her and that was bad enough; you didn't want to lose your freedom in the bargain."

"You're dangerously deranged," More shouted. "After you stop harassing me I'm going to get a lawyer and sue you and the police force for millions. You won't get a job as a crossing guard after I'm through with you." More knew he was trapped. He couldn't argue his way out of a murder conviction. The best he could do was bargain for something less than the rest of his life in prison. But foolishly, he still seemed to believe that he could protest his innocence.

"Dean More," Gaston began again, "let me tell you what I know and what I've surmised. Your wife was preparing to leave you. She told us that she had not yet asked you for a divorce, and I believe her. She thought you knew nothing. But you suspected, or knew, that she and Hilliard were getting back together again. Perhaps you accused her of it over lunch at the faculty club last week, and she denied it. But you knew that sooner or later Hilliard would win. You couldn't keep her by bringing up those old plagiarism charges, at least, not without embarrassing yourself, and she knew that. You had benefited from her stellar academic advancement as much as she had. Her plagiarism had become yours as well, and she knew your threat to expose her was an empty one.

"You didn't want to lose her. You thought that if you killed Hilliard she would stay with you. It's the stalker's mentality. Your ego couldn't accept that she just plain didn't want to be with you. You almost got away with it. If the cop investigating this case had been less familiar with the vagaries of the English language than me," Gaston said without even a trace of modesty, "you might actually have gotten away with double murder. It was Jane's e-mail to Hilliard that at first made me think she was the murderer and then showed me that she was trying to get out of your clutches. Your language can be ambiguous. When your wife wrote to Hilliard stating in effect that she would not give up her happiness, I thought that she was telling him to leave her alone and let her continue her life with you. But she was murdered and I had to re-examine the evidence and it was then that I realized I had misinterpreted the phrases from her e-mail. She was telling Hilliard that she was no longer willing to sacrifice herself to you. If you tried to ruin her reputation she and Hilliard would fight you and likely win. In other words she was prepared to call your bluff."

I was impressed at Gaston's ability to summarize a complicated series of events. When I joined Gaston in the investigation I had hoped that I would have a chance to confront the murderer and make a passionate accusatory speech. Obviously this was not to be the case. Gaston had the case solved and I didn't think I had anything to add to his solution. But I was curious about one thing: Did Jane discover that her husband was a murderer? Was this the real reason he killed her?

Following up on Gaston's précis of the case I asked, "Did your wife know that you killed the man she loved? Is that why you killed her?"

The question came out of my mouth a little more aggressively than my brain intended but the man had killed two people and I wasn't at all concerned about hurting his feelings.

Fred More looked at me. I was certain that he would not answer my question and I don't think he intended to answer it. But he did. "She had no idea." He spoke with the slow monotone of a man who can't fully control what he is saying, almost as if he was listening to himself saying something that he did not know was a fully formed idea. "But I couldn't take the chance that she would never figure it out. It became clear to me that she had no intention of changing her plans to leave just because Harold was dead. I guess I killed him for nothing. Even with him out of the way I was gong to lose my life. But I had no intention of losing my freedom as well. I realized that if Jane did not stay with me I would have to kill her to protect myself."

"So you marched into her office and killed her?" I prompted.

"I went over to her office to talk to her," he continued as if he had not heard my question. "I wanted her to agree to move to another city, to start over again. She refused. She told me that she didn't love me and that if she could not spend her life with the man she loved she would certainly not spend it with a man she did not love. I couldn't take it. I was not someone she could use and discard. I am a person to be reckoned with. While we were talking her phone rang. She turned to answer it and I grabbed her scarf and got behind her. The minute she hung up I strangled her. It was that simple. She must have known that I had killed her lover but by the time she figured it out it was too late."

Fred More stopped talking as abruptly as he started. He looked at us but said nothing. Gaston stood up and backed away from where More was sitting. For a moment I half thought More was going to get up and try to run away. And he did try to stand up but he couldn't. He pushed himself up with his hands on the armrests of the chair, but all the fight had gone out of him. He fell back into the chair. For a tense moment he stared pure hatred at Gaston and then he covered his face with his hands and began to cry.

This man was cold-blooded enough to kill two people, yet when his own life was in jeopardy he couldn't deal with it. He broke down.

Gaston pulled his cellphone out of his blazer pocket and punched in some numbers. After a moment he said, into the phone, "Please come inside now and make an arrest." He looked up and said to me, "My officers will be here in a moment. I have to make a few more calls.

Keep an eye on him. If he tries anything just push him back into his chair," and he turned away and punched in another number. I didn't know quite what to do. A career in bookselling had not prepared me for murderer watching but I figured that if he tried anything I would do as Gaston suggested. Anyway, More didn't try anything. He didn't even try very hard to stop whimpering.

Gaston must have called Steve's pager, because his phone rang the insant it snapped it shut, and from his side of the conversation I gathered that Steve and Dr. Young were anxious for news. He filled them in briefly and then asked Steve to bring Dr. Young over to More's house with her laptop and some extra cabling to create a network, as she had done with Hilliard's computer. His request surprised me at first but as I thought about it I realized that he knew More was the murderer based on a rational interpretation of the available evidence, but there wasn't much of that and a sharp defence attorney might have been able to get some of it excluded from a trial. Gaston wanted hard evidence to head off any attempts to create a convincing alternative theory for the rest of it. He needed documentary proof that Jane was on the point of leaving her husband and re-establishing her relationship with Hilliard in order to be able to present an unimpeachable motive for More to have committed a double murder. And he believed that evidence was concealed in Jane's computer.

Dr. Young and Steve Mandopolous arrived about ten minutes after the uniformed officers. A CSU technician showed up tight after them. Gaston turned Fred More over to the patrol cops and got the technician to take fingerprints from the computer. The techie made a move to remove the computer from the house but Gaston insisted that she, the same Constable Bouchard

who had been at Jane Miller-More's office, do her fingerprinting on the spot. It didn't take her long. Gaston
then asked her and her crew to investigate the rest of the
house and to leave us alone in the living room.

Barbara Young and Steve Mandopolous had trouble
restraining themselves while Constable Bouchard went
about her business and the second she left Dr. Young
virtually pounced on Gaston and me and demanded,
"Tell me everything. How did you catch the bastard?"

"You tell them," Gaston said to me. "I want to
make a few notes."

I brought them up to date. I hope I didn't embellish
the story but I sure didn't leave anything out. I acted all
the parts: sitting and sobbing for Fred and standing and
accusing for Gaston. It was an bravura performance if I
do say so myself.

The room was quiet after I finished the recounting of
events and it was during that quiet moment that I realized the meaning of the book order form Gaston found
in Hilliard's hand. I had theorized that it might point to
Jane. It was obvious I was wrong but it was only after I
reviewed our solution to the crime that I understood the
clue Hilliard had left for us. Jane Miller had talked to us,
when we first interviewed her in her office, about Henry
VIII, and his wives, and his *Lord Chancellor*.

It was the name of the Lord Chancellor that was the
clue: Sir Thomas *More*. Hilliard had pointed a direct,
accusing finger at the murderer, but we were too thick to
see it. I felt very sad and guilty about Jane Miller. If we
had been smart enough to understand what Hilliard was
trying to tell us we might have been able to save her life.

Gaston put away his notebook and went over to
observe as Dr. Young examined the computer. "Please
be very careful. We'll need solid evidence to get a
conviction."

"Don't worry. I designed the software. I'm sure I can figure out a way to crack it."

"Don't programmers usually leave a back door into their software?" Steve asked.

"Yeah, we do. But they're complicated and I only use them as a last resort. I'd rather use my brains to get into this thing than take a cheap shortcut."

She had wired the two computers together and got them booted. "Before I start this process, anyone want to take a shot at guessing her password?" she asked, looking directly at me. "What about you, Sam? You guessed the last one. Want to try for two out of two?"

I didn't really want to try. I didn't want to back away from a challenge but I couldn't do much without some information; after all, I hadn't *guessed* Hilliard's password. I'd figured it out from reading *Hamlet*. I didn't have anything to go on for Jane. "Do you know if she had a nickname? Or did she make a joke or pun on her name?" I asked. "Something based on More, more or less, much more, something like that?"

"Not More," Barbara said. "That was her husband's name, not hers. She did sometimes joke about *The Miller's Tale* being the start of her family's history."

"So try 'Chaucer,'" I heard myself say.

"Why not?" said Barbara. "The author of *The Miller's Tale* — it's got seven letters so there's room for that all important symbol that makes these codes so hard to crack. Let's try Chaucer1." She typed that in with Jane's login and got the error message.

"Damn it," she muttered.

"Keep trying," I suggested, looking over her shoulder. "Try Chaucer and the other possible symbols. It's worth a try before we give up on Chaucer."

She tried Chaucer combined with all the numbers on the keyboard and then went through the symbols on the top part of the number keys. We were beginning to think that we were back to square one when bingo! the asterisk worked.

"Way to go," she told me. "You could have a real career breaking into people's computers and stealing all their secrets. I better send out a memo telling folks not to be so obvious when they come up with passwords they think no one will ever guess." Normally I get a real rush when I solve a puzzle, but not this time. Jane's death made it impossible for me to take any pleasure in cracking her password. It was funny, but I hadn't felt that way about Hilliard's death. At that time I was just excited about getting close to a murder investigation. But now, well, I guess I'd had enough murder for a lifetime.

"Good work, Sam," Gaston said coming closer so that he could see the screen. "What have we found?"

"Well," Dr. Young explained, navigating thorough Jane Miller-More's e-mail box. "We found that she never deleted any messages. We've got a lot of communication with Hal along with a lot of professional, historian stuff."

"I'll want a printout of all her communications," Gaston said. "But for the moment let's read them."

The four of us — Steve, me, Gaston and Barbara — pulled chairs up to the table and read Jane's private e-mail. I don't know about the others, but I felt guilty at first, as if I was somehow violating her privacy. I felt better when I reminded myself that I was helping to find evidence to convict a murderer and that she and Hilliard were dead and could not be harmed by our prying.

We even found the original, complete version of the e-mail she sent to Hilliard. It said:

"I've thought very carefully about our conversations of the last few weeks. Very carefully. And I've come to a decision. It may not be the smartest decision but it's the one I feel most comfortable with and I'm pre-pared to face the consequences of having made it.

"I don't feel I can live a lie for the rest of my life. Whatever the short-term cost I'm determined to be happy and I don't intend to spend the rest of my life with someone with whom I'm not happy. Accepting the way things were just to avoid risk was horribly unfair to F and I won't go on with it. I wasn't sure I had the guts to say that but now that I see that I do I'm more sure than ever that I've made the right decision.

"The next step is to act on it. It won't be easy but I'll do it and I'll have to depend on your patience and understanding.

"I'm sorry, believe me, love,

"Sincerely,

"Jane."

If we had seen the whole message maybe we would have gotten to her office faster and saved her life. Who knows?

The rest of her e-mail pretty much confirmed what we had already deduced. That she and Hilliard had real-ized they were still in love. That this time he was ready to make a commitment to her, and she believed him. She was sorry to have to hurt Fred. She was fond of him and it wasn't his fault that she fell in love with Hal again. These were notes she wrote before he had revealed the full extent of his willingness to harm her just to keep her for himself.

At some point she must have confessed her plagia-rism to Hilliard. It seemed that he had assured her he didn't care, and would let past sins remain buried in the past. It was clear from her e-mail that she and Hilliard discussed how they would deal with the possibility of More's accusation that she was a plagiarist. Their solu-tion was simple: they decided to take the risk, betting on

Fred's not saying anything, because if he was believed he would look spiteful and petty, and, worse, if he was disbelieved he would look like a vindictive cuckold who spread ugly false rumours for revenge after his wife left him. Knowing his vanity about his reputation they thought he would make no public accusations.

Many years of experience working with the university crowd told me their strategy probably would have worked.

Jane's last e-mail to Harold, the one we found on his computer, made it clear that she was not planning to stay in the conjugal home for much longer. We all felt a sadness for her and Hilliard, emotionally exhausted, and anger bordering on fury at Fred More.

When we finished reading Jane's mail Gaston was the first to speak. "With these letters we'll have no trouble getting a conviction, I'm sure."

"It would be nicer still if he took a plea and spared the memory of his wife and Professor Hilliard the embarrassment of a trial," Steve opined.

We silently agreed with him.

"Would you like me to give you all this on a diskette so that you can print it out down at police headquarters?" Barbara asked Gaston.

"Yes, if you could. That would be best," Gaston agreed. "You may have to testify that the copy you give me is an accurate and true copy of the files on the computer. I'll keep the computer itself sealed and under lock and key so that there will be no question of the authenticity of the messages."

While Barbara fished in her computer case for some blank diskettes Gaston found the CSU people and told them that they could work in the living room and he gave them special instructions as to how he wanted the computer cared for.

"We can leave now," he told us.

We were standing on the front step feeling at loose ends. We didn't know what to say to one another. We had just come through an incredibly intense experience and we didn't know how to bring it to an end.

"I want to thank you all very much for all that you have done to help me," Gaston addressed us. "I could not have brought this case to a successful conclusion so quickly if not for all your help. We couldn't save a life, and that's too bad, but at least we got justice for the victims. Thank you." He solemnly shook each of our hands. "Would any of you like a car to take you home?"

"I think I'd like to walk," said Dr. Young. Steve and I said we would too and the three of us walked down the hill to Sherbrooke and east to McGill. That walk was more like a funeral procession than a stroll down one of Montreal's nicest streets. None of us looked at the art in the gallery windows or the expensive clothing in the shop windows. None of said a word till we reached the Roddick Gate. There we paused and before we parted we promised to keep in touch, the way mourners do after a funeral. I walked east and then north; it took about an hour to walk home, but the exercise helped to calm me.

I really wanted to be alone and get some sleep so I turned off the phone and my brain and crawled into bed.

chapter twenty-three

The next morning, after a long dreamless sleep, I actually managed to beat Jennifer into the store by about three minutes.

"Well, stranger," she greeted me. "Are you back for long?"

"Back forever," I told her. "The mystery has been solved."

"No kidding. Then the first thing you and I are going to do after we get the store open is go out for a coffee. You are going to tell me everything."

I took comfort at being back at my old routine, and in the normal opening procedures for a book store. We got the money out of the safe counted and into the cash register. We assigned tasks to the staff and checked our agendas to see what had to be dealt with immediately and who we would keep waiting. It didn't take long.

A few minutes later Jennifer and I were installed at a corner table at the Café Paillon with two large lattes, away from the noise of the ongoing battle between the Paillons. I brought her up to date, leaving out no detail, from the very beginning to the point where Steve and Barbara and I walked away from the More house on Irving Street.

I stopped talking only to sip at my coffee or to listen to one of the few questions Jennifer had.

"Wow," Jennifer said. "I hope they lock that guy up and lose the key."

Just then I noticed Arlene Ford at the counter buying a coffee to go. I jumped up and went over to speak to her.

"Hi," I said. "Did you hear what happened?"

"Yes, I did," she said. "It's all over the university." For the first time since the day I discovered Professor Hilliard's body she seemed cordial. Now that the crime was solved she was probably feeling less stressed.

"You must be pleased that it's over," I continued.

"Of course I'm pleased about that," she said and she even touched my arm in a friendly way. Then some of the fire returned to her voice. "But if you think I'm pleased that you and that cop virtually accused me of committing murder you've got another think coming."

"You didn't do much to co-operate, you know."

"I don't have to co-operate, now, do I? I lost someone very dear to me and before I could come to terms with that you guys turned me into a criminal. Let me tell you something: The next time you get ready to accuse someone of murder you'd better be pretty sure you know what you're talking about."

I would have apologized if I had had the chance but she turned and strode out of the café. I returned to Jennifer who asked, "What was that about?"

I explained, and her response surprised me a bit. "Well good for her. She probably feels a lot better for having told you off," she said.

We chit-chatted a while longer and returned to work.

epilogue

The case against Fred More was not resolved quickly. He opted to fight. Barbara and Steve and I and the other witnesses spent many hours with Gaston and the prosecutors before the case even got to court, as Fred hired a top-notch criminal lawyer in an effort to stay out of jail.

Barbara and Steve and I all wanted to be present in the court room for the trial, but were not allowed to, because we were going to be called as witnesses. We found this frustrating but accepted it as being in the interest of justice. While we waited we forged a close three-way friendship because of what we had been through together and because we were determined to see justice done.

In fact there wasn't much of a trial and none of us ever got to testify. The day after the jury was selected Fred copped a plea. He got twenty-five years with the possibility of parole after serving a third of his sentence for pleading guilty to two counts of murder. I asked Gaston why he thought Fred copped a plea at the last minute. Gaston believed that More took one look at the jury and realized that he'd never convince the eight women and four men that he was innocent. He realized that twenty-five years with the possibility of parole was better than life without the chance of parole. I wished I had seen the jury.

My life in the bookstore seemed boring for a while after the excitement of helping to solve a murder. Gaston continued to drop by the bookstore for his literary fix and we continued to go out for coffee once every week or two. The murders had the effect of adding another dimension to our friendship — they gave us something more in common than just books. Barbara and Steve also started to drop by the store from time to time and I always made sure I had time for coffee and conversation with each of them.

And then Gisèle came back from France. But that's another story.

There was one final irony to the case. About two weeks after Fred More's arrest we got a report on the book Jane had ordered for Hilliard; it was out of print.